Whispers
in the Wind

A SUNNY DAVIS MYSTERY NOVEL

VERONICA GIOLLI

PALM BEACH COUNTY
LIBRARY SYSTEM
3650 Summit Boulevard
West Palm Beach, FL 33406-4198

Whispers in the Wind
Copyright © 2019 by Veronica Giolli. All rights reserved.

Cover illustration courtesy of Leeland McMasters

Published by Pace Press
An imprint of Linden Publishing
2006 South Mary Street, Fresno, California 93721
(559) 233-6633 / (800) 345-4447
PacePress.com

Pace Press and Colophon are trademarks of
Linden Publishing, Inc.

ISBN 978-1-61035-329-8

135798642

Printed in the United States of America
on acid-free paper.

This is a work of fiction. The names, places, characters, and incidents
in this book are used fictitiously, and any resemblance to actual people,
places, or events is coincidental.

Library of Congress Cataloging-in-Publication Data on file.

In loving memory of
Norene La Rae Wilson

You were a true best friend and a beautiful person.
Your encouragement kept me going in the early years.
Yes, I did use your name as you asked.
Rest in Peace, dear friend.

There is no death, only a change of worlds.

WHISPERS IN THE WIND

SUNDAY, MARCH 1985

The wind is coming. I feel the cold air.
My hair is caught up, whirling round and round.

The wind is taking me.
My body's light as air. What's happening?

I choked on my own blood.
Did I hear a gunshot? I smell gun oil—hot metal.

I'm rising. Stop.
What's pulling me?

Where are my boys? Where am I?
Am I dead?

Help! Someone help me!
Sunny! What's happening to me?

I want my boys. Where are my boys?
You know I would never leave them.

And Gina's spirit rose with the wind.

CHAPTER ONE

MONDAY, MARCH 1985

Sunny reached out to touch the pillar of fog as it formed into the familiar shape of her best friend, Gina. It was cold as it curled around her hand before the vision dissipated into the wind. The phone on her nightstand startled her awake. She stared in fear at the receiver before picking it up. Gina's husband, Jesse, delivered a brief brutal message. "Gina killed herself."

Stunned, Sunny Davis leaned back against the pillows as the dial tone hummed in her ear; she bit her fist to keep from crying. "My God, Gina. No! Why?" Tears stung her face. Her heart felt on fire. "How could Gina kill herself?"

She threw off the covers and paced blindly in her bedroom, the phone hot in her hand. She threw the receiver on her bed and looked for something else to throw. Stumbling to the dresser, she grabbed her hairbrush and bounced it off the wall.

Gina killed herself. Jesse's words tumbled over and over in her head.

The clock on her nightstand, the only light in the room, glowed, reading 3:14 a.m. Her hand shaking, she lit the small ceramic lamp on the dresser.

For a few seconds she leaned into the dresser. Then, remembering, a wave of guilt assailed her. "Oh no! Was it because of me . . . because of our conversation? No, Gina, no. What have I done?"

The weight of her realization made Sunny buckle. Not knowing what else to do she rubbed her palm against her chest. She picked the brush up from the floor, flicked the bristles with her thumb, and put it back. The front door slammed. Wiping her eyes, she hurried from the bedroom to look down the stairwell. Her husband fell against the door.

"Drunk!" she uttered. "Screw him." She couldn't deal with it now. Moving back to the bed she waited for him to come up the stairs. *I can't think straight. Gina's dead and he should have been here with me. I don't know what to do. It's all too much.* She clasped her hands and watched the door.

Listening to Barry stumble up the stairs, banging into the walls, her anger rose. He swore and staggered into the room, then flipped on the wall switch. His black hair hung low on his forehead. Part of his shirttail hung out over the top of his slacks with blotched stains down the front. The stale smell of booze and smoke hung on him like the morning fog. He squinted and gazed around for a moment. "Uh-oh," he said. "I know that look."

She sat on the edge of the bed, blankets around her legs, and glared at him. "Something horrible has happened, and of course, you weren't here."

Her face felt hot as she pushed the blankets aside and stood. She stretched her small barefoot frame taller so her forehead was level with his chin. Her long black hair hung in front of her shoulders, some of it over her left eye. She yanked it out of the way and braced for a fight.

"I'm sick of this crap, Barry. I needed you tonight. I thought I was going to lose my mind." Her legs ready to give way, she sat back on the bed.

Barry swayed and fell onto it too, then sat up and tried to pull her close. He draped his heavy arm over her shoulders. "What're you . . . talking about? A bunch of guys from work went out and the time got away from me. Is that why you're crying?"

Shoving his arm aside she stiffened. "Jesse called." She took in a breath. "Gi . . . na killed herself." Sunny collapsed on the bed, weeping.

His head jerked backward. "What? When? What . . . happened?"

She sat up and fidgeted with the blanket. "Late yesterday." Her shoulders drooped. "She shot herself. The BIA and the Reno Tribal Police were at their house most of the night."

"That's rough, Sunny. Oh man, that's terrible. I'm sorry. Her poor kids."

"I told him we'd be there as soon as we can," she gasped, fighting back sobs.

"Okay. Sure. That sounds good." He sighed.

"Even my special pot roast dinner was ruined." *Why am I thinking about a dinner now?*

"Damn . . . I'm sorry."

"The call scared me. It was late. My stomach knotted. I'm always afraid it's about you. I felt weird all day yesterday, like something was going to happen, you know, how I do sometimes. I thought it was you, but it wasn't. It was Gina. The two people I love most."

He was nodding off. "Nah, not me, babe," he slurred.

"I hate it when you're out drinking." She pinched her lips. "By the way, the bars close at two." The clock's red numbers glared accusingly. 3:45. "So, where were you?"

"Ed and I got something to eat and I took him home." He raked his thinning hair out of his eyes. "Since when do I have to punch a time clock?"

"That's how you want to act? That's what you want to say to me right now?"

"What can I say?"

He untied his shoes, climbed out of his stained white shirt and beige pants, and reached for her trembling hands.

She yanked them away. "Don't start with a long line of excuses again." Her eyes burned into his. "I warned you; if you don't stop drinking I'm leaving. Yet you're still out boozing. I won't live with an alcoholic husband like my mother did."

"I'm not . . . an alcoholic. I just like to drink. There's a difference."

"No. No, there's not."

Sunny picked at the blanket. "Your drinking, on top of Gina's . . ." She shook her head and chewed on a piece of her hair. "It's too much for me right now. I love you, but I can't live like this anymore."

Barry raised his hands in the air, palm side up. "I'm sorry, babe. How was I supposed to know about Gina? Let me get a couple hours' sleep and I'll be ready to go to Reno with you."

He sat on the edge of the bed as his head swung back and forth. "Why the BIA? Aren't the tribal police good enough?"

"Have you forgotten?" She looked over her shoulder at him. "Gina lives on the reservation. Federal land makes it a federal crime. The Bureau of Indian Affairs is called whenever there's a death. What kind of Indian are you?"

He gave her a side-eyed glimpse and stretched. "Yeah, I forgot." He yawned and lay down.

"It doesn't seem real." She reached for a tissue on the nightstand. "Gina was my best friend."

"It'll be all right, babe," he mumbled and just like that dropped off to sleep.

Sunny looked at him, cringed, and whispered, "No, it won't. It'll never be right again."

Unable to go back to sleep, she watched the Bay Area fog roll through, obscuring the city's skyline, and then disappear.

She pulled at a tendril of hair. She never guessed it could be this horrible. Guilt overwhelmed her. How could she tell Barry or Rita about their last conversation? What if they blamed her?

Her gaze rested on the framed wedding pictures on the dresser. In one, Gina smiled back in a pink matron-of-honor gown. Waist-length hair hung down her back like a shawl. The sides of her hair were twisted and tied with a headband of pink baby roses. Her tan face glowed. It was hard to imagine Gina as anything but a sister . . . a living sister. Thinking about her wedding day—her and Barry's—Sunny chewed on the ends of her hair as her eyes settled on the happy faces of Gina's three boys. A moan escaped her lips. "Oh my Lord, what will happen to them now? They were her world. She adored them . . . and they adored her."

Her vision blurred again as she went into the bathroom, slipped out of her nightgown, and stepped into the shower.

I have to find out what happened. She hit the shower wall with her knuckles and cried out, "Why, Gina, why?" Even the scent of the lavender soap couldn't relax her.

As she sank to the shower floor she clasped her arms around her chest and pressed her head against her knees until the water ran cold.

Finished, she toweled off her trembling body, moved to the bedroom, and put on her underwear, then opened the window and took in a deep breath. The damp air chilled her as she stared at the Bay Bridge spanning the San Francisco Bay.

The sweet, sad sound of a foghorn intruded on her thoughts. The click of metal rods attached to electric buses hit the wires as they drove along her street. She loved the music of her San Francisco neighborhood. It calmed her, like the moaning whistle of a faraway train.

Looking out her window she thought about the day before. Her intuition had made her restless. She'd felt that something was going to happen, but certainly not this.

Dressed in blue jeans, she added a crimson sweater and jean jacket. Her jeans were tight, right out of the dryer, and hard to button. She was as thin as tissue paper. Looking in the mirror, she said, "Oh, Gina, what have you done? My eyes are red and swollen. I'm forty-two and I look a hundred and two."

I have to pull myself together. Grabbing her long wet hair, she twisted and pinned it into a knot on top of her head. Dashing around the room she threw clothes, shoes, and toiletries in a suitcase.

Behind her, Barry stirred and stumbled out of bed, then tugged his robe on. "I'm going downstairs to take two aspirins and start the coffee. You okay?"

She refused to answer right away. *How can I be?* She cleared her throat. "I'll be there in a minute."

It always amazed her how he could come home falling-down drunk, get a couple hours' sleep, and wake up sober, ready to go.

Sunny headed down the hall to call her daughter in Reno. Because Gina was closer in age, she and Rita had been like sisters, sharing secrets and laughing over everything. Rita would be devastated if she heard about Gina from someone else.

She dreaded making the call but knew she couldn't wait until they got to Reno. Her hands felt heavy. They shook as she started to dial.

Midway she stopped. "I can't do it. Not like this." Her head down, she turned to Barry. "How do I tell her Gina killed herself, when I don't believe it? I feel like I'm having a breakdown."

"I know this is hard. It shouldn't take us long to get there. Four hours, maybe less."

Her stomach turned over. It had been too much for her. She didn't know what she would do if their argument on the phone was the reason.

The strong aroma of coffee and cigarette smoke greeted her as she came into the kitchen. She picked up her mug and joined Barry at the round maple table where he sat smoking his first cigarette of the day. He'd opened the window halfway to let his smoke disappear. The breeze sent the curtains swaying. Silence filled the room.

Sunny looked around at her teapots atop the cabinets, the copper molds hung on the wall. How Gina had loved this old Victorian house. She'd walk around admiring the wood moldings on the doors and windows, especially the spindle staircase winding to the top floor. Barry had bought the house for Sunny when they got married.

Gina once said, "I love the mauve guest room. It's my favorite. I could sit for hours on the window seat and read or watch the squirrels playing in the park." Sunny's eyes glistened and she smiled remembering Gina saying, "My room has the best view."

Sunny's thoughts came back to the present. She pushed herself up and went to contact her supervisor, Carol. She explained the circumstances, voicing her shock and disbelief.

"I'm so sorry for your loss. If anyone can find out why this happened, it's you. Use those instincts of yours. You've always had more intuition than anyone I've ever known."

Sniffling, Sunny thanked her and hung up.

Now dressed in Levi's, a long-sleeved red plaid shirt, and his favorite eagle bolo tie, Barry was ready to leave. He struggled to put on his blue down parka. She hated that jacket. It made him look like the Michelin Man.

He fidgeted with the zipper. "I'm ready. I left a message at work."

"You don't have to come with me. Stay home. I can do this myself. I don't want to worry if you're drunk, or whatever. I don't have the patience to babysit you, especially now."

He scratched his head. "I'm sorry about last night. I know Gina's suicide is a shock. I promise, we'll talk about the two of us later."

Sunny hated screening her thoughts from Barry. She just wanted him to cut down on the drinking. She decided not to tell him about her last conversation with Gina. Not yet.

He picked up his keys from the coffee table. "I'm going with you. You're in no shape to drive. Sunny . . . I'm sorry about the pot roast."

"I know, I know."

"I've packed the car. I even grabbed your sketchpad and pens."

"Thanks, I completely forgot."

"Don't worry. It'll be fine."

Sunny lowered her eyes. "I don't know how." *God, Gina, what am I going to do without you in my life?*

[8]

Barry maneuvered the car out of the garage and backed cautiously onto the street. Sunny said, "Wait. Go back. I have to get something." She jumped out and ran into the house, up to their room, and threw open the closet door. There, off to one side, hung the dress Gina had always loved: a red wool knit her mom had made by hand. Sunny pulled it off the hanger, folded it, and raced back to the car.

"What'd you forget?" asked Barry, shifting into reverse.

"This dress." Sunny held it up for him to see.

"Why do you need it?"

"I'm wearing it for the funeral."

"You're kidding, right?"

Sunny shot him a what-the-hell-how-dare-you-question-me look.

"I mean," he went on, "it's not appropriate."

"Oh, so now you're Chief of the Funeral Fashion Police? You get to tell people what they can or cannot wear to a funeral?"

"C'mon, honey. I just meant you might be more comfortable in something that's not so . . . uh . . . bright."

"Look, Gina loved this dress," Sunny stated. "She even told me I had to leave it to her in my will. So, to my way of thinking, this is the most appropriate thing I could wear to her funeral. Just as we were leaving it dawned on me that since Gina loved it so, I should wear it for her. I know she'll be looking on from above and when she sees me walk in, she'll be smiling."

Barry shrugged. "Whatever."

CHAPTER TWO

The sky in the direction of Reno looked like a canvas painted in shades of gray. It was March and the weather was cold and unsettled.

"Hope we don't hit snow over Donner Summit," Barry said as he drove on Highway I-80 East. He slid two fingers in his shirt pocket for a pack of Marlboros, tapped out a cigarette on the steering wheel, and offered one to Sunny.

"Get that out of my face. When I quit at New Year's I said not even stress will make me smoke again. I meant it."

"Sorry, I forgot. It's a habit. Will it mess you up if I have one?"

"Not at all."

Barry lit one for himself and dropped the pack into his pocket.

While he drove, "Tired of Being Alone" by Al Green came on the radio. Gina had played the song over and over when she lived with Sunny. Blinking back tears, Sunny focused on the blur of scenery between Vallejo and Sacramento while music and memories washed over her.

"You've been quiet." Barry tilted his head and brought her back to the moment.

She shook her head. "Damn."

"What?"

"I keep seeing Gina in my head, the first time I ever laid eyes on her. She was standing on the porch of her foster home, waving with one hand, holding her suitcase in the other. It was her eighteenth birthday. She'd aged out of the system and had no place to go."

Barry kept his eyes on the road. "She was so young."

"Yeah, she'd been there ten years. My friend, Barbara, you remember, she used to be a CPS worker? She talked me into taking Gina as a live-in babysitter."

"That was before we got married. But you just let her come to your house to watch Rita? You didn't know her. You didn't know what she'd do."

"I trusted Barb. And I trusted Gina, right away, as soon as I met her."

"Child Protective Service worker or not, that was foolish."

"No, I knew she'd be fine, and she was."

Sunny remembered Gina sitting in the car. She had said, "Thank you for letting me babysit. I won't disappoint you." Sunny went with her gut feeling.

As she leaned her head against the window the cold from outside seeped into her ear. "I feel so helpless."

"I doubt you can do anything. When someone commits suicide it's hard for the survivors to believe or understand. It leaves the people who loved them guessing." Sunny could tell Barry was referring to his brother's suicide years ago. "Sometimes we never do know the reason. We just learn to live with it and keep going."

"How could she do it . . . and leave her boys?"

"I wish I could give you an answer but I can't."

In her purse, she looked for a tissue and ached to feel smoke curling in her lungs, the nicotine working its way to her brain and numbing her for a while. It was an all too familiar pattern. She fought the urge.

Then she surprised and hated herself for saying, "I'll take that cigarette, after all."

"Sure? You'll be back to square one."

Sunny raised and lowered her shoulders and half smiled. She'd thought she was strong enough to resist her body's "raving craving" for nicotine. In the end, her fingers decided for her and reached for the cigarette.

"You've gone this long. I don't think it's a good idea."

"Just give me a damn cigarette!"

"Sunny, you said nothing could make you start. Think about it."

"I have."

Her mental resolve shattered like a quail egg fallen from the nest. *I'll have to quit again and rebuild my strength when all this is over.* When and if she would ever be able to stop again was the unanswered question. She couldn't believe she'd given in so easily. The guilt and pain of Gina's death caused her determination to collapse.

He shoved the cigarette between his lips, lit it, and passed it over to her, brushing her fingertips with his.

As she inhaled, the sweet taste of nicotine and the slight burn in her mouth and throat soothed her frazzled nerves. She couldn't resist. The pain was too much. She thought about the death of her mother, and how that had affected her for many years.

CHAPTER THREE

An hour or so into the trip, Barry patted her on the leg. "We're close to the Nutt Palm. Do you want to stop for coffee or a bite to eat?"

"We have to get to Reno."

"My head is killing me."

She ground out the butt of her cigarette in the ashtray. "Really? I can't imagine why."

He furrowed his brow and didn't respond.

The restaurant parking lot was almost full. He found a space at the end of the lot. The Nutt Palm was known for its diverse colored birds. Once inside Sunny was glad they had stopped. She loved the different types of birds housed in large glass cages. Wire mesh stretched across the open top.

As they waited for a booth, she and Barry watched the birds flutter their rainbow plumage and listened to them chirp.

After ten minutes, a disheveled waitress seated them. She had a just-jumped-out-of-bed look with rumpled hair and smudged mascara. She seemed to be on autopilot as she served them coffee and took their order: eggs Benedict with fresh-baked sourdough toast. She didn't flinch at Sunny's puffy eyes.

Sunny leaned forward and whispered across the table, "Looks like she also had a hard morning."

He smiled. "Or a late night."

When they finished, the waitress refreshed their coffee and cleared the table. Through the window Sunny watched smiling families pile out of their cars ready to start their morning. Their happiness, their normality, seemed wrong. Everything seemed wrong.

How can anyone be happy? My best friend is dead. She pulled a strand of her hair and chewed on the ends.

Barry's eyes softened as he stared at her over his coffee mug.

She hadn't noticed but she'd let hers get cold. She picked up her cup and drank. She didn't care. Silent tears trickled down her face.

He touched her hand and offered her a napkin.

Sunny wiped her eyes and cheeks, wadded up the napkin, and tossed it on the table. "I'm hurt. And I'm pissed. I feel like I'm in a nightmare and can't wake up. Gina's death brings back the pain of my mother's. My mom, I can understand. She was so sick. But Gina? I just don't get it." *I should have called her back. Maybe I could have changed things.*

Barry's hand lingered on his napkin. "I'm so sorry, on both accounts. Hard to understand why she'd do this."

The waitress came by, reheated their coffee, and dropped off the check.

With her elbows on the table, Sunny cradled her forehead in her hands.

Barry started to reach for her as she looked up, then pulled back and shifted the subject. "I don't remember, did Gina meet Jesse when she was living with you?"

"No, she had her own place, but she still watched Rita for me. They met when we went to a sweat."

He took money out of his wallet and paid the bill. "You ready to go?"

He helped her into her jacket, put on his Michelin Man parka, and left the tip. "It's almost nine. We'll be in Reno around noon, unless we run into snow."

Out of habit, she slipped her arm through his as they walked to the car.

"You were starting to tell me about Gina and Jesse getting together . . ."

"One Sunday, we were at the sweat when Jesse showed up and flirted with Gina. As soon as he walked toward her, with his good looks and his long black hair swaying in the wind, she fell hard for him."

He smiled. "Love at first sight?"

"Yeah, I guess so. Sadly for Gina, when she got pregnant with her first son, Tommy, she was involved with a white man. When she told him she was pregnant, that jerk told her he was married, and that was that. Asshole stayed with his wife. Gina loved him. It was hard on her."

"Oh, I didn't know that."

"He never came around to see his son."

He shook his head. "Wow, that's tough."

"Jesse was so lovestruck he accepted her son along with Gina. Package deal."

Her heel caught in a crack on the concrete and she stumbled, lurching forward. Her arm tightened on his.

"Watch out!" He steadied her.

"Thanks. They need to fix that. It's dangerous." *Sometimes he is there for me.* She checked the heel of her boot. It wasn't broken, but her ankle hurt.

"Pay attention. You could've broken something."

"Wasn't my fault." She was so out of it, so emotional. She had to be careful. She couldn't afford to get injured.

"Oh man, I left my lighter on the table. Here's the car keys. You go on ahead." He hurried back into the restaurant.

As she strolled to the car, a family with a dark-haired little girl walked by, playing and twirling. She accidentally bumped into Sunny. For a brief second, the girl looked up at her before she ran away. Sunny could see Gina's same strong look in the child's eyes, and started to panic. She couldn't picture Gina's face. She couldn't breathe.

Running to the car, she unlocked it and got her sketchpad from the back. Sitting at the nearest picnic bench, she took out her pencils and drew frantically. Being unable to remember Gina's face scared her. Her chest was tight, her forehead felt hot. She could feel droplets of sweat along her hairline. *I need to be strong and get my head together.*

Returning, Barry said, "Found my lighter." He sat next to her. "What's the matter? You feeling all right?"

She just kept drawing. He lit a cigarette and waited.

When she was done she was exhausted. "I was afraid I wouldn't remember Gina's face." She smiled at the picture she'd drawn.

Barry's smoke swirled around and around the sketch. "That's nice, babe. You captured her eyes."

"The eyes are the hardest to get right." Standing tall, she flexed her ankle as she put her pad in her purse. "Thanks, I don't know what came over me."

He held her arm and changed the subject. "Finish telling me how Gina and Jesse got together."

Eyes glued to the concrete, she looked down at her boots as they walked back to the car. "Anyway, I think I was saying, Jesse impressed her because he had a good job, and he was single. How could Gina resist?"

When they reached the car, Barry helped her in.

She scrunched up her nose. "I never cared for him. And I *really* never trusted him."

"Why not?"

"He's too pretty. Eventually, Gina knew he drank and even cheated, but she liked that bad-boy mystique and married him anyway." Sunny played with the button on her jacket. "You'd think she'd have known better. Like I said, he was hard to resist. I warned her and warned her, but she wouldn't listen. Not many women could, or would, I guess."

CHAPTER FOUR

They drove over Donner Summit in silence. The wind twirled large snowflakes around the car. Pine trees were covered with snow that hung like rolls of cotton, casting dark shadows off the limbs. The smaller trees looked like fluffy white monsters, with snow plopping on the ground.

Sunny tried to get her emotions together. She wanted to be optimistic, but it came out sounding like she was trying too hard. "Look, Barry, it's like someone sifted powdered sugar over the whole area."

She placed her fist over her heart. "How can it be so beautiful and silent when I feel so damn angry and hurt?" She shook her head. "How could Gina do it?"

He turned to look at her. "You'll get through this. You're strong. Hell, you're Wonder Woman."

"Don't call me that! It's not true. I don't do everything myself. You know I hate th—"

THUD.

"What the hell?" Barry gripped the steering wheel with both hands and pumped the brakes. The car shuddered as it skidded into a small snowbank.

Sunny gasped and grabbed the hand grip. "Was that a flat?"

Barry looked in his rearview mirror and saw a small whitetail doe lying in the road.

"Shit! We hit a deer. Wait here. I'll go check." He got out of the car, forgetting he'd worn tennis shoes. Sunny watched him sink into the snow. "Damn it!" he yelled.

Her stomach churned as she opened the door to help him.

"Stay in the car, it's too cold. I'll take care of it." He sloshed behind the car, bent down to look at the lifeless doe.

She turned and watched as he dragged it to the side of the road, then walked around and checked the front of the car, shook the snow off his shoes, and scooted back into the driver's seat.

Her chin trembled. She knew it sounded childish but she couldn't help it. "Why does everything around me have to die?"

Sighing, he ignored her remark. "I looked at the front of the car. Only the headlight and bumper are damaged. It's drivable. I can get it fixed in Reno, but I have to get out of these wet shoes before my feet freeze."

He grabbed his boots from the back seat and changed into them, then tossed his tennis shoes onto the floorboard behind his seat.

He started the car and turned the steering wheel while stepping on the gas. The tires spun in place, roaring round and round. He stepped on the brake, then the gas, then the brake, rocking the car back and forth. He hit the gas again and pulled out of the snow and onto the road to the hum of the tires grinding through the icy slush. "We're lucky the roads were plowed and there's no traffic," he said.

CHAPTER FIVE

The rhythm of the tires on the ice filled the silence once again. The snowbanks and trees were behind, with the snow blowing off the branches onto the windshield. Past Truckee, Verdi, and Boomtown into Reno, everything was covered with white patches of snow pillows on roofs. The other parts of town looked dry and barren with yellow-brown sticks, sagebrush, rocks, and hard ground. It was a dismal morning with dark clouds darting in and out under gray skies.

Sunny struggled. She was on the verge of telling Barry about her last conversation with Gina, then changed her mind. She didn't need an argument. *Would he blame me? Why did I say what I did to her? I could have fixed it. Now it's too late.* She watched the scenery. "I never noticed how dead the desert looks."

He glanced at her. "Especially in late winter."

Seeing the flat-faced buildings pass by, down the streets of Reno, knowing Gina would never see these places again, she swallowed hard. Several sights came into view: Bill Fong's New China Club, the Comstock Casino, and Harrah's. As she passed a bar called Rae's, she pointed and tapped her fingernails on the window. Rae's was boarded up.

Sadness was in her voice as she clutched her throat. "That was the Indian bar where everyone hung out. Remember when I came up to Reno to help Gina, when she had Jesse's first baby?"

Barry nodded. "Yeah, you were so mad when you came home."

"Did I ever tell you about the night Martin was born?"

"Probably, but I don't remember." He pulled out a pack of Marlboros, nudged two cigarettes out, handed her one, and pushed in the cigarette lighter.

She hated that she took the cigarette, but she did.

Staring out the window she said, "I went looking for Jesse and found him in Rae's Bar. There he sat at the bar, on a stool, with some girl on his lap, their arms wrapped around each other and his face buried in her breasts."

Sunny stopped talking long enough for him to light her cigarette. "I walked up behind him and slapped him on the back of his head. Surprised the crap out of him." She sighed, her mouth turned up. "I told him, 'Your wife just gave birth to your son, and here you are with your face all up in some bitch's chest. Let's go!'"

"What did he say?"

"He didn't say anything. Got up, rolled his eyes, shrugged, and walked out. I admit I enjoyed the hell out of breaking up that little love scene."

She leaned her head back against the seat and took a long drag, blowing out the smoke, and gazed at clouds drifting across the sky.

With a slight cough she said, "I guess he never changed."

A short time later Barry drove past the police station and turned left on Park Street. They pulled up in front of a little brick house, shutters trimmed in black, with a red porch.

Sunny jumped out of the car practically before it stopped.

"Hey, slow down," he hollered, then turned off the engine and followed her up the steps.

She knocked hard and waited for Rita to open the door.

"Mom! This is a surprise. I just got home. Hi, Dad." She gave each a hug.

Her daughter looked like a teenager instead of a twenty-two-year-old, with her brown hair pulled up in a ponytail. She stood eye to eye with her mother, both less than five feet four.

Tears welled in Sunny's eyes. She pointed to the beige couch in the living room, behind which Rita stood. "Sit down."

"What's wrong?" Rita's eyes widened, accentuating their gold flecks.

Sunny sat on the sofa next to her, grabbed her daughter's hands, and held them to her chest. Barry sat in the recliner across the room and leaned forward.

"I have some terrible news." Sunny's voice cracked on the last word. Tears flowed. "Gina's dead. She . . . ki . . . killed herself. Last night."

"What?" Rita jumped up, looking from her mother to her dad and back again, her eyes begging them to say she'd misunderstood.

"No! She couldn't! I don't believe it! Why would she do that? Oh my God, Mom!" Rita made gagging noises. She could hardly catch her breath.

"Breathe. Do you hear me? Take a deep breath." Sunny's cheeks were damp, her nose ran. She stood and put her arms around Rita, making motherly noises and pats.

Barry hurried to the kitchen and came back with a wet paper towel that he gave Rita. "Here, wipe your face." They sat on each side of her as she sobbed.

She grabbed a tissue. "I don't understand. That's crazy."

Two hours passed during which they discussed Gina's suicide, trying to understand through their shock.

After Rita calmed down, spent from her pain and bewilderment, Sunny and Barry got up to leave. "We'll see you at Gina's."

"Okay, I'll pull myself together and be there in a while."

Sunny felt horrible, having to tell her daughter about Gina. It had crushed Rita. And made her look so young. Again, she hoped her conversation with Gina wasn't the cause. Damn, this was hard.

"Mom?"

Sunny paused at the door. "Yes?"

Rita put her hand on the arm of the couch for support. "Is Jesse okay? How did he sound when he called you? He must be in shock."

Sunny's stomach tightened. It was all too much for her. Sunny didn't have any idea what she answered, or if she did.

She walked out the door, then took a few minutes in the car to wipe her face. "That was rough."

Barry nodded deliberately. "I know. It was awful to see Rita so devastated. She loved Gina. We all loved her."

CHAPTER SIX

Sunny grabbed Barry's arm. "Wait! Stop here." They were about to pass Sunny and Gina's old hangout—Liquid Emotion—on Virginia Street.

"Here? You want me to stop here? It's a bar."

"I know it's a bar. It's where Gina and I hung out. I want to see it once more, for old times' sake, to remember the good times."

"Are you kidding? It's a waste of time."

"Just do this for me, will you? Please."

He turned into the small asphalt parking lot in back of the bar and shut the ignition off.

When they walked through the door, the strong odor of stale beer, cigarettes, Pine-Sol, and sawdust smacked them in the face. It was still the same bar atmosphere with glistening bottles stacked neatly in front of a wall of mirrors. Flashing neon signs told customers Coors beer was "the best." Gone were the ripped, cracked seats patched with duct tape. In darkened corners, smooth black leather booths had replaced the outdated, torn raspberry ones.

Sunny lifted her eyebrows. "This is where Gina and I spent our time, laughing, enjoying each other's company, and talking with friends."

On the jukebox, Willie Nelson and Johnny Cash wailed "On the Road Again" as she and Barry crossed the sawdust-covered floor.

Sunny pointed around the room. "Well, the scenery hasn't changed much. I'm glad I have." Hands on hips, she looked up at him. "At least one of us quit drinking."

"You should talk, Miss I'll Never Smoke Again. Hmm?"

Her eyes darted sideways at him. She ignored his remark.

A loud argument between two men and the bartender caught their attention. A silky haze of smoke lingered around them. It was noon and the rest of the place was empty.

Barry took it all in and smiled. "Maybe we could sit and have a beer."

Her mouth hardened and she shot him a look. "And maybe we can't."

CHAPTER SEVEN

EARLY MONDAY AFTERNOON

When they reached the Reno Reservation Barry turned right, off Forrest Lane and drove to Hayes Street, maneuvering down the gravel road, around potholes and rocks. "Damn! This is some road. It'll tear the hell out of a car."

She smiled. "Well, at least it's drivable now."

He leaned into the steering wheel. "Barely. It's still the shits," he observed as the car bounced on its shocks.

"We used to have to park at the end of the road and walk in." She twisted her head to look out the window. "There's my old place, where I grew up. Look at it now. All boarded up."

Barry glanced at the house. "Yeah, damn shame."

"I swear it looks worse every time I see it. It always makes me sad."

Barry reached over and patted her hand. "I know. I remember we met after you and Rita moved to that little white stucco off Wells Avenue."

"Yeah, I think so. I forgot about that place."

"I'll never forget the first time I saw you. I was lecturing on law enforcement to the County Social Services. You were sitting in the aisle seat, in the second row, taking notes as fast as you could write. When you looked up our eyes met and boy, were you hooked." He gave a short chuckle.

Sunny punched his arm. "Oh yeah, well, I remember it the other way around. You couldn't take your eyes off me." Her sadness lifted for a moment.

He grinned.

Barry parked in front of a faded yellow house with peeling green shutters and a yard that was more dirt and weeds than lawn.

"I'm lucky to find a parking spot. Looks like they have a crowd in there."

They walked along the driveway. The neighbor's dog lifted his head, looked, and went back to sleep on his blanket.

Barry tilted his head toward the dog. "Eee-e-e. Maybe he's too cold to bark."

"It's so like you to think about the cold dog." Barry had always been good with animals and children.

He raised his nose. "Someone is making fry bread. Reminds me of my mom's house. Her kitchen always smelled so good." They sniffed the familiar aroma filling the air.

He sighed and took her arm. "You okay?"

She didn't answer. Instead, she hung her head and looked at her shoes. They climbed up the three stairs to Gina's last address. It was less than twenty-four hours since Gina had died. Sunny needed to find out exactly what had happened. She just couldn't accept suicide, not for Gina. She didn't know when she had decided this, but she had. Despite the cold desert air, her hands were wet with perspiration.

She took a deep breath, braced herself, and then rang the bell. The door opened. "Gerald!" she gasped and stammered. "Of all people. What a. . . a . . . surprise."

The years had treated him well. Silver threads flowed through his short black hair. A dark green turtleneck complemented his olive skin; gray slacks hung nicely on his hips. His waistline, in her opinion, indicated a few too many beers. She'd been engaged to him over twenty years ago, before Barry. Panic stirred in her stomach and floated up her throat. Her body tensed.

Her face felt heated as she introduced the two men. "This is my husband, Barry Davis."

Gerald shook his hand and leaned down to give her a polite hug. "It's been a long time," he whispered in her ear.

She hesitated, hoping he couldn't feel her heart beating like a tribal drum. After the usual pleasantries, Gerald led them through the house.

Barry touched her arm, looking at her with eyebrows raised. "And?"

Her face felt frozen in a smile. "No big deal. I knew him long before I met you."

Sunny nodded to people she knew. A few gathered around Gina's half sister, Eva. She seemed shorter and heavier than Sunny remembered. Her bobbed hair shone like patent leather.

With a new interest and uneasiness she stared at Eva. She'd never trusted the woman, who was sneaky . . . and mean-spirited. When Eva pointed to the ceiling Sunny's eyes followed; she sucked in a breath. Her mouth gaped, and she stared in horror at the small pieces of flesh and splatters of blood. A few long black hairs clung to the cottage-cheese ceiling. Eva showed it off like it could be squashed bugs, seemingly unmoved by it all. She gave Sunny a smirk and a low "Humph."

"My God!" Sunny grabbed her stomach. Her lips twisted in repulsion, her eyes narrowed.

"What the hell?" Barry murmured.

"That turned my stomach upside down," Sunny said. "She's Gina's half sister, such a bitch we call her Evil Eva."

Barry shook his head. "What's wrong with her?"

"I hope it's because she's in shock," Sunny hissed under her breath.

"I think it's 'cause she's nuts." He made his way into the kitchen where the men were gathered.

Sunny walked around the living room. It had a familiar feel, as if frozen in the 1960s. In the corner sat an antique rocker. When she walked by she couldn't help reaching out to touch the apple-green-and-orange paisley print upholstery. A threadbare matching ottoman stood alone.

She looked across the large room at the brown love seat, the same one she and Gina had sat on many times. As she stood by the wall and listened, she imagined she heard Gina laughing. Sunny remembered when they had gossiped about Maggie, the old drunk down the street who chased them whenever they walked past her yard.

The memory made her smile. She leaned against the wall and gasped, then backed away. Someone had tried to wash the spattered blood off the wall, leaving pinkish-brown streaks. Regaining her composure, she moved away and walked around.

A quilt covered the other sofa. Her first thought was that the couch was shabby and torn. Taking another look, she saw the quilt had been pulled back to reveal the large dark blood stain that ran along the back and over the side.

The worn avocado shag carpet clashed with a dark blotch that had dripped beneath the couch. It smelled like death, and felt to her as if the blood had dried in midair. *I feel like I'm in the House of Terror.*

Realizing the horror of her thought, she wandered through the large living room to look for Jesse. She noticed the basketball-size hole in the television screen. "Did Gina take a practice shot?"

On the coffee table, ashtrays overflowed with bent cigarette butts, and ashes heaped up like a volcano. The odor of stale, burnt tobacco rose from the table. A lump stuck in her throat. She swallowed hard.

"Hi, Sunny." The familiar voice was almost a whisper.

Startled, she turned and found herself face-to-face with Jesse. They exchanged a quick awkward hug.

Still handsome, the sun lines around his eyes and scruffy beard gave him a weathered look. Long black braids hung over his shoulders. His Marine-like posture made his six-foot stature even more impressive.

"Will you please tell Eva to stop the show-and-tell? Now! Do you see what she's showing them? What the hell is wrong with her?"

"Eva, knock it off!" he shouted across the room.

His sister-in-law shot him a defiant look, then a condescending smile. She stopped and shrugged.

Watchful, Sunny's gaze flitted around the room. "I'm so sorry about Gina. Let me know if I can do anything. But right now, I need to know everything: the how and why."

Glancing at the roomful of people, Jesse took her elbow and guided her toward the bedroom. "We can talk in there."

When they walked past the kitchen, she saw empty Coors cans on the counter and piled in the sink. The air was dense with the yeasty tang of stale beer, which had spilled on the floor and mixed with dirt brought in on shoes and boots, smearing muddy footprints across the linoleum.

Barry stood in the corner holding a coffee cup while he talked with Gerald and another man. Her heart skipped a beat. She hoped they weren't talking about her. She caught her husband's attention, motioned toward the bedroom, and mouthed, *I'll be right back.*

In the bedroom, at the sight of Gina's photo on the dresser, she choked back a sob. The picture showed a woman turned sideways, her face toward the sky, with flawless dark olive skin. Her hair swirled in the air, caught by a breeze.

Sunny's chest was tight, her head heavy. Torment consumed her. On display around the room were pictures of Gina's three boys, the oldest, twelve-year-old Tommy, and the two younger ones—Jesse's—Martin and Patrick.

Sunny snatched up a marble off the dresser and rolled it in her hand. "Where are the boys?"

"My mom took them. She's going to keep them with her. It's too much for them. They're the ones who found her. They were playing outside."

"What? Oh my God!" She covered her face. Sunny's heart felt like glass shattered into tiny pieces. She dropped onto the bed. "Gina was crazy about her children. I can't imagine she would kill herself, especially with them in the front yard."

She stared at Jesse's face. The muscle in his jaw twitched as she sat across from him. They were seated on the edge of the bed when he started to say something. She jumped to her feet and walked over to a small table and grabbed up the brown box with an advertisement for gun shells. She picked it up. "What's this?"

"I keep my pistol in it. After she shot herself, I buried it out in the field."

"What!" Her face twisted in disbelief. "Why?"

He rubbed the back of his neck. "I don't know. I wasn't thinking."

She walked to the window and looked at the tall weeds behind the house before giving her attention back to Jesse. "Why didn't the police take it? Don't they need it for evidence?"

"Gina used my twenty-two rifle. The pistol was under a board in the closet. Maybe, because it was a suicide, the cops didn't look there. I took it out after they left."

His knee was bouncing. "I wasn't thinking straight."

"What the hell happened here anyway? This is crazy. Things don't make sense." She rubbed her forehead. "I just talked to her a few days ago. Was she upset? Was she drunk? Did you guys fight?"

He didn't answer her last question. "Gina was upset after she called you. She started to cry, ran to the bedroom, and slammed the door. Something hit the wall and broke. What happened between you two?"

She looked down at her lap, crossed and uncrossed her hands. Her stomach had a lead ball in it. "It was . . . a huge blow-up."

His jaw dropped. "What? Why?" He pushed one of his braids behind his shoulder. "You two were like family friends forever."

[26]

Pacing, she picked up a pack of cigarettes, tapping out one for herself. *Should I say something now or keep quiet?* Anger churned though her body.

She took a deep breath. "I can't keep it to myself any longer. Gina accused me of knowing you and Rita were having an affair. Why would she think that, Jesse? She was talking divorce."

He flicked his lighter and watched her lean toward the flame. His shoulders lowered as he looked away. "Who knows where she got her crazy ideas?"

Sunny inhaled, then blew the smoke out. "When I said I didn't know about anything like that she called me a lying bitch. She said, 'Eva knows.' Then I got mad. We called each other some choice names. She said, 'I can't believe my two best friends would stab me in the back.'"

His eyes widened. "I don't get it."

She took another drag. "She knows us. We've always been there for her. How could she think that? I told her she could keep her lying, troublemaking sister to herself. And I said I didn't want her in my life anymore. When I said, 'Don't call me again,' she hung up on me."

Tears welled in Sunny's eyes. "I should have been calmer and more understanding. I've done social work for years. I've dealt with people's emotions every day, for God's sake. Now I've lost my best friend, and it can never be fixed." Her lips quivered. "I pray that wasn't what sent her over the edge."

Elbows on his knees, he hung his head and stared at the carpet.

Did Jesse's face show any signs of deceit? She couldn't tell. His face was free of emotion. "Why don't you answer my question? Did you have an argument? Were you seeing someone else?" Her voice rose as she went for the ashtray. "Why did she think you were cheating on her?"

His hands trembled as he shoved the sleeves on his sweater up. "Now you sound like Gina."

Sunny's eyes tracked his gesture. "Rita doesn't know about Gina's suspicions. So it's all on you, Jesse. I want the truth. Did she confuse Rita with some other woman?" Sunny took in a breath. "What the hell is going on with you?"

He avoided direct eye contact. "I don't know where she got such a crazy idea."

"Maybe it's not so crazy. You collect women like a black suit collects dandruff."

"Eee-ee. That's cold. Yeah, I care a lot about your daughter. I used to tease Rita a lot. I'd say Gina and I were going to wait for Rita to grow up and catch up to us. But I was kidding. Gina knew that, even she got a kick out of teasing Rita. She loved Rita."

She scanned Jesse for some sign of guilt. "Humph."

"I have a feeling Eva started the rumor. Sounds like her," he said. "She was always telling Gina I messed around with this woman or that one. She's jealous and a troublemaker. She's like a pesky gnat."

"Or a rattlesnake," Sunny murmured. She looked at her nails as her cigarette burned itself out. "Gina said Eva was the one who told her. I know one thing; my daughter wouldn't do that to Gina, not with you of all people."

She took a deep breath. "Now you listen to me. I haven't told Rita about any of this. Don't you say anything. I'll tell her myself." Sunny rolled her shoulders waiting for the weight to lift. But the guilt over her part in the call last week kept it from happening. She had to ask herself if what she said was the reason Gina killed herself? A suspicion niggled at the back of her mind.

A loud knock on the bedroom door startled Sunny. The door opened and Eva barged in without waiting to be invited. A cloud of dime-store perfume filled the room. Sunny sneezed and whispered to Jesse, "Does she bathe in that stuff?"

Eva gave him a quick smile and looked Sunny up and down. "Rita's here . . . with some guy," she snarled and left, mumbling to herself.

Rita came in, her eyes watery. A man followed behind as she gave her mother a hug. She crossed over to Jesse and did the same. In Sunny's opinion, their embrace lasted a little too long. He too, seemed moved, his cheek twitched, and the vein throbbed in his temple, he dropped his arms to his side.

This left Sunny wondering. She had hoped for a clear signal that they were not involved, which she didn't get. But how could she doubt her only daughter? Rita wasn't that kind of girl . . . or friend.

"What's up with Evil Eva?" asked Rita.

Sunny rolled her eyes. "Who knows? Just being her usual bitchy self."

Rita pulled at the arm of the young man beside her. "Mom, Jesse, this is Lee."

"Hello," Sunny and Jesse said.

Lee was in his early twenties, like Rita, with short dark auburn hair, mustache, and eyebrows. He reminded Sunny of a cop: like the ones she dealt with at work. They were cut from the same pattern, stocky, arrogant, and forceful. He stood a good seven or eight inches taller than Rita. He shook hands with Sunny and offered his hand to Jesse, who turned away and didn't acknowledge him.

What was up with Jesse? Why was he so rude? Did he care more about Rita than he let on?

Rita also noticed his behavior and scowled at him. With a shaken voice, Rita asked, "What the heck happened here? That sofa made me sick to my stomach."

"I was just going to explain to your mom what I know. Have a seat." Jesse waved his index finger in the air at Lee. "There's a chair in the corner."

Lee shook his head. "No thanks. I'll go to the kitchen and get something to drink. You have a lot to talk about." He bent and kissed Rita. Jesse half closed his eyes and crinkled his nose.

Sunny noticed but said nothing.

A little later, the creak of the bedroom door stopped the conversation as everyone turned toward it. Barry came in. "Sorry to interrupt." He took a drag from his cigarette and looked at Sunny. "I'm going to see if I can get the car fixed before they close."

"They don't fix cars in the bar, you know."

He brushed her remark aside. "I'll be back," he said and walked out.

Rita moved over to the dresser and picked up a picture of her and Gina. There was a large diagonal crack on the glass from corner to corner. "What happened here?"

"Gina got mad and threw it at the wall last week," said Jesse.

Sunny felt her cheeks flush and looked away. *Gina must've been really upset with me.*

Rita stared at the photograph. In it she stood beside Gina. Rita was a petite girl, with shoulder-length dark cinnamon hair, squinting at the sun and smiling for the camera. She wiped her eyes. "I remember the day these pictures were taken. We had so much fun."

Sunny looked at her daughter and then strolled over to a chair, struggling to swallow the lump in her throat. *Oh God, don't let me be responsible for Gina's death.*

Rita sat on the bed and hugged the picture close to her chest, head down, looking up at Jesse under her lashes. "It makes me feel close to her."

"Sure."

"Earlier that day, you and Gina argued right here in the bedroom." She patted the bed. "You pushed her on top of this bed. Right?"

"Yeah." Jesse's eyebrows drew together as he shifted positions.

"Gina jumped back up and said, 'See I'm just like a rubber ball. I keep bouncing back.' It's when you grabbed her by the shoulders and shoved her to the floor."

Sunny couldn't believe what she heard and interrupted, "You shoved her to the floor? Jesse, what the hell is the matter with you?"

"Wait, Mom." Rita turned and looked again at Jesse. "When you shoved her to the floor, you said, 'Bounce back, now, bitch.' Gina sat and rubbed her butt. You both started to laugh and you two made up."

Jesse smiled and rubbed the back of his neck.

"Remember?"

He closed his eyes. "Uh-huh."

Rita's chin shuddered. "Gina and I cracked up over that story. It was a day of fun." Tears blurred her vision.

Sunny sat back in her chair and adjusted the cushion.

Jesse put his arm around Rita's shoulder as she shivered. "I'm so sorry I did that."

CHAPTER EIGHT

Jesse rubbed his hand down his pants leg. "I'll tell you what I know. On Sunday some coworkers and friends came over for a party. They stayed here all day. This one guy, his name is Victor, he works with Gina. He wasn't here at the party, but she acted different after she talked to him. I don't know what was going on 'cause he kept calling."

Sunny's mouth hardened. "Like all the times you call Rita?"

"Mom!" Her daughter glared at her, then turned to Jesse.

He ignored them. "I asked Gina what was going on with this guy, Victor, and she got mad. Said he's a friend. They talk about work. Eva asked her about him and Gina told her it was none of her damn business. Anyway, I hung around awhile. All of us were drinking and acting Indian. You know how it goes, telling stories, laughing, putting each other down, making fun of each other."

Sunny had forgotten the old term "acting Indian." It had been a long time since she had been to the rez.

"Yeah, it's what we always do." Rita looked down at her feet.

He laced his fingers together. "Eva gave her too much booze. When Gina said no, Eva teased her in front of everyone and dared her to have another drink, so she did. And then another. I couldn't talk to Gina when she was drinking and in one of her moods. I left and walked down the road to visit my cousin, Louis. You know him. We call him Moochie."

Sunny stared at him. "You went off and left the boys here with a bunch of drunks?"

"They were playing outside with the neighbor kids." He twisted his wedding ring.

"Moochie. Why do I know that name? There's something about you and him, but it's not coming to me right now. . . . Anyway, you're telling us you stayed at his place all day and left everyone partying at your house so they could tear it up?"

He looked out the window and didn't respond.

Rita brushed her hair out of her face. "Mom, let him finish."

His eyes moved back and forth at them and repeated, "I got mad and took off. Like I said, I left the boys outside with their friends."

"Okay, so you left. We get it. What else?" Sunny asked.

"About four o'clock, Frank Allen came to get me. That's when he told me what happened. Frank went inside the house after he learned about Gina and called the police. Helen called my mom. Mom told her I might be at Moochie's. Well, when I heard I ran back to the house. The tribal police and BIA were here. The ambulance came and parked outside as I ran up on the porch."

Rita's perfectly arched brows rose. "How did Frank know about Gina?"

"When the boys found her they ran over to Frank's house."

Rita's hand flew to her throat. "Oh my God!"

Sunny's eyes widened and her mouth dropped open. "No!"

Jesse sucked in a long breath. "Some cop stopped me at the front door. Other officers were securing the scene, putting yellow tape all around the house and yard. Everything was moving too fast. I couldn't get inside."

Jesse eyed her with a downturned mouth. "The police kept me from going to her. I hollered, 'It's my wife in there.' They questioned me about what went on at the house earlier and where I was, and what I was doing. I shouted questions back at them at the same time.

"I could see Gina on the couch. Her hair hung over the side with blood splattered all over the floor and wall. A couple of BIA agents were kneeling beside her.

"They were all talking at once. When they saw me the house got quiet. Everyone who'd been at the party was gone, including Eva. Later, the guys from the ambulance took her off the couch, put her on the gurney, and covered her. My rifle lay on the living room floor. One of the tribal cops told me he believed Gina had stuck the rifle under her chin and shot herself."

Sunny shoved her hands between her knees to keep them from shaking. Beads of sweat formed on Jesse's forehead.

Rita's eyes were closed. Her shoulders drooped as she bit her lower lip and shook her head from side to side.

"Why? Why'd she do it?" Sunny felt sick to her stomach. She couldn't think straight. Acid rose in her throat. She focused her attention on the garbage truck out the window.

"I don't know. I couldn't believe what I saw. It seemed like a frigging nightmare. Everything moved in slow motion."

Rita looked at the ceiling, her face wet with tears. She whispered, "What about the boys?"

"I could see them out in the yard, crying. One of the neighbor's older girls wrapped her arms around Tommy. Frank and his wife took the younger two. I tried to get to them, but the police were in my face. I couldn't understand what had happened. I was in a daze."

Jesse crossed over to the table and picked up a cigarette pack. Hands shaking, he took one for himself and offered one to Sunny.

"No thanks," she said, though she desperately wanted one.

His hand shook as he leaned against the dresser. "The kids heard the shot and ran into the house. They found her and rushed over to Frank's. Thank goodness he was home." Jesse looked around the room as he shook his head.

"I can't believe she would do it with the boys right outside," Sunny said. "That doesn't sound like her. Not when it came to them."

He scratched at his neck, not looking at them. "Maybe she was so pissed off or drunk she forgot they were outside."

"I can't believe it either," Rita said.

Sunny picked up Gina's bracelet off the nightstand. It felt cold as a steel blade. She thought, Gina is the same way now. She got more than a prickly neck; she got a powerful vision. It was so overwhelming it took over her sight and hearing. For a moment, she left her reflection behind, looked through the window, watched Gina's youngest son, Patrick, standing, screaming bloody murder. She felt the boys' pain and confusion when they discovered their mother.

Tommy had blood on his hands. He pushed on his mother, trying to revive her, while the middle boy ran off screaming. Tommy went pale, rubbing his arms absently. He turned and looked through the window at his brother, Patrick, frozen in one spot in the yard, choking on his sobs. She was sure the whole thing took only a few seconds, but it was so powerful she felt drained.

She'd never had this happen before, an image so strong and painful. She recoiled and pulled herself out of the vision.

Back in Gina's bedroom everyone was staring at her. The image gradually faded and the grinding, clattering garbage truck across the street returned her to normal consciousness.

Rita had moved from the bed to the corner chair and fixed her gaze at her mother.

Sunny wished it had lasted longer. If she could have controlled it, she might have picked up more clues or seen what actually happened. Anger rose in her chest. She had no knowledge how to handle it or what to do with this vision. If only she could have found out Gina's reason, *if* she did it.

She heard Jesse say, "What with the empty lot between our house and theirs, and the loud music, the Allens told the police they didn't hear anything. They'd gone shopping and just got home when the boys hollered and banged on their front door. The neighbors on the other side were not home."

Sunny's eyes widened. Sadness overwhelmed her. "Oh God! What's this going to do to the boys?" Jesse's eyes darted around the room and Sunny wondered why beads of sweat were popping out along his hairline.

"The tribal police were called. It took 'em only a few minutes to get here."

Queasiness rolled from Sunny's stomach to her throat. She excused herself, hurried into the bathroom, put the toilet seat up, and hurled. Then she sat with her knees on the floor and rested to regain her composure.

Seeing a wastebasket wedged behind the porcelain sink, a certain feeling caused her to press her two fingers against her hot neck, and then her stomach knotted up again. Her gaze was drawn again to the basket.

Sunny bumped the wastebasket with her leg and tiny pieces of pink paper fell from a rumpled tissue. Curious, she gathered them up and put them in her pocket. Once again her neck grew warm. Searching in the medicine cabinet for something for her stomach, she was surprised to see prescription sleeping pills. *This makes no sense, with these in the cabinet, why would she use a gun, especially a rifle? She could have gone out peacefully instead of taking a violent way.* She looked up at the wall in the bathroom. Pictures of Gina's children lined the shelves on the wall unit.

Returning to the bedroom, she slipped her hand inside her pocket and felt the torn pieces. Her fingers tingled. She gave them a little pat, uncertain why she'd bothered to pick them up, or why they gave her a strong reaction.

She wasn't used to having visions. She knew she had psychic abilities, like her grandmother, but never visions. Those confused her. Sunny joined the others again in the bedroom.

Jesse looked at her. "Are you all right? Do you want to hear the rest?"

Sunny rolled her eyes. Her chin quivered. "Yes, of course. Keep talking. I didn't mean to interrupt."

"Rita, is it too much for you?" he asked.

She repositioned herself in the chair. "Yes, but I need to hear it."

He rubbed the back of his neck. Sunny wondered if it was hard for him to tell about what had happened, or if this is what he did when he was nervous. *What does he know?*

"Well, Eva told the cops that Gina took the rifle and ordered everyone out of the house." His hand shook as he took a drag.

"I can't understand why she'd have a gun. She never wanted to touch one," said Rita. "Maybe someone else got it out."

"Her glasses are on the kitchen counter. She was blind without them," added Sunny. "Did you put them there?"

"No, I guess it's where she left them when she wrote me a note. The letter was on the table next to her."

"Why use a rifle when there were sleeping pills in the medicine cabinet? She always said she couldn't tolerate pain," Sunny said. "And you had a handgun in the closet. It doesn't make sense."

"I don't know." With short jerky movements, he stubbed out his cigarette. "I don't know." He changed the subject. "I'm sorry. You guys want something to drink? A beer maybe?"

"No, I quit," said Sunny. The front door opened and closed. She wondered if Gerald had left.

"Sorry, I forgot." He smiled at Rita. "What about you?"

"No thanks. When I'm all grown up, Mom stops drinking," Rita complained.

Sunny scowled at her. She wanted to focus on the facts around Gina's suicide, rather than her own problems.

"What's this about a letter?" Rita asked Jesse. "You said she wrote you one. Did the police ask if she left one?"

"They'd found her note before I got here." Jesse frowned. "They were the ones who showed it to me."

Changing her mind about the cigarette, Sunny walked over to the table and tapped one out while he talked. Lighting it, she looked Jesse in the eyes, a mixture of sympathy and disgust going through her. "Tell us about the note." She blew out her smoke.

"Gina said, 'I can't live like this anymore.' With me, she meant. She was tired of the drinking and fighting. All she wanted was to be left alone and in peace." He paced around the room. "The rest of the note said, 'If this is the only way to get peace, then it's what I'm going to do.'"

"She didn't say anything about the kids?"

He rolled his tongue inside his cheek. His voice rose. "No. I'm not a mind reader. I can't tell you what she was thinking."

Sunny stood with her back against the wall and exhaled smoke, taken aback by his abruptness. "No, something's not right here. Gina couldn't even talk without mentioning the kids." She looked at him. His jaw twitched. *Is he upset or is this talk making him nervous? Is he hiding anything? What about those papers I found? Could Gina have written a practice letter?*

Could the boys have written a letter? I remember Gina saying they had done that before, like when they wanted to go to Circus Circus for Christmas and their birthdays. In fact, she used to call and read them to me. These questions hung in the air like her cigarette smoke. She shuddered. *I can't take this. My brain is on overload.*

Rita's boyfriend, Lee, tapped on the bedroom door and came in. "I have to go to work. I'm on the late shift."

Rita turned to her mother. "You guys want to stay at my place tonight?"

"No, you two go on. We've got a room at Super 8. Room 5."

Sunny watched from the bedroom as Rita and her boyfriend passed Eva in the hall. Everyone avoided eye contact.

Eva's perfume announced her arrival before she came through the bedroom door. Sunny coughed into her fist. Eva shot daggers at her, then smiled sweetly at Jesse.

"The mortuary called," Eva said in a monotone. "Gina will be ready for viewing in the morning. I already told your daughter and that guy she's got with her." She turned back and dipped a shoulder flirtatiously at Jesse, then sauntered out.

Sunny grabbed her purse and told Jesse good night. Hearing about the mortuary was too much for her. She just wanted out of there and headed toward the front door to meet Barry, who waited in the hallway. He leaned toward her ear. "Remind me to tell you what I found out."

They were the last to leave. Sunny had hoped she'd receive a sign, another vision or a prickle on her neck, but nothing happened. She didn't know what to make of the vision she'd had of Gina's boys. A thought occurred to her: her vision didn't show any images of Gina in the house, or with the gun.

Why not?

CHAPTER NINE

MONDAY NIGHT

Exhausted, Sunny and Barry picked up takeout at the Chinese restaurant near their motel. Moments passed as they ate silently. Sunny's stomach was so upset she hardly tasted the noodles.

Barry took a bite of fried rice. "Remember, I wanted to tell you something?"

She fumbled with her chopsticks. "Yeah, what is it?"

"I talked to this guy in the kitchen, Gerald. You know, your ex?" He grinned. "He was at the party."

She hoped Gerald hadn't said anything about them being engaged. That was a long time ago, and she didn't want Barry to know anything about him, and vice versa, but she had to say something.

"I was surprised," she finally answered. "Why was he there?"

"He and Eva are dating."

Sunny almost dropped her chopsticks. "What? Oh no. Not her." She stuck out her tongue. "Yuck."

"Hmm, jealous?" he teased.

"Stop it. Just tell me what he said."

"He said that Gina and Eva got into a big argument about Jesse. After a screaming match, Eva told her, 'You're lucky to have him.' Gina said, 'He's a liar and a cheat. If you want him, he's all yours. I don't care anymore. There's someone else who cares about me and wants to help me and the boys.'"

"Oh, wow. Maybe she was serious about leaving him for this guy at work. None of us thought she'd do it."

"That's not all. Here's the ass-kicker. Before he left, Jesse said something to her. Gerald told me he couldn't hear it, but he saw Jesse's hands draw into fists."

"He hit her?"

Barry shook his head. "No. Gerald said she hollered, 'Take your lying, cheating-ass temper and get out of here.' Then Jesse shouted back, 'I don't need you, bitch. You need me, and don't forget it.'

"At least, that's what your ex told me."

Sunny looked up from her food. "This is so weird. Jesse said he didn't talk to Gina because she was drunk. Why does he act like nothing happened between them?"

Barry gathered their Chinese restaurant food containers and stacked them on the nightstand. "Obviously, something did. Your ex went on to say Jesse slammed the door and left. Gina screamed, 'It's my turn now,' and threw an ashtray across the living room. It hit the television."

"That explains the hole in the screen. By the way, my ex has a name. Gerald. It was a long, long time ago, so get over it. Anything else?"

He looked at her. "No, I don't think so." He broke open his fortune cookie and crunched bits of it in his mouth.

She took a strand of her hair and swiped it across her mouth. "They sound like us."

Barry stood and slowly exhaled. "Yeah, I know, except you don't break things." He winked at her and dumped their takeout boxes in the trash. "I'm going to take a shower."

She got out her notebook to record and analyze everything she'd seen and heard. She wondered why Jesse lied, and if it was he who was the cause of Gina's suicide. Or if it could have been her conversation with Gina. Or if it might be something else entirely.

Why did Jesse say he didn't talk to Gina before he left the house?

A few minutes later she slipped into her nightgown and got under the covers. The motel room was small, with spare furnishings, but clean and comfortable. Barry came out of the shower, a towel around his waist, and stood at the sink outside the bathroom. He brushed his teeth as she watched appreciatively.

His firm biceps were proof he pumped iron on a regular basis. With such a strict regimen, she couldn't understand why he drank like he did. "If only he'd quit drinking," she whispered. "Our life would be great."

He caught her gaze in the mirror and turned to smile at her, his teeth so white and shiny it looked like he'd applied Vaseline. Her cheeks felt hot and tingly. The feeling made her think of the color of rosé wine and even though she'd stopped drinking she hadn't stopped wanting a drink to calm her nerves. But then again, she'd been a disaster at trying to stop smoking. She felt divided, wanting her addictions, wanting to be free of them. Wanting her husband, wanting to be free of him.

Barry dropped his towel and crawled into bed next to her. She gave in, loving the masculine blend of Zest and Old Spice. He pulled her to him for a deep kiss. She felt the hardness of his body and tasted the freshness of toothpaste.

With one hand he lifted her nightgown over her head and in one movement had slipped off her panties. He withdrew his lips from hers and slowly moved his mouth from her neck down to nibble her breast. She ran one hand though his hair and wrapped the other around his manness. He spooned up behind her, one hand cupping her breast.

The shrill ring of the phone made them jump.

"Damn," they said in unison.

Out of breath, Barry picked up. "Okay, hold on a minute." Obviously irritated, he handed it over to her, mumbling into the receiver. "Here's your mom."

Sunny talked to her daughter for a few minutes and then hung up. "Rita wants to meet us at the coffee shop across from the mortuary so we can go in to the viewing together."

The mood broken, they shared a few moments of talking before he turned over and went to sleep. Sunny lay awake considering her feelings for Barry. She couldn't handle his drinking anymore. They were talking divorce, yet her body wanted him. Her heart wanted him. *Well, it has to go on the back burner for now.* But she knew she couldn't ignore her feelings forever, good or bad, right or wrong. It was hard when the love was still there.

CHAPTER TEN

TUESDAY MORNING

Up and out early, they met Rita at Vara's Coffee Shop on Becker and Ninth, and maneuvered their way through a collection of booths and tables. Smells of bacon and coffee lingered in the air.

Rita stood and gave each a hug. Sunny hung her coat on the back of her chair and they ordered from the menu. After the waitress brought their breakfast, Sunny spoke. "Rita, when's the last time you talked to Gina?"

Rita cut into her eggs. "Quite a while ago. She told me she wanted to take the kids and move in with a guy she worked with. She talked a lot about him, said he was so nice. I thought it was just a crush. She was always threatening to leave Jesse, so I didn't believe her."

"Well, I felt the same way. Gina'd get mad at Jesse and say she was moving out. I didn't think she meant it either."

Barry's gaze bounced back and forth from Sunny to her daughter as he reached for the little container of grape jelly.

"A couple of weeks before Gina died, she started acting different towards me." Rita mashed her eggs and potatoes. "She didn't call me. And when I called her, she made excuses to hang up."

Barry finished his breakfast and washed it down with coffee.

Sunny studied her daughter's face and thought for a long moment. She didn't know if now was the right time, but before she could stop herself she blurted it out. "Maybe it had to do with our argument."

Rita's forehead wrinkled in a puzzled expression.

Sunny went on. "Eva told Gina a terrible thing."

Rita's lips parted and her eyebrows inched upward. "What are you talking about?"

"She told Gina that you and Jesse were sleeping together."

Barry smacked his mug down, causing coffee to slosh out on the table. "What?"

"That's crazy." Rita picked up her muffin and waved it in the air. "Jesse and I are old friends, nothing else. Gina had met Lee and knew I cared about him." Her voice rose.

Her mother put her finger to her lips. "Shhh." She looked around. "The last time I talked to Gina was our big argument. Gina told me, 'I can't believe you and Rita could stab me in the back.' She said I knew all about it and didn't do anything to stop you. I told her it wasn't true. I reminded her that you could never do anything to ruin your friendship, and she knew it. If she believed her crazy sister over you or me, then I didn't want her for a friend. When I said that, it really upset her."

Rita sipped her coffee. "We've always been there for her."

"I told her that. It was terrible. I should have called her back and made her listen."

"How come I never knew about your fight with Gina?" asked Barry.

"You didn't tell me what bar you'd be at."

He exhaled, his chest deflating. "Cheap shot."

Rita's face crumbled like the muffin on her plate. "How could Gina think that about me?" She stood abruptly and made a beeline to the ladies' room.

"Aren't you going after her?" he asked.

"No, she needs time alone." She couldn't eat any more.

Barry had no problem eating off of Sunny's plate. After he finished he paid the check. In the lobby they waited for Rita, then walked out into the cold air and crossed the street to the funeral home.

CHAPTER ELEVEN

Sunny felt sick. She hoped to have another vision but had no idea what she'd do with it. Nothing was making sense. Nothing at all.

The bone-chilling wind picked up, whipping at their hair and coats. Sunny pulled the scarf tighter around her neck. Silently, they walked up the steps. Barry pushed open the tall heavy Spanish-style wooden door. Carnations, gladiolas, and other floral fragrances hit Sunny's nostrils. The silence was intimidating. They passed small rooms to the left, larger ones to the right. They tiptoed to the bookstand in the corridor, which indicated Gina's viewing was in the second vestibule on the right.

"Is it okay if I go in alone first?" Rita asked.

"Go ahead, we'll wait here." They watched her walk along the hallway and hesitate at the door. She took out a handkerchief and went in.

Sunny eased herself into a fabric-covered chair and waited. Her eyes focused on the plants and flowers in the foyer. The interior reminded her of an old Victorian home. The walls were cream colored with a chair rail of dark wood molding. Mahogany framed the doors. Wainscot, the color of bittersweet chocolate, finished the room. The inside looked surprisingly different from what the plain gray stucco exterior suggested.

Sunny had always thought of Gina as her older daughter and best friend rolled into one. Her mouth felt dry. She dug in her purse for a stick of gum. Her hands shook as she took her time unwrapping the paper and foil. While she waited she watched people come out from other rooms dabbing their eyes and hanging onto each other.

Her thoughts went to her daughter. "Barry, will you check on Rita, please? Then we'll go in."

A few minutes later, he came out with his arm around Rita's waist. She went to Sunny, wrapped her arms around her neck and sobbed.

"Oh my God, Mom, this isn't real. It can't be. Why? Why did she do it?"

"I don't know, I just don't know." There was nothing Sunny could do but hold her daughter close, their feelings blending in mutual sorrow.

Rita composed herself and Sunny helped her to a chair. She and Barry went in.

In the hallway, she began to tremble. Barry grabbed her and held her close. Their footsteps on the hardwood floor made a sorrowful sound. They stopped outside the door and signed the guest book. Their names were not the first. Victor John, the man Gina was supposedly leaving Jesse for, had left his signature.

Sunny opened the door and approached the walnut casket, inhaling the sweet fragrance of the many bouquets surrounding it. She placed her hands over her mouth. She moaned as she looked in. A few pieces of black wig were woven in to cover the part of her head that was blown away. Gina's lashes lay on her cheeks like butterfly wings.

"They did a great job. She looks beautiful," remarked Barry.

Taking a second look at the way Gina was dressed, Sunny was paralyzed by anger. "What the hell?! They've got her in a motel maid's uniform."

The smock was covered with blue and white flowers. It had short sleeves, and a zipper up the front, with a pocket on each side. It wasn't right for a funeral. And it definitely wasn't right for Gina. Sunny's eyes were drawn to her left wrist.

"What's this?" Sunny's stomach reacted. The top layer of skin was rubbed off. Sunny pointed to it. "It looks like someone gave her a horrible Indian burn. See there?"

The mortician had tried to hide it with cosmetics, as he had the spot beneath her chin. Sunny's neck prickled and her stomach knotted up. She was unable to breathe.

Barry also took notice and scoffed. "Ask Jesse."

"You better believe it. I want to know how that happened to her arm. And I want to know why the maid's outfit."

Her husband stepped out and called Rita in. Mother and daughter stood side by side to take a last look at their friend. They said silent prayers of goodbye, each in her own way. They held each other, sharing their pain and sadness. Sunny needed to leave the funeral home and get some air.

On the way out they ran into Eva. Rita tightened her jaw and looked at Eva like she was something to scrape off the bottom of her shoe.

Sunny put her hand out and abruptly stopped Eva. "Why is Gina dressed in a maid's uniform?" she demanded.

"That's what Jesse wanted."

"She'd hate it. I'll buy her something pretty."

"No, you won't. That's what she's going to be buried in," Eva declared. "Now get out of my way."

Rita stepped closer, a cat with its back up. "I see you've turned your dial to hate."

Barry pulled Rita back and placed his hand on Sunny's arm to calm both of them. They stared at Eva like she might be crazy, which Sunny believed to be true.

CHAPTER TWELVE

Rita's driveway was unoccupied. Rita explained that her boyfriend was using her car again. Sunny could tell she was upset but said nothing. Rita brewed a fresh pot of coffee and served it with a plate of oatmeal raisin cookies. Sitting at the kitchen table, they talked about the events at the mortuary.

Barry added cream to his coffee until it was caramel colored. "Gina did look beautiful."

Both women agreed. "Yes, she did."

"It was awful to see her in that horrible getup, and the skin rubbed off her wrist," said Sunny. "To top it off, we had to run into Evil Eva."

"She makes my blood boil. Needs to get her ass kicked." Rita took a bite of cookie.

Barry reached for another cookie. "Wouldn't solve anything. It'd just make things worse."

Sunny added sugar to her cup, licked the spoon, and set it on the table. She wondered about Gina's wrist and why she'd had those feelings. She'd hoped for another vision; it was so confusing. She scooted her chair back. "I'm going to call Jesse. I can't stand to wait any longer. I want to know about Gina's wrist, and that stupid uniform they put on her."

She dialed his number. After several minutes he answered, out of breath.

"Jesse, it's me. Sunny."

"Oh, hi. I was getting in the car when I heard the phone ring. We're headed out to the rez to prepare the grave."

"When's the funeral?" she asked.

"Day after tomorrow. Louis, my cousin, and a couple of other family members are helping. So we should be ready by then. It's at the church on Green Valley Reservation. Thursday morning at ten."

"Good. We'll be there. Um, by the way, I don't remember Gina ever working as a motel maid."

"What?"

"You heard me, a motel maid."

"She didn't."

"Then why is she being buried in a maid's smock? It's terrible. I'll buy her something else."

"No, it's okay. Eva told me Gina liked it."

"Like hell. She told me it's what *you* wanted." Sunny snorted. "Eva must have bought it. Gina'd never wear something so ugly. She had better fashion sense."

"What difference does it make now?" said Jesse. "She's going to be in the ground. Who cares?"

"'Scuse me? Did I just hear what I think I heard? *Who cares?* Is that what you said? *Who cares?*"

"Huh?"

"Well, I care! That's who cares. And you should too. She was your wife! You should friggin' care! But since you don't, I'll take care of it. I'll get her something that won't embarrass her spirit if she's looking on at her own funeral."

"Nah, leave it alone, Sunny. Eva's in charge."

No, Eva's not in charge. I'm taking over!

Sunny was getting nowhere with Jesse. "Did you see her left wrist? It was an Indian burn, like someone twisted her arm."

"I never noticed. I haven't been to the mortuary yet. Anyway, I gotta go. I'll catch you later. Talk to Eva if there's anything you want to know."

"T' hell with Eva."

"Sunny, I have to go."

Sunny slammed down the receiver. "Asshole! This is a frigging nightmare. The more I talk to him, the worse it gets. He hasn't even gone to the mortuary. His whole attitude seems to be 'Who cares?'"

"Try to calm down, babe. There's nothing you can do about it."

"The hell there isn't. Just watch me."

She repeated her conversation with Jesse, then said, "I'm so mad I could spit nails. Rita, let's you and me go to Park Lane Mall first thing tomorrow and buy something nice for Gina. She is not going to her grave in something she wouldn't be caught dead in!"

"My mother the comedian," said Rita with a chuckle and a roll of the eyes.

Sunny grinned wryly and turned to her husband. "Barry, you've never lived on the reservation but, you know, when someone from the rez dies it's the family members who dig the grave."

"Sure, my grandparents and my father are buried in the Maidu cemetery, over by Quincy. It's up to my family to maintain it. Right?" He grabbed a beer from the refrigerator, sat back, and lit a cigarette.

Sunny shot him a pissed-off look but continued. "Yeah, Gina's family's reservation is about twenty miles from Reno."

Rita put another cookie on her plate. "Mom, I think Eva is up to something. She's always flirting with Jesse and trying to hang out with him. She even bought a silver Mustang to match his. I don't know if he feels the same, but with him, you never know. She was sneaking around and watching Gina and me all the time. I don't trust her."

"Me neither. She can be vicious." Sunny changed the subject. "At the funeral home, I saw in the guest book the first person to visit was Victor John. Isn't he the guy Gina was leaving Jesse for? Odd that he went to the mortuary, but Jesse didn't. Strange. I hope I get a chance to talk to him."

Rita finished her cookie and brushed a crumb off her mouth. "Good idea. He wasn't at the party, but maybe he knows something that might help us understand why this happened. Gina was always scared to leave Jesse. Maybe this guy was the reason she got so brave."

Sunny moved to the wall and turned up the heater. "I thought of something. It was when I finished college. Gina called and wanted to stay with us. Remember? She said Jesse was drunk and locked them out of the house. When she tried to get in, he hit her. She and her oldest boy, Tommy, ended up sleeping in an old junk car on their property."

Rita looked at Barry's long ash and pushed the ashtray in front of him. "I didn't pay much attention when it happened. I was young."

He put his cigarette out. "What I want to know is, if Jesse was abusing her, why didn't she call the police?"

Quickly looking at him, Sunny said, "Wouldn't do any good. Not in his territory. It was the Wentworth Reservation, where he grew up." She shrugged one shoulder. "The tribal police are all his good buddies."

Barry picked at the label on his bottled beer. "I don't see how they can look the other way."

"But they do." Rita's cat, Floyd, rubbed against her legs. She lifted him and stroked his silky fur. "They always do."

"Anyway, Gina got away. She ran a half mile to the store to call me," said Sunny. "Her lip was cut and she had blood all over. By the time I picked them up her eye was turning the color of eggplant and puffed up. She looked terrible."

"I was young but I remember when you brought them to the house. She held little Tommy in her arms. His hair was all matted and their clothes were filthy. They were a mess," Rita said.

"He didn't hit Tommy, did he?" asked Barry.

"No, Gina told me he never did. She and Tommy stayed with us for a few weeks. Jesse began to call. He finally convinced her to come back home. He promised he'd straighten up. What a joke! I didn't like him then; I don't like him now."

"I wish we could have talked her into leaving him for good," Rita said. "But Gina was love blind. She believed him, and gave birth to his two boys."

Her spirit sagging, Sunny said, "We can't change anything now." She shook her head sadly. "We better get going back to the motel. It's getting late."

"Mom, why don't you two stay here? I can go to Lee's apartment for a few days. I don't mind."

"I bet you don't." They grinned at each other.

Sunny turned back to Barry who seemed preoccupied. "Well, do you want to stay here?" She stared at him. "Is it okay with you?"

"Fine," He twirled his beer in his hands. The cold sweat from the bottle had made a ring on the tablecloth.

Rita packed some clothes and showed her mother where she kept the linens. "I'll need a ride. Lee has my car."

Barry said, "Sure. I'll drive you." Rita picked up Floyd, hugged him, and left with Barry.

The cat took over Sunny's lap. Eyebrows squeezed together, she shook her head in concentration. "What is it about his cousin, Louis? There's something I ought to be remembering. They call him Moochie, 'cause that's what he does. He mooches food, tools, money—whatever's moochable. Hence the name. I can't put my finger on it, and it's driving me crazy. Well, I better call work and let them know what's going on." She placed Floyd on the floor. He stiffened his legs, looked up and gave her a short angry *meow*, which made her laugh. Because of the thoughts that kept coming to her, she needed to get ahold of her supervisor, Carol.

Sunny explained some of what she'd learned and added, "It might take longer than I thought. I'm having strange feelings about this."

"Well, your instincts are usually right on. Go ahead, stay awhile and finish up with the loose ends," Carol said.

"Thanks." Sunny hung up.

By the time Barry returned, it was arranged for Sunny to stay in Reno to look into things. "Carol said they could handle everything for me. I have vacation time on the books," she relayed to Barry.

"Good. You know I'm leaving after the funeral. I assume you're staying?"

She nodded. "I want to poke around a little."

"I understand. That investigator's instinct is coming out in you."

"Maybe so. There are too many things out of order, and I feel I owe it to Gina."

Still somewhat upset with him, the words tumbled out. "You can go back to your bar buddies. Stay out all night without a nagging wife wondering where you are and who you're with. I won't have to see you hung over or smell your stinky booze."

He cleared his throat. "I don't want to leave you upset and here alone."

She could tell she'd hurt him. "I won't be alone. I have Rita. You know you clear your throat every time you get nervous. Are you lying to me about anything?"

"No, I'm not lying. I've never been with anyone else, if that's what you're suggesting." The veins in his neck bulged. He walked to the refrigerator and grabbed a soda. "I know you want a divorce, Sunny, but I don't. Because I drink doesn't mean I don't love you. It didn't bother you when we first met. You were right there beside me, chugging one for one."

Sunny's face felt flushed. "You're throwing over ten years ago in my face now? Okay, I got a little tipsy."

"A little tipsy? You were in the parking lot puking your guts out. I brought wet paper towels to clean you up. And if I remember right, you ruined your new dress."

"Yes, but I quit right after that, didn't I? I'm sick and tired of fighting about this all the time. It's always about the same thing. Your drinking."

"Sunny, stop pacing and sit, or stand still."

She leaned forward and gripped the edge of the table where he sat. "You're out with your buddies more than you're with me." Her eyes narrowed. "Even my friends say if you loved me you'd stop."

Barry jumped up, pounded his fist on the table and looked her in her eye. "I don't give a damn what your friends say. They're not paying our bills. It's not about your friends, relatives, or even Rita. It's only about us, you and me."

"Once the love is gone, Barry, I won't get it back. When I'm done, I'm done. I don't know what to do about the drinking anymore. I can't live like this. It brings back memories of me growing up. My dad was a sloppy drunk. I watched him fall flat on his face on the living room carpet, or sit in the rocker sobbing, and saying the same thing over and over again. I won't put up with it. I can't."

Still standing, he studied his hangnail.

"Are you even listening to me?" She hated when he tuned her out like that. "Do you hear me talking to you? Answer me! I hate that about you." Fists clinched, nails digging into her palm, she glared at him. Her voice reached a higher pitch. "Barry, answer me."

"Why?" he asked softly, nudging the cat, so he could sit in the chair. "Sounds like you've already made up your mind. You have all the questions and all the answers. Can't this wait until we get home? You have other things you need to deal with first. Okay?"

Everything felt like it was breaking inside her. She needed time to think, time to calm down, and time to ask more questions about Gina. "You're right. I can't do this now. It's too much."

"Sunny, please, don't make yourself sick. We'll work it out." He reached out and touched her sleeve. This time she didn't try to pull away.

She turned to him with misty eyes. "Promise you'll think about us when you go home, all right?"

"I will. I don't want to lose you."

She grabbed a tissue and wiped her nose. "It's not what I want either."

A few hours later, she'd calmed down and composed herself. Both were in the living room watching television when she announced, "I forgot I have to go to the store to get a few things." Picking up her coat, she paused at the door. "You don't have to go. It won't take me long."

"No, I'll drive you."

CHAPTER THIRTEEN

At the grocery store, Barry was pushing the cart when Sunny stopped and reached for a can of Folgers coffee. A familiar voice behind them drew her attention. Sunny turned and came face-to-face with Eva and Gerald.

"Well, what do we have here?" said Gerald. He shook Barry's hand and smiled as his eyes roved over Sunny.

Eva wrenched hard on his arm. "Let's go!" she snarled.

Gerald stepped back. "All right, calm down. See ya." They walked away.

Sunny giggled. "There goes the odd couple."

Barry agreed and looked at his watch. "I didn't realize how late it's getting. I'm hungry."

He pulled his knit cap over his ears. "Let's go to that pizza place across from the mall."

"Hey, while we're there, I want to go in and see if they have anything for Gina's final fashion statement."

Barry and Sunny crossed the parking lot. The wind had picked up and snow flurries swirled around them. Heads down, they picked up the pace and headed toward the yellow-and-red building.

Inside Santo's Pizza Parlor, Barry picked up a pepperoni and sausage pizza with mushrooms and olives, paid, and brought it to the table. "Is Eva always such a bitch?" he wanted to know.

"Always. Who knows why? She's just nuts. She does things different than most people, and takes no responsibility. Likes to stir up shit. That's why we call her Evil Eva." She handed him a napkin to wipe the cheese off his chin. "As long as I've known her she's been a total bitch."

Finished, he tossed the napkin on the table. "I think she's jealous of Gina and Rita, and even you."

"I don't know why. They had this love-hate relationship going. You know, she and Gina never even knew about each other until ten years ago, when Gina married Jesse. They had the same father, different mothers. Eva is the oldest, by two years. They ended up in foster homes at opposite ends of Washoe County.

"Eva met Jesse and was with him first. It got complicated because then Jesse met Gina and fell like a ton o' bricks. I guess Eva never forgave him . . . or Gina, for that matter."

"You're kidding."

"No, it was a long time ago, but it seems like Eva's more in love with him than ever."

He took a big bite. "Wow."

They finished their meal and scooted out of the booth. As they exited Santo's they passed Eva and Gerald coming in the door.

Sunny couldn't believe it; Gerald and Evil Eva right in front of her. Again. Had they followed her and Barry? Sunny wanted to punch her lights out.

Eva smiled sweetly. "Hello again."

Gerald half nodded.

Sunny and Barry ignored her and kept on walking. Outside, he whispered, "Now I know she has a screw loose."

At the mall across the way they visited a few boutiques, holding up one outfit after another. None seemed suitable, though, and Sunny, knowing how Barry hated shopping, especially in women's clothing shops, cut it short.

Sunny shook her head as they left the bright lights of the mall. "I thought we could just run in, find the perfect outfit, and be done."

"What kind of outfit are you looking for?" asked Barry, unlocking the passenger side door for Sunny.

"I don't even know," answered Sunny. "But I'll recognize the right one when I see it."

The snowflakes had stopped falling. The clouds were high and the air windy and soothing.

They burst out laughing. It reminded Sunny of their early years together and how happy they'd been. It could still be that way, except for his drinking, which had gotten worse these last few years. She missed those moments and was eager to have those times back again.

CHAPTER FOURTEEN

Sunny's thoughts tumbled down different paths as the moonlight glowed through the window. It was nine o'clock. She had a lot to do after the day's events. She planned to write about all of it. Even though she was overwhelmed, she continued recording in her notebook, contemplating what she'd learned. This would include talking to the people who'd been at the party. She kept a journal on everything. She thought about the phone conversation and how she should have made Gina listen to her.

Barry settled in front of the TV, engrossed in *Death Wish 3* with Charles Bronson.

At ten thirty, she said, "I'm too tired to think. It's late. I'm going to bed."

He got up. "Yeah, my movie's over. Bronson won again, just like last time. I think I'll go to bed too. Want me to get the lights?"

Before she could reply, the phone rang. She snatched up the receiver and listened, hearing only a dial tone. She shrugged. "Another wrong number."

Her intuition was on high alert, but she couldn't figure this out. A wrong number was what these calls were. For now, she didn't know what was going on. It was all too hard. She missed her friend, her Gina.

WEDNESDAY MORNING

It was eight thirty when they got out of bed. Exhausted from the day before, they slept in later than usual. Barry sat at the kitchen table and read the newspaper while Sunny put the coffee on and fixed breakfast.

"Maybe we should buy a new car," he said. "The Celica GT-S costs nine thousand dollars."

She put the fried eggs, bacon, and toast on the table. "We don't need a new one."

"How long are they going to keep writing about Reagan's movie with the chimp?" He looked up over the paper. "Oh, look, here's Gina's obituary."

"Let me see." She put her hands on his shoulders and leaned over to read:

RENO GAZETTE-JOURNAL
OBITUARIES

Gina Henry Wilson, 33, died Sunday at her residence. A Nevada native, she was born February 28, 1952. Mrs. Wilson worked for Sierra Pacific Power Company. She was a longtime Reno resident. Survivors include her husband, Jesse Martin Wilson, sons, Tommy Henry, Martin and Patrick Wilson, and sister, Eva Marshall, all from Reno.

Visitation and funeral details to follow.

Barry looked up. "Hey, you okay?"

Sunny's tears fell on his shoulders. "It doesn't seem possible." She moved to the counter, wiped her face with a paper towel, and poured him another cup of coffee as Rita came though the back door.

Poor Rita, Sunny thought. She'd loved Gina as much as anyone. Sunny felt she needed to be strong for her. But right at that moment she didn't know how. She wiped at her eyes so Rita wouldn't see them.

"Hi. I forgot my makeup," said Rita, throwing her purse and jacket on the chair.

"Coffee?" Sunny asked, turning and grabbing the coffeepot.

"No thanks. I'll just have toast. Mom, can you believe Jesse called me at Lee's? He said he wanted to be sure I was okay and to tell me his uncle is having a special sweat in Gina's honor, after the funeral."

"Why would he call you at Lee's?"

"I don't know. But it made me uncomfortable. He sounded strange. I felt like there was something else he wanted to say."

"What's the matter with him?" asked Barry, handing Rita the paper. "Gina's obituary."

She read the article and tried to nibble her toast. Rita blanched, her toast dropping onto the table. "It's so hard. Makes me want to throw up." She pushed away and got up. "I'm going to go take a shower. Then we'll go to the mall."

Sunny joined her husband. Minutes later, a loud noise echoed from the bathroom.

Barry squinted up from his coffee. "I guess she dropped her shampoo."

A shout came from the hallway. "Mom, hurry, come here!"

Sunny pushed her chair back and darted toward the bathroom. "What's wrong? Are you okay?"

Steam covered the bathroom mirror as water cascaded down the shower wall. Breathless, her daughter leaned with her back against the sink, wrapped in her pink terry-cloth robe, her wet hair dripping onto the bath mat.

"What's the matter? Tell me, are you okay?" Sunny reached across her daughter and turned the water off.

"When I was in the shower, I felt a cold breeze. I got out and opened the bathroom door to see if the window was open. It wasn't. All of a sudden, the picture Gina gave me fell to the floor. As I bent to pick it up, a draft of frigid air brushed across my shoulders and around my neck, wrapping itself along my body. It scared the heck out of me." She started to shake. "What's going on, Mom?"

"It's Gina's spirit. She wants your attention."

"If it's Gina, then do you think she might have come to Jesse too? I'm going to call him to see if anything strange has happened at his place," Rita said. Calming herself as she dried her hair, she got dressed, hurried, and phoned to ask him.

Sunny didn't think talking to Jesse was a good idea. She didn't know why; it was just a feeling she had. But she held her tongue and went into the kitchen. She sat at the table and explained to her husband what had happened in the bathroom.

A few moments later, Rita hung up and relayed her conversation with Jesse to them. "Jesse said he hasn't seen or felt any presence. He told me I needed to smudge the four corners outside of my house with sweet sage to keep her spirit away."

"I thought that was to cleanse your home and body, and keep away bad spirits, not Gina's. I'm going out to have a cigarette." Barry set the newspaper down and went outside.

"What do you think, Mom?"

Sunny had mixed emotions about the smudge. In one way she wanted Gina to come to her, because she needed to find out the reason behind her suicide. Also, she wondered what was with the abrasion on Gina's wrist.

"Do you have sage? Or do we need to pick some?" asked Sunny.

"I have some, but I don't know if I want to keep her away."

"She's troubled; some spirits hang around because they can't accept death or have some unfinished business. I think hers is the latter, but she needs to start her journey. We'll pray for light for her spirit. Do a loving cleansing of your home. Then maybe we'll know what to do. "

Once again Floyd meowed, jumped up, and made himself comfortable on Sunny's lap. She petted him as she told Rita, "Why don't you sew little prayer pouches instead and put them in all the rooms? That way you can bless both the inside of your house and her spirit. I'll help you hang them."

"That's a better idea. What do I need?" Rita had paper and pen ready. "We'll get it while we're out getting something for Gina. We'll buy white cotton material. And small remnants of red, yellow, black, and white, for the four directions. Usually, you use colors according to the person's illness, but this time it's different. It's for her soul. We'll need tobacco to fill the pouches. Also heavy thread."

Sunny had practiced this form of spirit healing for decades. It was a common tribal practice. She hoped it would help Gina's suffering spirit, also help her on her journey. Sunny was raised with these ceremonies. She had taught some but not all of them to Rita and certainly not the ones used to help a spirit travel to the other side.

Barry walked in. "I need a shirt for the funeral and I gotta replace the broken headlight before we get a ticket. Yesterday I only had time to fix the bumper."

"Go ahead." Sunny got up. "We'll pick up a shirt for you at Gottschalk's. White okay? Or striped? Colored?"

"You pick. I trust your good taste." He kissed her, hugged Rita, and left.

At the large department store in Park Lane Mall, Rita and Sunny shopped, remembering times they'd each gone shopping with Gina. Gina had loved the perfume and makeup counters where you could try on stuff for free. Rita remembered the day—long before Gina married Jesse—when they pretended to be bride and flower girl and tried on wedding dresses, trying not to laugh and give away their mischievousness. Sunny recalled shopping with Gina for baby things before Tommy was born. Gina had held the soft baby blankets and sweaters and booties to her cheek and sighed happily, though it was not a totally happy time, with her being pregnant and single.

After picking up Barry's shirt and a tie, they set out to find the perfect thing for Gina—a shroud that was anything but a shroud. Gina always loved bright colors, so it had to be bright and cheerful. She loved soft materials, so it had to be fluid and comfy. She insisted that everything she wore, even from thrift stores, be chic and fashionable . . . or kooky retro. She had a way of putting things together so she always looked like a magazine cover model. Sunny and Rita scoured the store, becoming more and more frustrated.

"I never even thought about how to dress a dead person before. It's not that easy," said Sunny. "It has to be perfect . . . but what's perfect?"

"Let's just get something, Mom. Anything would be better than that maid thing Eva stuck her with," said Rita, checking her watch. "I have to get to work. Three of my regulars are coming in this afternoon."

They settled on a print dress—purple, fuchsia, and turquoise in a soft silky knit—and hurried home. As soon as she dropped her mom off, Rita drove to her salon.

Sunny settled down to wait for Barry, notebook and pen in hand. Her mind wandered to Gina. She felt that Gina was close. Maybe if she shut her eyes.

When the front door burst open and Barry lumbered in, she awoke surprised that two hours had passed, and no Gina.

"Hi. Got the headlight fixed. And the tires rotated. I never have time to get it done at home. What's up?"

"Bought you a shirt. We got a dress for Gina. I'm not thrilled with it, but it's better than what they've got on her now. Maybe that's the best we can hope for. And we got material for the tobacco pouches."

"What do you have the rest of the afternoon?"

"I want to update my notebook on what has happened so far, before I forget. I'll start with when we first got to Gina's house, including what happened with Eva, Jesse, and his cousin, Louis."

He smiled. "Uh-oh, I see the 'investigator' taking over."

"Barry, this is serious. Something is off. I still can't remember what I heard about Jesse's cousin, Louis, but it makes me uneasy."

"Did you see him at the house?"

"No. I haven't seen him, but when I hear his name, something jars my insides."

She jotted down things that troubled her, and names of people at the party. It was odd that Gina loaded a rifle when she hated guns. And the raw skin on her wrist was still troubling to Sunny. She concluded her notes with Jesse's and Eva's strange reactions to everything. Sunny looked up at the wall, watching dust motes float in the sunshine as her thoughts went in all directions.

"So, when are you taking the dress over to the funeral parlor?" asked Barry.

She shook her head to come back to the here and now. The clock on the wall indicated that the time was three already. "Right now."

CHAPTER FIFTEEN

Sunny went to her room to change from jeans and a sweatshirt into gabardine slacks, a tailored blouse, and a blazer, such as she wore to work. She'd have to "dress for success" if she were to carry this thing off. She'd need to exude authority to convince the undertaker to change the clothes of a "dear departed" in his care.

Pulling the jacket from the closet, her eyes rested on the red wool knit dress, the dress Gina had begged to inherit, the one Sunny brought to wear to her funeral. "That's it! That's the one! She'll be buried in my red dress that she loved."

The more Sunny thought about it, the more excited she became. She held the dress up to her, watching her reflection in the full-length mirror in Rita's room. "Yes, that's perfect. That way, we'll be together through eternity. My dress, and the faux gold jewelry I always wore with it, on my best friend. I don't know why I didn't think of it sooner."

At the funeral home, Sunny made her way down the long hallway to the office at the rear of the building, her arm wrapped tightly around a parcel. She knocked. A man's voice called out, "Come in."

Squaring her shoulders and taking a deep breath, then exhaling all the way from her toes, she opened the door and walked in.

"How can I help you?" asked the man from behind his desk. His deep James Earl Jones voice seemed out of place coming from his sallow, skeletal frame. His charcoal-gray suit and pale gray tie suited him, however.

"I'm Sunny Davis, here for Gina Wilson." She spoke with calm authority, extending her hand.

"Ralph Kendall. How can I help you?" he repeated, rising and placing his bony hand in hers. He came round the desk.

"Gina was my best friend. She always told me she wanted to be buried in this dress," she fibbed. "Of course, we never thought it would happen this soon." She set the parcel on his desk and unwrapped it, revealing the red dress and costume jewelry. "But her sister, Eva, didn't know about that and put her in something different. I promised my Gina I'd see to it that she wore this dress to her grave, if she were to die before me, that is."

"This is highly unusual," said skull-face in his undertaker voice. "Once a. . ."—he cleared his throat—". . .person . . . is prepared for burial and placed in the casket, we don't make changes."

"Oh, but surely you can make an exception," stated Sunny with as much confidence as she could. "I'd be glad to pay for the extra time it takes, or whatever you need to make it work."

He shook his head. "It's not a matter of money, Mrs. Davis. It's policy. Besides, you're neither the deceased's spouse nor a blood relative."

"That's true. But a best friend is often closer than either of those. A best friend is a confidant with whom you share your deepest secrets. A best friend is the one who will fight everyone, and everything, for you. I'm here to keep my promise to my best friend."

"All the same, you are not a family member."

"As I'm sure you're aware, Mr. Kendall, 'family' has many definitions. There are families related by blood, and there are 'intentional families,' in which members choose who they want to claim. Gina and I chose to be 'family.'" She paused to let that sink in. "I'm sure you have blood relatives to whom you're not close, and perhaps a friend who's very close."

Kendall nodded almost imperceptibly, signaling to Sunny that he was beginning to thaw.

She said, "Perhaps you could find a way to help me keep my promise to my best friend . . . my chosen sister."

He looked away noncommittally, then glanced at the red dress on his desk. "My boss would not approve. It's against the rules."

She laid her hand on his arm and smiled into his eyes. "If anyone can find a way I'm sure it's you, Mr. Kendall . . . Ralph."

He coughed. "I'll try, Mrs. Davis. No promises, you understand, but I'll do my best."

Late that afternoon, Sunny arrived at the same time Rita and Lee pulled into the driveway. After they brought in everything, Lee helped Barry build a fire in the woodstove, and they moved to the front room where *Cheers* was on the TV.

Sunny began cutting three-inch squares of the cotton material while Rita got the tobacco ready to put in the center of each pouch. Its aroma filled the room. Both took deep breaths before folding the ends of white fabric, said a silent prayer of purification, love, and light, then stitched them closed. Stringing the pouches together, they sewed in silence.

"Hey," Sunny hollered into the next room. "Will you guys come help us hang these?" The women said prayers while the men tacked the strings of pouches in the corners of every room. Lee had questions about the ceremony, but Sunny silenced him in order to finish her prayers. They walked through the house as Sunny said one prayer to help Gina's spirit pass over to the other side and another to keep them all healthy. Outside they found a small tree with bare branches by the rock on which Rita often sat for meditation. The wind was now a breeze and the smell of wet dirt filled the air. The men strung the colored pouches on the swaying branches, north: white; south: red; east: yellow; and west: black. The men bowed their heads while Sunny and Rita said a prayer to Mother Earth.

When the job was done they went into the front room where they sat and made idle chitchat. Lee didn't say much. Sunny thought maybe she had offended him when she silenced him. He looked out the window, disinterested. Of course, Sunny smiled; maybe it was because of Barry. When he got started it was hard to get a word in.

Lee's eyebrows lifted; he stood. "Let's go," he told Rita and barely said goodbye.

As they walked out, she shrugged and gave her mother an exasperated look. "Good night." She closed the door behind them.

It was clear to Sunny that her daughter was embarrassed.

Barry's mouth gaped. "Was it something I said?"

"No." Sunny got unfriendly vibes from Lee. She couldn't put her finger on it . . . but he was Rita's choice and she was an adult. Rita would have to deal with him.

In the car Rita turned to Lee. "What is the matter with you? What did I do?"

"Nothing, it's me."

"That's bull. Is it my parents?"

"No, it has nothing to do with you or them. I'm tired and I want to go home. What's wrong with that?"

"Okay, but you were rude. You've been acting strange lately—preoccupied, like," she said. "Does it bother you that I'm staying at your house?"

"Just leave it alone, okay?"

They were quiet the rest of the way.

CHAPTER SIXTEEN

THURSDAY MORNING

The morning of the funeral was overcast. Barry was first to finish dressing. He heard the phone and hurried down the hall to pick it up as Sunny came out of the bedroom. He answered and handed the receiver to her.

"Hi, it's Jesse. Is Rita there?"

"No, she's over at her boyfriend's. What's up?"

"Humph," Jesse snorted. "Well, after the funeral my uncle is holding a sweat in Gina's honor. I know Pine Creek is a long way for you guys, but I hope you can make it."

"No, it's fine. Rita already told us. We'll be there."

Sunny turned and told Barry what was said. "For some reason when I talk to Jesse lately I feel like I want to throw up."

A half hour later, Rita and Lee came in. Sunny remarked how nice Rita looked, and she returned the compliment. Sunny wore a long-sleeved black midi cinched at the waist and black boots.

Barry spoke up. "Let's take my car, it has more room."

"Hurry up," Sunny said. "I want to sit where I can watch Jesse and Eva to see how they act together."

"You are one suspicious lady."

"Yes, I am." Sunny thought maybe Jesse and Eva were up to no good but couldn't put her finger on anything.

She especially wanted to see the expression on Eva's face when she saw the red dress on Gina in her casket. Certain that Mr. Kendall had managed to make the switch, she smiled in anticipation.

CHAPTER SEVENTEEN

The twenty-mile ride to the reservation church seemed to take forever. Sunny stared out the window in silence. It was the worst trip she could ever remember. She studied the landscape, looking at the dry, dead floor of the desert. She felt as dry and lifeless as the desert.

Rita tapped her mother on her shoulder. "You know, Mom, I never told a soul, but Gina tried to kill herself once before . . . before her last baby. She took a bunch of pills to Paradise Park because it wasn't messy and she didn't want her kids to see. But she started thinking about her boys and couldn't take it. So what changed?"

"I don't remember when that happened," Sunny said. "It makes things more confusing. Why would she do it with the boys right outside? I know she hated guns. It doesn't add up. I just have to find out what happened."

Barry looked over at his wife. "Be careful what you say. And who you say it to. You don't know what really went on. It could be dangerous."

"I am, but I'm going to keep my eyes and ears open."

"And your mouth shut."

Her eyes darted sideways at him. She said nothing.

Pulling into a parking space in front of the church, Barry pointed. "Look." Two red-tailed hawks circled above the area as they got out of the car.

Sunny looked up at them. *They could be messengers bringing Gina to us.*

She fell into step as the four walked in silence up the paved pathway.

Entering the small frontier church, Sunny's stomach did a flip-flop. She tasted bitter saliva. Even in the coolness, she felt beads of sweat form along her hairline. She looked around at the large somber room constructed of wooden planks. The floors were scuffed and badly worn. Large stained glass windows lined both sides of the walls. The other smaller windows had clear glass.

Baskets of flowers surrounded the podium and filled the room with a florist smell. Six rows of hard wooden pews were divided by an aisle into two sections.

Hushed conversations filled the little church. Sunny wasn't surprised to see a large crowd. Some mourners were dressed up while others wore jeans and Western boots. A couple of men sported traditional Native shirts with ribbons across the front, the ends hanging loose, and cowboy boots and sweaters.

Rita turned to Lee. "It's nice how everyone comes out to pay respect for the deceased, whether they knew them or not."

Sunny caught the eye of Jesse's mother in the front pew. Both gave an understanding nod. Gina's children weren't with their grandmother. Sunny's heart felt broken imagining what those boys were going through. The Allen family sat in the back. The church filled up quickly. The organ music played in the background. Soon the minister came in, dressed in a navy blue suit and a white shirt with a silver bolo tie. Gray braids hung over his shoulders.

During the service, Sunny's gaze bounced back and forth between Jesse and Eva. Next to Jesse sat a man who was built like a bear. He was dark-skinned, with a face that made you want to play connect-the-dots on his pockmarks.

Sunny leaned over and whispered in Barry's ear, "That could be Moochie, Jesse's cousin."

Two of Gina's friends faced the coffin with their backs to the congregation. They sang a prayer in Gina's native Paiute language. Sunny barely took her eyes off Jesse and Eva. Jesse looked straight ahead, stone-faced. Eva's chin rested on her chest, her fingers playing with the strap on her purse. Next to her, Gerald raised his head in greeting. Eva yawned several times and checked her watch every couple of minutes.

Sunny nudged Barry. "Look at them. Bored to death, like they just want this to be over."

Barry tilted his head and nodded.

When the preacher finished, everyone stood and, starting with the first row, walked past the coffin. Sunny whispered to Barry and Rita, "Watch Eva. Let's see what she does." Jesse and his mother went first. Jesse looked down into Gina's face and touched her cheek almost tenderly. His mother's shoulders shook and she wiped her eyes, viewing Gina's lifeless form.

When Eva got close enough to see what Gina was wearing she gasped and stiffened, then turned to glare at Sunny. As her face darkened with rage she mouthed coarse profanities in Sunny's direction. Her body convulsed with fury. Her eyes blazed like hot coals. Sunny returned her stare with a small satisfied smile before dropping her gaze.

Sunny, Barry, and Rita stood at the casket, the two women weeping, Barry in between with a consoling arm around each. No words came. Words could not convey their feelings. They turned and made their way down the center aisle of the simple church, heads bowed, past the other mourners, and out. Just outside, Eva waited on the church steps.

"Bitch!" hissed Eva, her hands balled into fists. "You had no right."

"No," Sunny replied, walking on. "*You* had no right."

Eva followed. "She was my sister."

"And you hated her."

Barry led her toward the car, speaking softly. "Watch your mouth, Sunny. She's not somebody you want to mess with."

"It's too late for that. I already messed with her by changing Gina's dress. And I'm glad I did."

Eva, a coiled snake ready to strike, continued swearing at Sunny, with cursing asides at Rita.

Barry told her, "Eva, I know you're upset. This is not the time or the place. We're all upset. Please just back off, okay?"

"I'm not done with you bitches," she hissed and continued cursing out Sunny and Rita as she retreated to the crowd gathered on the church steps.

They stood by the car, Barry and Sunny smoking Marlboros. Rita said, "Well, that was intense."

"Big surprise," said Sunny. "Evil Eva shows her true colors."

"I'm not happy about this, Sunny," said Barry. "She looks like she doesn't get over things easily."

"Well, I'm not sorry I did it. I couldn't let Gina look bad at her own funeral. And I'd do it again, a thousand times over. She'd've done the same for me."

"I'm just saying, be careful."

Wanting to change the subject, she spied her good friend, Barbara, and waved. When Sunny caught her eye, Barbara waved and hurried over. "Good to see you."

Barbara, a tall platinum blonde, appeared fresh out of a Neiman Marcus showroom. Sunny admired her friend deeply. Barbara had worked hard to become a therapist. Sunny remembered, over ten years ago, when Barbara was just starting out. She was a social worker, then director, and finally, after twelve years, she had her own practice. Sunny was so proud of her.

The women hugged. "Barbara, you remember my husband?"

"Sure." They shook hands.

Barry ground his cigarette out on the sidewalk. "I'll go get the car and see if Rita and Lee are ready. It's good to see you again." He walked away.

Barbara lowered her voice and her gaze. "This is so horrible. I can't believe it. Gina was a little girl, just six years old, when I placed her in foster care. Fortunately, we found her a placement with a Paiute family. Remember, I had you pick her up the day she turned eighteen?"

Sunny looked down at her cigarette. "Doesn't seem that long ago, does it?"

"No. She turned into a sweet woman and a wonderful mother. It hurts to think she was having a bad time and I didn't know. How did this happen? Do you know?"

Sunny flicked her cigarette out in the street. "No, I was shocked. I didn't have a clue either. But I plan to find out. I'll tell you later about my last conversation with Gina."

Barbara stepped closer. "I was surprised to see your ex here. And with Eva . . ."

"Yeah." Sunny smirked. "What's up with those two?"

Barry drove up with Rita and Lee in the back seat. The two women hugged goodbye. "I'll call you, Barb. There's a lot I have to tell you." Sunny opened the passenger door and got in.

Barry turned the headlights on and followed the line of cars as they drove to the cemetery. The trees were restless. Sprigs of squaw tea and tumbleweeds swayed to nature's rhythm as gloomy clouds spread over the landscape.

At the gravesite they clutched their coats closed against the icy wind.

As birds flew overhead Barry looked up and whispered, "There are those hawks again. I think they're following us."

"They're following Gina." Sunny watched the birds awhile, then looked around at the other graves. Some had flowers, most were covered with golden sticker weeds. A few nameless white markers stood alone. Others had rocks piled on like blankets, to keep the occupants warm.

"It feels like the raw cold ate through my gloves. My ears ache from the wind," said Sunny.

The minister said a few words on Gina's good mothering skills. Her childhood friend recited a prayer for Gina, first in Paiute and then in English, and finished with a song.

Eva's eyes shot daggers at Sunny and Rita. When they walked close, she kicked dirt and rocks toward them, but they ignored her as much as was possible.

Jesse had fashioned a simple cross out of two twigs and placed it at the head of the grave.

"Look at that. It's not right. She deserves a decent headstone," uttered Sunny. "Jesse's too cheap . . . or doesn't give a damn. I'm going to talk to him."

"Sure, go ahead. But be careful, and watch your mouth. Remember, you don't know who you can trust."

"Humph." Her eyebrows drew together. It gave her a bad taste in her mouth as they got in the car to go to Pine Creek for the sweat.

CHAPTER EIGHTEEN

An orange-streaked cloud lit up the mountains against the gray afternoon. As they drove east of Reno, they passed the Painted Rocks in their natural beauty. Sunny studied the green, gold, and lavender rocks, which glistened along the highway en route to River Bend Reservation. The beige desert haze was interrupted only by dry weeds and sagebrush. Out there, seen by passing cars, owls, hawks, and coyotes hunted the jackrabbit for their main course. Boulders lined gravel roads.

Barry turned the car onto the paved road that led to the reservation and passed houses with old cars growing roots in the front yards. Dogs ran beside their car, kicking up dust and barking in the wind.

Rita nudged Lee in the back seat. "Look, the old general store still has its hitching rail."

"Looks like a movie set," he said. "One of those old Westerns."

When Barry drove past the park, Sunny inhaled sharply. "Stop the car! Let me out!" *I can feel Gina. I hear her. Our memories are here.*

"Why, what's going on?" He pulled over and stopped; she hopped out.

Rita and Lee got out and leaned against the car. "What's wrong, Mom?"

"The park brings back memories of me and Gina. I'm taking a breath of time. I feel her here beside me."

Sunny cocked her ear as if listening to Gina's spirit whispering in the wind. Sunny realized she had a connection to the earth at this place, and that Gina had made her presence known.

"Every year we came here to the Pine Nut Festival. It was so much fun. We sampled everything: soups, breads, cookies, all made with pine nuts."

The others followed as Sunny walked over to a table and explained the festival.

"My aunt always served pine nut soup with fry bread." Sunny laid her hand down. "This was her table. If she got too busy, Gina and I jumped in and helped her."

"Mmmm. Fry bread sounds good," said Rita.

"The aroma lingers among the trees. It can break through a dream," said Sunny. "Over there is where we gambled all night playing hand games."

Lee pulled on his mustache. "Playing what?"

"Hand games. Players sit in a row on both sides of a mat. One team has a small bone or stick. The first team passes a bone along behind their backs."

"Where's the gambling come in?" Lee asked.

"When the other team thinks they know who has the bone one or all stand up, point to that person, and the others bet. The one chosen shows their hand and hollers yes or no. It keeps going 'til the sticks are all gone. Sometimes it lasts all night."

Barry looked at the road. "We better get going. I see cars filing past."

They returned to the car and took one last look, then fell in line and followed the procession to the medicine man.

Rita was telling Lee, "Jesse's uncle ran the sweat for years. After he died, his brother Alvin took over as medicine man."

They found parking among the many cars. Everyone except Sunny got out. "Give me a minute." Memories of a happy Gina flooded her mind. She saw her best friend's spirit dancing and laughing. It stopped, looked at Sunny, and waved. Sunny covered her eyes and wept. "Why, why would you do it?"

Barry rushed back, slid onto the seat, and took her in his arms, rocking her gently. It was what Sunny needed at that moment.

Standing in the yard, Lee pointed up. "Hey, those look like the same hawks from the cemetery. They followed us."

"Yeah, I see them." Rita turned back to the car and opened the door. "Mom, are you okay?"

"She'll be all right," said Barry.

After a few minutes, Sunny stopped crying and wiped her face, reapplied her lipstick, and tied her hair up on top of her head, then stepped from the car. She held her head in the air watching the red hawks. "They are sacred, and they're waiting for Gina's spirit to rise with them."

Eva lurked around the corner of the house; she watched Rita like a cobra ready to strike. Rita looked Eva up and down, closed her eyes, and shook her head. As everyone entered the house Eva mouthed, *Bitch!* at them.

Jesse's uncle Alvin stood in the middle of the large room, hands clasped above his head. "You know it's only been seven years since the Indian Act of 1978, that we're able to have our religious ceremonies with no worries. Today, this sweat is in honor of my niece. Please say your prayers to guide her to the ancestors. Let her journey be swift and smooth. We want to send her to Grandfather Spirit with lots of love."

Jesse stood with his back to the partition, his left foot placed up against the wall, arms across his chest. Eva sat in one of many folding chairs and rolled her eyes. Both she and Jesse stared at the others, as all said their prayers of goodbye.

Sunny watched through the window as the red hawks flew away; she hoped they hadn't taken Gina's spirit. Not yet. Suddenly, sadness fell over her. She was torn between knowing Gina needed to journey on, and needing Gina here with her.

CHAPTER NINETEEN

Sunny and her daughter were ready to go into the sweat. They entered the outdoor shower room made of wooden slats, with back-to-back showerheads. Colorful Hawaiian muumuus hung along one wall. On the left were two small shelves, one with towels, and the other with swim trunks, for men who weren't comfortable wearing only their undershorts. The two women stuffed their undergarments in the bags that were provided and slipped on muumuus, ready to go in.

The medicine man was talking to Barry and Lee. "Will you stand outside and open and close the flaps? Each thirty minutes is called a round. We go three rounds."

"Sure, no problem," each man answered.

He pointed to a nearby bush. "People can pick mint leaves from the bush before they enter."

"What's that for?" Lee asked.

"They hold it up to their nose and inhale. It helps them tolerate the heat."

"You have to open the flaps early for people who can only do one five- or ten-minute session," said the medicine man. "Some people come for help with back problems or their joints, but today is only for my niece."

Sunny and Rita bent down to enter the five-foot-high willow-and-canvas sweat hut. Barry and Lee held back the heavy canvas flaps to let the others in.

Sunny sat next to an elder who sang prayers for Gina's spirit. The smell of musk, mixed with mint, damp straw, dirt, and sweat filled the hut. Perspiration ran from Sunny's forehead, down her neck, and between her breasts, dripped from her hair, and stung her eyes. They listened to the mumbling of prayers to the Grandfather Spirit, the land, Mother Earth, and nature. Everyone took a sip of water from a metal cup attached to a long wooden handle as it passed by. The remaining water was poured on the rocks, creating intense steam and heat.

At the end of the third round both women gave a big sigh. "We did it, and without the mint." Sunny smiled at Rita.

"I didn't know if I could make it all the way. I hope Gina can find some peace. I forgot how hot it gets," said Rita. "It's been a long time since I went in."

Afterward, they showered and joined everyone in the house for a light lunch of Indian stew and fry bread. Prayers were spoken before and after eating. Alvin, the medicine man, sang a prayer in Paiute, then concluded with one in English. "Good for your body and good for your soul. Ah-eee. All eat."

CHAPTER TWENTY

Because they were tired and felt drained, the drive back to Reno seemed extra long. "That was a nice crowd for Gina," said Rita. "I was surprised to see Jesse's family all showed up. Mom, did you notice he and Eva never went in to sweat . . . ?"

Barry nodded. "Yeah, I thought that was strange. When Lee and I were handling the flaps, Eva was standing by a tree smoking. Her eagle eyes watched Jesse and his cousin over by the cars. I was glad she stayed over there. If she'd gone inside I'd have had to worry about you. No telling what someone like her might do when she gets her dander up."

Sunny grimaced, then twisted around to face everyone and loudly interrupted. "Now I know who Louis is. Moochie, or whatever the hell they want to call him."

Rita wrinkled her forehead. "You explained before but I forgot, why do they call him Moochie?"

"Because he's always borrowing something: food, tools, whatever . . . I had already moved away from the rez, but when Jesse was seventeen or eighteen, he and two other guys took a white man out in the desert, robbed and beat him, and left him to die. Louis gave Jesse his alibi. Said he was with him the whole time, at his house. He lied and Jesse got away with murder. Everybody knew it."

Barry shook his finger at his wife. "It was never proven. So please be careful what you say. You didn't know for sure then, and you don't know now."

"Well, I'm pretty sure, and I'll find out. At the time, Jesse got drunk and someone overheard him bragging about it."

Barry mumbled, "Hearsay. Inadmissible in court." He cocked his head, cautioning Sunny with his eyes.

Rita ignored Barry's remark and turned to her mother. "Wow, I never knew that." She glanced at Lee, who was staring out the window, and whispered, "I guess you're not interested in anything we do or say." He didn't respond.

Barry warned Sunny, "If something is going on, you need to watch your step around everyone. I go home tomorrow."

Rita leaned forward and put both hands on the back of the front seat. "Why are you going so soon?"

"Well, I have to. You know how busy our probation department is. I have to check my cases. Besides, I'm due in court next week, and it's one case I need to handle myself."

"What about you, Mom?"

Barry broke in and answered for her. "Your mom is staying until she buys the headstone. You know how your mother is when she gets her strong intuition and a hot neck. Her investigator skills kick in, and look out!"

"Yeah." Sunny knew he was being sincere but she couldn't help it. She was still upset by the loss of Gina.

As they drove back to Reno in silence, Sunny felt fatigued and her imagination or intuition was stirred up.

THURSDAY EVENING

The night air was cold and clear, the black sky alive with winking stars. Barry pulled into the driveway and turned off the ignition. An unfamiliar red GMC truck was parked in front of Rita's house.

Rita's forehead crinkled. "Whose truck is that?"

A strange man sat on the porch swing beneath the light. Dressed in gray sweatpants, a red jacket unzipped, showing his tight 49er jersey. Shoulder-length hair hung loose around his tanned face. He stood and extended his hand as they walked up.

"Victor John." He shook hands with Barry and Lee first.

Rita stared at the stranger and took his hand. Gina had mentioned him to Rita. Sunny was surprised. So this is the man Gina was leaving Jesse for.

"I wanted to come by and talk to you about Gina," he said.

Rita showed him into the front room. "She talked about you often. It's nice to meet you."

"Same here," he said. "Gina showed me your pictures and told me all about you and your mother and how important you were to her."

Barry offered Victor a beer and grabbed two more for Lee and himself. Sunny lowered her eyebrows and pinched them together in disgust. He shrugged it off.

"I'm glad to meet you too," Sunny said. "I saw your name in the guest book at the funeral home." Sunny paused, then asked, "Do you have any idea why all this happened? What would make Gina kill herself?"

"That's why I wanted to talk to you. When I called Gina, people had been there partying since early in the day. I talked to her several times on Sunday. The last time was in the afternoon, within hours of what happened. At that point Eva was the only one who was still there."

"Was Gina drunk?" asked Rita.

"Buzzed. Gina said she and her sister got into it because Eva kept forcing drinks on her. She'd just found out that Eva lied about Rita and Jesse having an affair. Gina told Eva to get out. She said both Eva and Jesse were liars. She was finished with them and their lies."

"Thank God she found out the truth before . . ." Rita's gaze fell to her lap. "I would never do anything like that to hurt her."

Sunny patted her daughter's hand.

Victor looked at them. "Gina told me she and Jesse had fought, and he left. She wrote him a letter to let him know that the drinking and fighting were too much for her. She was going to leave, take the boys, and get a divorce."

"According to Jesse," said Sunny, "Gina never mentioned anything about leaving him or getting a divorce, in the letter or anywhere else." She raised an eyebrow. "What does that say about him? Why would he keep that quiet? Did she change her mind after she talked to you? Or did he lie about it on purpose?"

Rita shrugged. "Maybe he was embarrassed."

Barry looked at her. "Jesse?" He *humphed*. "I don't think so."

Lee picked up a magazine and flipped through the pages, seemingly bored with the conversation.

Victor ran his fingers through his hair and continued. "I asked Gina about her plan to come live at my house. I wanted to help her get out of her situation. She's a sweet person . . . was. I got to know her at work. Her friend Patty would tell me when Gina had a black eye or swollen lip and couldn't make it in to work. I'd call her up and we'd meet for lunch and talk."

Sunny looked at her hands. "She was lucky she had good friends at work who cared about her."

"I never knew what to do for her," Rita said and bit on her lip. "When it was bad I'd let her and the boys come stay, but then Jesse would come and talk her into going back, which she always did."

Victor took a sip of beer. "I thought everything was fine. My wife and I had divorced. Now that I have a practically empty three-bedroom house I offered Gina a safe place for her and her boys. I wanted to help her out of her situation. But, right there at the end, she said she wanted her own space."

Victor shook his head and exhaled sharply. "I got mad and hung up. Now I'm mad at myself. It was our last conversation and we ended it arguing. I wish I could do it over. Does either of you know what changed her mind about moving in with me?"

Sunny wondered if Jesse had threatened her. Why she wouldn't just leave if she had a safe place to go to. She might've felt trapped. Of course, if she was drunk enough, maybe she *had* forgotten about the boys playing outside. That was too much for Sunny to swallow, though. She could never imagine Gina doing something like that.

Rita rubbed her eye. "No. She talked about leaving Jesse. That's all we know. Except that she often talked about leaving him."

"Did she sound like she was about to kill herself?" Sunny asked, thinking that his last conversation with Gina sounded like hers.

Victor took a swig of Coors. "No, it doesn't make sense. Not with the kids there. She wasn't depressed. She was mad, as in furious. I don't know what she was thinking."

Rita reached down to pick up Floyd. "No it doesn't, not at all. And why didn't Jesse mention anything about Gina getting a divorce? Why so closemouthed? I don't understand him either."

Sunny listened to everything and turned it over and over in her mind like rocks in a tumbler. She still had more questions than answers.

Victor finished his beer and said good night. "I'll be in touch."

Rita and Lee said their goodbyes and left too.

Lee was very quiet as they headed for his apartment. Rita didn't talk either. She thought he acted tired. Maybe he liked his space and didn't like her staying with him. But it was his idea. If he didn't want her there why didn't he tell her? He had acted different lately. She didn't know what was going on with him, but didn't feel comfortable about it.

After everyone left, Sunny helped Barry pack for his trip home. "I don't want to admit it, but I hate to see you leave." She half smiled and turned her face up to him.

"I'll be in touch every day." He looked in her eyes, and brushed a lock of hair over her shoulder. "You know, I'm only three and a half hours away. If you need anything . . ."

"Feels farther." Her eyes started to mist.

"You and Rita, be careful what you say and do. Please. I don't know what's going on, but I agree with you that things aren't adding up."

"Thanks. I thought it was just me."

"I understand you have to find out why Gina killed herself, babe. But I don't think it was your conversation with her. She had a lot of other things going on. Why not look somewhere else?"

She had mixed feelings: sad, mad, and confused.

"How about we spend the rest of the evening thinking of something else?" He flashed his grin, the one that always made her feel warm inside.

He's right. I don't want to feel like this. Not tonight. Tonight I need to forget everything and get lost in the moment.

Barry got into bed and Sunny crawled in and snuggled next to him. She felt his body heat surge through her.

They shared a good last night together, and after they were spent, they lay there talking over the events of the day before both fell asleep.

Sunny bolted upright screaming. Barry reached for her. "Sunny, Sunny, wake up, you're okay. I'm right here. I have you." He held her close and stroked her back.

Her breath came in gasps. "I had a dream. A nightmare!"

"It's all right now. Do you want to tell me what happened?"

"It was terrible. I heard Gina crying. I tried to go to her. She sat on her couch drenched in blood. It was everywhere; pools of it overflowed onto the floor, and started to bubble, then boil. I felt the heat. I checked my arms and feet. They had blisters. It was horrible."

"You're okay, I'm right here." He took her arm, "Look babe, no blisters."

She held up her hands and turned them over. Satisfied there were no blisters, she nestled against his chest.

"Try to go back to sleep." He rocked her in his arms.

Her dream faded away and soon she was asleep.

FRIDAY MORNING

Barry was in the kitchen when Sunny came in.

"How are you feeling?" He got up and kissed her cheek.

She smiled and gave him a hug. "Fine now, but what a terrifying dream."

"Sit down, I poured your coffee, and fixed your favorite blueberry bagel."

She couldn't help looking once again at her arms, "Just making sure no blisters."

At nine a.m., with their breakfast finished, Barry sat and fiddled with his keys. "Are you going to be all right?"

"Yes, I'm fine now."

"Are you sure? I can fly home, and leave my car for you. I'll ride BART to work."

"No, you might need the car. I'll rent one. Besides, I have errands to run and don't want to depend on Rita." Sunny grabbed the phone book and looked up the number for Hertz.

In the industrial part of the city, they pulled up to the nondescript buildings next to the airport. The sun peeked around the clouds as they walked to the small building, with a yellow-and-black overhead sign. Hertz Rental Cars.

"How long are you renting it for?" Barry asked.

"At least a week."

"What! I thought you were only going to be here a day or two."

Exasperated, she blurted out, "Barry!"

He threw his arms in the air. "All right, all right. We'll talk later."

She fiddled with her scarf. "I'll go in and get the car" At the office door she pivoted to face him. "Meet you back at Rita's."

When Sunny pulled in, Barry was on the porch smoking, wearing the ugly blue parka she detested. He greeted her with, "What's this about? Let's have it. Why did you rent the car for a week? You didn't have any intention of staying just long enough to buy the headstone, did you?" He threw his unfinished cigarette in the dirt, meeting her eyes with his.

"Please don't get so upset. It's just that I know this thing with Gina isn't right. With my neck and the tingly feelings, I can't believe she'd kill herself, especially with her boys so close by. She wasn't depressed, so that can't be it. I have to get to the bottom of it, Barry. Please don't be mad."

She put her arms around him and nestled her face on his chest. "I don't want for us to be apart, but I have to do this."

"You don't know how much I want to stay. Last night felt like old times." He pulled her closer.

She inhaled deeply of his wonderful male aroma: shower soap and Old Spice, the woodsmoke smell in his shirt. It felt like old times to her as well.

She nodded and kissed him goodbye. "Will you think about what I said before? Please, Barry. Your drinking's too much for me."

CHAPTER TWENTY-ONE

Sunny relaxed in the recliner with Floyd snoozing on her lap. Her head back, eyes closed, she was thinking of Gina and what could've happened. *Maybe it wasn't me. Why didn't Jesse tell me Gina was leaving him? Or was she?*

The door banged open. Startled, she opened her eyes. Rita rushed in, her face ashen, and eyes wide.

Sunny sprang up and dumped Floyd off her lap. "What's wrong?" Sunny asked. "Sit down. Did you and Lee have a fight?"

"No. I had a terrible dream about Gina. It scared the heck out of me. Gina spoke to me. She said, 'I didn't do this. It was—' then Gina's hand flew over her mouth, and she said 'Don't let . . . get away with it.' She covered her mouth again. I hollered, 'Who? Who, Gina? Who did it? Tell me!' I couldn't get what she was saying. I woke up sweating and upset."

"Her spirit is restless. She can't pass over until we know the truth," said Sunny, sitting back down. She reached for her cigarettes and lit one. "Maybe we should use the sage to help her spirit."

"Good idea. I have smudge sticks in my room," Rita shouted to Sunny. "I'll get them. I have one in an abalone shell, along with the feather."

Outside, Sunny struck a match to the bundled, tied sage. "I wish I knew what Gina wants. What is she trying to tell us?" She held one end of the burning sage in her hand, then blew it out. The sweet fresh scent found its way to her nostrils. Rita's large eagle feather fanned the smoke into the four corners of her house. It formed a white cloud in the shape of a long tail. They smudged both inside and outside the house, including all the rooms and each other. They said a prayer of love to help Gina on her journey for peace and to cross over.

After the ceremony Sunny opened her eyes. "I almost wish she would come to us first and help us find out what happened before she crosses over.

She's having a hard time, and fighting. There is something I have to find out."

The phone rang and Rita ran in to answer it.

Ending the smudging and seeing the smoke encircle the house, Sunny picked up the abalone shell, went in, and put it away. "Who was that?"

"Another hang-up."

"I wonder what's going on. It's been happening a lot." Sunny headed into the kitchen, stopped, smiled, and crossed her arms. Once again, Floyd was in her favorite chair. "Get out of my chair." She grabbed the cat and dropped him on the floor. He stared up at her with his tail in the air, and gave a loud, long, resentful *mee-ow* before sauntering away.

Rita giggled at Floyd and, pulling a chair next to her mom's, plopped down and leaned in close to the table.

Sunny looked at her watch. "It's getting late. We should go see about the monument before they close. Will you dial Jesse for me? I want to ask him what he wants on her headstone."

Rita punched in his number. "Hi, Jesse." She jerked the receiver away from her ear and looked at it, then scowled before returning it to her ear. "Uh . . . my mom wants to talk to you. Hold on a minute."

Sunny took the phone from her, grabbed Rita's arm, and mouthed, *What's wrong?*

Rita shook her head.

While she spoke she watched her daughter. "Jesse, I'm going to get a headstone for Gina. Do you want anything special on it?" She was just being polite. She didn't really care what he wanted.

"I guess you could put her name . . . oh . . . and her birth and death dates." He hung up.

Sunny stared at the mouthpiece in disbelief. "Asshole!" She hung up and looked at Rita. "What did he say to you?"

"I was surprised. He called me 'my babe,' like he was coming on to me. What does he think he's doing?"

"With him who knows? Maybe he's drinking." Sunny remembered Barry telling her to be careful. She checked her watch again. "Come on, grab your coat, and let's get going. It's almost four o'clock."

Rita struggled with her coat. "I'm just going to ignore him. I never know what's going on with him or Eva."

She locked her doors and they left.

CHAPTER TWENTY-TWO

The wind howled as tumbleweeds raced across the road in front of them. Sunny drove to the south end of Reno, pulled up, and parked in front of a brown shingled building. A sign read, Nevada Monuments.

She pointed into the air. "We'd better hurry. The wind can bring rain or snow to the valley floor before we know it." They grabbed at their coat collars, holding them closed beneath their chins.

Along the walkway of red rock slabs, they strolled, looking at monuments propped up against the building: granite, bronze, and marble.

Sunny found an oyster-colored granite monument with an angel etched into it. "What do you think of this one?"

Rita bent over and looked closely at the angel. "Perfect."

In the office, Sunny brought in the tag that described the headstone. She requested the headstone be engraved with the inscription May Grandfather Spirit Guide You On Your Journey.

Sunny filled out the form with Gina's name and the dates of her birth and death, and then added Mother and Friend, deliberately leaving out Wife.

Rita picked up the form. "You left out—" Sunny stopped her.

She cocked her head and shrugged. "Jesse said, 'Only her name and dates.' So that's what I did. Only her name and dates . . . so far as he's concerned, anyway."

Sunny gave instructions to the clerk and arranged to have the headstone delivered to the minister at the church on the reservation.

FRIDAY EVENING

By the time they got back to the car, the rain had started. The streets were dark and slick. The only sound was the soft music from the radio and the slapping of the windshield wipers. The rain caused Sunny to slow down on the freeway.

Bright lights in the rearview mirror caught her attention. "What the heck?"

"What's wrong?"

"The car behind us has its high beams on. It's coming up on us too fast." As she sped up so did the other car, coming closer and closer. Her eyes widened, her heart raced.

Rita squirmed around in her seat to look out the back window. "Mom, get in the other lane and let them pass."

The panic in Rita's voice unnerved Sunny. She swerved into the other lane, tires squealing. But the other car was right on her bumper. Sunny moved over into the near lane. Back and forth, no matter what she did to shake it, the other car followed.

Sunny's heart was pounding. "Look, they won't pass. They're right behind us." All she could see was the glare of lights on the road. The rain made it impossible to see who the driver was. Sunny watched in shock as the headlights came racing toward her car.

"Oh my God!" she screamed. "They're going to hit us. Hang on." They lurched forward as the car hit them from behind, causing them to fishtail. She fought the steering wheel to stay in her lane and keep the car on the road.

"Mom!"

"Hang on!" Sunny's hands gripped the wheel; she changed lanes again.

The car behind them slowed, changed lanes, and speeded up. *Bang!* Another hit from behind. Heading toward the guard rail, fighting the wheel, she pumped the brakes. The streets were wet and slick.

Rita grabbed the hand grip above the door as her body jerked forward.

"I can't see! Damn it!" Sunny's hands tightened, her knuckles white. "The lights are blinding me!"

"What the hell? Move over, Mom! Move over!"

Sunny watched in the rearview mirror. She thought the car behind her slowed down and turned off as they passed an exit. The rain came down in sheets, visibility was nearly zero.

Rita looked again out the back window. "I think they're gone."

Sunny looked for a turnout, pulled over, and stopped. She could hardly talk. Her mouth felt dry. Her hands shook. She wasn't going to worry about the bumper or the damage right now. Besides, the fierce rain kept her from stepping outside. She tried to slow her breathing but was badly shaken.

"I thought they were going to run us off the road."

"Me too." Rita patted her chest and took a deep breath. "I think they tried."

Sunny gasped. "That scared the crap out of me." Adrenaline rushed through her like a train racing down a track. Her hands on the steering wheel, she put her head between them. A long sigh followed. She concentrated on taking deep breaths and waited to calm down.

She looked at Rita. She had leaned her head back, eyes closed. "How are you doing? Y' okay?"

"I think so. Just scared."

When Sunny felt able to drive, she started the vehicle again. She looked behind her, to make sure the other car hadn't returned, and pulled out.

Rita held tight on the hand grip. "Dang! I'm still shaking."

They discussed how scared they were and whether the repeated impacts were on purpose. "Could it have been kids, or a drunk? Is that possible?"

Sunny began to relax. "I don't know who would want to do that to us. I can't report it to the police because I wasn't able to see what kind of car it was, only I think it was a smaller model. I couldn't tell if the driver was a man or woman. I know I'd need some kind of facts. What could the police do?"

As they got closer to town and the rain let up, Sunny felt more comfortable.

Rita let her hand off the grip and shifted the topic. She told her mother how uncomfortable Jesse's words made her feel. "Maybe I'm overreacting but it bothers me. He never called me 'my babe' before, and the way he talks to me now is different. He's called me more times than I've told you."

"You think he's drinking more now? Could he be the one responsible for all those hang-ups?" Sunny questioned Jesse's innocence. "Why would Jesse do something like this to us?"

"Who knows?" Rita shrugged. "Nah, I can't see him banging into our car."

They drove on in silence until Rita spoke. "Can we stop by Lee's apartment? He asked me for a loan."

"Really? How often does he ask for money?"

"A lot lately. He uses my car once or twice a week, and he's always short of cash. I don't know what's going on."

"You loan him money and your car? Doesn't he have a job?"

"Yeah, he's a shift supervisor at Harrah's."

"Then he should have money. What's he doing with it? Gambling? Drinking? Drugs?"

"I don't think so. But when he takes my car it always comes back empty. So far he hasn't paid me back any money I loaned him."

Sunny kept her eyes on the road. "That's rude."

"Sometimes I can't get a hold of him, or he doesn't call when he says he will. If I ask where he's been he cops an attitude. He's not like he was when we first got together. He seems cold. Standoffish. I wonder what I'm even doing with him. It's hard, never knowing what mood he's going to be in."

Sunny tried to lighten things up. She didn't want to badger her daughter. "How'd you meet this guy?"

"I was in the bank and dropped my deposit slip. He was behind me and picked it up. We started talking."

"Maybe he thinks you're loaded. Or it could be he needs a little space. You've spent every night with him. Things might be better now that you're home."

Rita rubbed her finger across her nose. "Could be, we'll see." She hurried out of the car.

While Rita was in Lee's apartment, Sunny got out of the car, using the light from the carport to check the back bumper. She ran her hand across a large dent. She also noted smaller dents that hadn't been there before. "Damn, the asshole dented my car."

Soon Rita came back, chewing on her bottom lip.

Sunny knew that sign. Rita was upset. "Why so quick? Is everything all right?"

"He took my money, thanked me, and acted like he wanted me to hurry and get out. I wonder what the deal is with him. He seems so weird. I don't seem to know him anymore."

Sunny looked down at her hands. "Maybe you're into him more than he's into you. Sounds like he's a user. Maybe you should kick him to the curb."

"Mom, I'm not sixteen. I'll handle it. Okay?"

"Okay, fine." Sunny was reluctant to meddle, which was sure to start a fight. They'd been through enough already that day.

"I looked at the car. A few dents. I have to contact the police. Because it's a rental it'll cost me. I can only tell them what I know, which isn't much."

Rita got out of the car. "I want to see what happened." She looked at the bumper. "It could be worse. We could be the ones who got dented."

Sunny nodded. "So true. There's nothing I can do at this time." Maybe I'll try and cheer her up. "Are you hungry?"

"Yeah, I am."

"Let's go have Mexican. Javier's stays open late."

LATE FRIDAY EVENING

Sunny treated her daughter to dinner at her favorite Mexican restaurant. She loved its ethnic feel, Spanish tiles on the stairs and floor, colorful piñatas hanging from the ceiling. Portraits and pictures framed in red on the yellow walls. The smell of fresh-made corn tortillas, roasted peppers, and chilies filled the room. The waitresses wore long green-and-blue ruffled skirts with snowy-white peasant blouses.

Sunny ordered the enchilada combo plate, with extra cheese, and fruit-flavored iced tea. Rita had chili rellenos and a glass of sangria. While they waited for their orders they talked about the events of the last few days, also recalling memories of Gina and some of the good times. Sunny mentioned the papers she'd found at Gina's house.

"I can't remember where I put them. I keep moving them to different places."

Rita took a drink of her wine. "Why do you think they're important?"

"It's the feeling I got when I saw them."

They ate in silence. Sunny was lost in her own thoughts. Why did she have that strange feeling about the papers?

Finished, Rita talked about how her feelings toward Lee were changing.

Though Sunny was tired of that topic she listened. She knew her daughter wouldn't listen to her, though.

Rita was speaking. "When I stayed at his house, nothing I did was right. He seemed mad at me the whole time. I don't know what his problem is. I don't want to put up with his mood swings anymore. I have enough to think about. "

"Well, you know what I think. But you do what you want. After all, you're not sixteen."

Smiling, Rita stuck her tongue out and crinkled her nose.

"Ready to go?" Sunny picked up her purse and left the tip.

When they approached the rental car in the parking lot, Sunny was reminded how lucky they were. The damage was only a couple of dents. It could've been so much worse. With Gina gone, she couldn't imagine something happening to Rita too. She unlocked the car's doors and made a mental note to call the police when she arrived home. She didn't know what she could tell them, but at least there'd be a report on file for the rental company.

Rita got in on the passenger side. "I'll have to go to the salon tomorrow," she said. "It's my day to check supplies and do the paperwork."

"That's okay. I have things I want to work on at home," said Sunny. "Did I ever tell you how proud I am of you? A business owner at your age!"

"Well, you remember, if my godmother hadn't left the hair salon to me, I might not."

"Yes, but you've kept it going and made a good living from it." Sunny leaned over and squeezed her daughter's hand.

Sunny and Rita were home, relaxing with their shoes off when the ringing started. They stared at each other.

Rita rushed to answer it. "Mom, it's Barry." With a sigh of relief, glad it wasn't another hang-up, she handed the mouthpiece to Sunny.

"Hello?"

"I made it home okay," Barry answered.

"Was everything all right?"

"I don't know if someone broke into the house, or if a kid threw a ball, but the window in the front bedroom is smashed. Nothing seems to be missing, and everything else looks okay. The rain and wind caused a tree to fall over. It's small. Maybe caused by the storm. The backyard needs some cleaning. I'll get it done."

"Oh, damn. What else got trashed? Should I come home?"

"No. I said I'll do it. I've already called the police and our insurance. You don't have to do everything . . . Wonder Woman."

She grimaced. "Don't call me that. You know I hate it." It made her feel as if people viewed her as controlling and bossy. "I'm not in 'Wonder Woman' mode. But I need to trust you. Can you do it?"

"Give me some credit, okay? I can take care of things."

"I guess."

"See, there you go."

She sighed. "Okay, it's all yours. Call and let me know."

Sunny placed the receiver on its hook and turned to Rita. "Do I try to do everything myself?" Not letting her reply, she answered her own question. "It's only because of the drinking. I can't depend on him."

"Is it possible that you don't give him a chance? You act like he drinks day and night." Rita handed Sunny a cup of tea. "He holds down a responsible job, remember. I think he just wants to feel needed or appreciated. Everyone does."

"Maybe. We'll see. When did you get so wise?"

"Why didn't you tell him about the car hitting us tonight?"

"I didn't want him to worry. We don't know who hit us or why. It could be kids, old people, a drunk. Even if I think someone did hit us deliberately, what can we do about it now?"

Rita bit her lower lip. "I know. It's complicated. I wish we could've seen the license or even the color of the car—"

Sunny butted in. "Or if it was a man or woman. There is probably nothing we can do, except be thankful we weren't hurt."

"Yep." Rita hugged her mother good night and called Lee. He had her car and she needed it, but there was no answer. Shaking her head, Rita said, "I'm not going to worry about him. Night, Mom."

Sunny sat awhile longer. More time passed. She was exhausted. "It's been a long, hard day. Maybe I'll have a glass of wine. I deserve it," she noted. "I've gone years without a drink. What would it hurt?" She opened and closed her hands. A desperate need to check out the pantry built inside her. "I fell back on my promise to stay a nonsmoker." She closed her eyes tight. "I'm not going to do the same with drinking. If it's not one drink, it will be two, three, four . . . Besides, Gina needs me now."

In the kitchen she stopped and looked at the pantry. The wine bottle and bottles of beer on the shelf beckoned, as if they could somehow save her. "No," she decided. "No." She turned off the lights. Empty-handed and sober, she went to bed.

During the night something shook her bed. Surprised, she sat up. Sitting there as if she were real, on the edge of the bed, was Gina. Her long hair fell over her shoulder, covering half her face.

Sunny teared up, overwhelmed. "Oh, Gina, why did you do this?" she stammered.

"I would never leave my boys," Gina stated.

Sunny opened her eyes and was surprised to find she was alone, lying on her pillow. *Was Gina a dream? It was so real. Gina came to me. Now I know she needs me. Is this a dream now, or am I talking in my sleep?*

She turned onto her stomach and placed the pillow over her head. Sleep wouldn't come. She was up, tossing and turning, most of the night. She kept thinking about what Gina said. She vaguely remembered her saying that before. Somewhere.

I would never leave my boys.

What had Gina meant when she told me that?

Gina, please come back.

Sunny wondered if she was sorry she'd done it . . . or if she hadn't meant to leave her boys.

Then why had she done it?

Damn, I can't figure it out. She's drifting.

CHAPTER TWENTY-THREE

SATURDAY MORNING

Rita was ready to go to work, but Lee still had her car. "Damn it. He knows Saturday is my busy day. I can't be late." Annoyed, she called him again. It was both a surprise and a worry when there was no answer. She didn't want to wake up her mother because when she was up at one o'clock to get a drink of water her mother was engrossed in writing in her notebook. She never looked up.

Rita called Lee once more. This time he answered, bright and cheerful. "Lee," she said. "I need the car now. It's Saturday and I have to get to work. Supplies come in today. Remember, I told you?"

"Sorry, I'll be right there."

Rita held off asking why he wasn't home earlier. She wanted to see his reaction. Maybe he'd been in the shower. She blew on her coffee and watched for him out the window. He didn't take long. She set her cup in the sink and rushed out the door.

Sliding in the passenger side she smelled perfume. Sweet and flowery. "Why do I smell perfume? Where were you? I tried to call you last night." Nausea rose in her stomach. Her heart beat hard. She studied his face, watching the vein in his neck throb. Would he tell her the truth? Or was he lying to her?

"Hey, hold on," he said. "I was at my friend's house while he worked on my ride. If you smell anything it's aftershave." She tried to identify the smell when a can of WD-40 rolled out from under her seat. She knew that old Indian trick. WD-40 hides perfume. "I don't care. I told you, I need my car. Now you've made me late."

He averted his eyes. "Let me use it today. I have some important papers I need to sign. I'm buying a condo," he said. "I'll bring it by later. I promise."

"What the hell are you talking about? A condo! If you have money to buy a condo why do you need money from me? Never mind. I'm running late. I don't have time to drive you home. I'll call you when I'm finished, and be there!"

In front of her salon she got out and waved at him. He didn't say goodbye. *Shithead.* He didn't kiss her or return her wave. She assumed he was mad because she'd questioned him. She didn't deserve to be treated like this and would let him know about it.

Furious, Rita busied herself to keep from screaming, stocking supplies and a few shampoo sets, and then took a break as her employees caught her up on all the gossip. Looking around the reception area, Rita was proud of the changes she'd made in the salon. The walls were a cream color, and she'd added wood-grained stations. The chairs were either turquoise or ivory. Indian prints hung in turquoise frames on the walls.

The hairstylists wore black pants and black smocks. Rita wore a turquoise smock coat over black pants. She felt good about what she had accomplished. But it was nice to have her mom notice too.

Later, in the afternoon, ready to leave, she called Lee. Nothing. Sighing, her stomach flipped.

A few minutes later, one of the girls called her to the front reception desk. "You have a patron."

"I don't have any more appointments." She walked to the front of the salon.

Victor was in the reception area. Rita's gaze rolled over his forest-green sweatshirt. It brought out his seaweed-green eyes. Even though she wasn't familiar with him, she liked what she saw. "Hi, Victor. This is a surprise."

"Hi." He had a great smile. "Your sign says no appointment needed. Got time for a haircut?"

"Sure. I was ready to quit, but it won't take long."

He sat in front of the mirror; she put a towel around his neck. He had great shoulders. When she looked in the mirror she also noticed his bow-shaped mouth and cleft chin. With his sleeves pushed up, dark hairs shaded the curve of his forearms. Nice, she thought. Her hands were sweating. Why did she feel nervous around him?

He winked at her. "Just a little off the top."

Rita smiled back. "Half inch?"

"That's good." He glanced around the salon. "Nice place. I like the pictures."

"Thank you. Turquoise and cream are my favorite colors. I added the Indian theme to give it authenticity."

She looked at his face in the mirror, then away, when her pulse quickened. You have a boyfriend, she scolded herself. Or was he just a stranger who had conned her into buying a condo for?

"Excuse me a minute. I have to call Lee to pick me up." Rita left Victor and went to the phone; it rang and rang. She felt sick. Then she sucked it up and returned to her station. Her heart sinking, she tried to sound casual. "He's not home."

Her face in the mirror had lost some color.

Victor must have noticed. "I'll give you a lift."

Now embarrassment flowed across her face. "Thanks. He should be home by the time I finish." She picked up the comb and scissors, absorbing herself in her work in order to calm her mind. The *snip snip* of the scissors was soothing.

"I didn't see you at Gina's sweat," she said. "Did you go?"

"No, it didn't feel right. I did go to her funeral. I sat at the back."

Shaking her head, she murmured, "It's all so sad." Silence fell.

Rita finished his haircut. "Okay, done. How's that?" She gave him a mirror to view the back. "Could you wait a minute? I'll try to call Lee again."

Rita called one more time. No answer. "I guess I'll take that ride, if you don't mind."

Hanging up her smock, she grabbed her jacket and called out goodbye to everyone.

Rita thanked Victor as they left the salon. "I could have called my mother to come get me, but she needs to rest. Gina's death has been too much for her."

"It's fine. I'm off today, and it's not out of my way."

As they walked to his vehicle she remarked how nice his truck was and climbed in. "Isn't this the new '85 GMC?"

"Sure is. Right off the assembly line." While he was driving they talked about his truck, the weather, mundane things. But soon they were absorbed in conversation. He became animated and wasn't paying attention to where they were going. He took the wrong exit.

As soon as they came to the next stoplight Rita spoke up. "We were talking so much, you missed my exit. I missed it too." She slapped her forehead. "What's wrong with me?"

"Sorry," Victor said. "I tend to get gabby. I'll get us back to the highway, no problem." He drove steadily in the unfamiliar neighborhood looking for signs back onto the highway. He turned onto the next street. Each block had a row of brown stuccoed apartments or brick duplexes with small clean yards in front.

Rita tried to help. "I think this road goes to the freeway."

He wasn't so certain. "Feels like I'm driving in a circle. Not as quick and easy as I thought." He traveled a little farther to find an easy place to turn around.

Finally, Rita saw a car that looked exactly like her blue Mazda. "Slow down," she said. She realized she wasn't the only person in the world with a blue Mazda. When they neared the row of apartments, she looked at the car parked in the carport. Same color. Same everything. "There!" She pointed. "That's my car! What's it doing here?"

Victor turned his attention to her. "Are you sure? Wait. I'll pull over."

She jumped out almost before he came to a stop and ran to the carport. Peering inside the window of the vehicle, she saw an unfamiliar scarf across the front seat. But her favorite to-go cup was in the holder, and her half-finished paperback novel lay on the back seat. Confused, she checked the one telltale sign, the dent by the handle on the driver's side, and checked the license plate. Maybe she read it wrong? No. Definitely her car. Her heart beat faster.

Looking at the space number where her car was parked, she matched it up to the corresponding apartment. She located number 121 in black metal numbers next to the door. Rita knocked hard and heard movement inside. Standing tall, with arms down at her sides, her hands drew into fists.

The door opened and a small, frail, white-haired lady appeared, leaning on a cane. "May I help you?" the woman asked.

Rita stood stiff-legged, folded her arms, and stared at her. Flustered, she said, "I saw my car in space number 121 and I want to know what it's doing here."

"Oh dear, I don't know. The space numbers don't coordinate with the apartment numbers." The woman's hand shook on her cane. "They do that for safety reasons. I'm sorry."

Rita stood a minute looking at the closed door, uncertain what to do. She wanted to go bang on all the doors in the complex, but there were too many. Plus, she was with Victor, so she couldn't search through the area the way she wanted to. *Should I leave a note on the windshield? What would I say?* In the meantime, she decided to go home and wait for Lee. She'd talk it over with her mother.

Victor sat in his truck, listening to the radio. "What did you find out?" he asked. "Is that your car?"

Rita scooted in. "Yeah, I guess this is where Lee has been the last few days. Maybe it's his friend's place." Her voice cracked.

He asked no more of her. He started the truck and turned it around, to find the right on-ramp and take Rita home.

He cocked his head and looked at her. "Are you okay?"

"Yeah, I'll be fine. Thanks for taking me home. And the little detour that turned out to be a big detour." She tried to smile.

They drove on until Victor found his way to the highway. Farther along, she pointed. "This is my exit."

Even though her thoughts were jumbled and her stomach in knots due to finding her car in a strange neighborhood, she couldn't help but stare at Victor from time to time. She hated for their ride to be over. He was so nice. Those dark green eyes seemed to look right into her. She was sure he knew something was wrong, but she couldn't tell him what she really thought. She was too embarrassed to say, Lee is cheating on me. And even if he wasn't, she was done. He was too moody, and now she knew for sure that he was using her.

Victor kept chatting. "I don't know how I got lost. Sorry. I didn't have any trouble the other day. It's strange the way you found your car. I can see you're worried about it. But we don't have to talk about it. I just want you to know I care. You're a friend, Gina's friend."

"It's fine." She smiled. "I appreciate it. Thanks again."

In front of Rita's house, Victor got out and opened the door on her side of the truck. She wanted to flash a smile. But she was so tired and upset about finding her car where it shouldn't be that she couldn't manage it. She invited Victor in but he declined. She felt empty. There was nothing to do for it at the moment.

CHAPTER TWENTY-FOUR

Her mother was wiping off the kitchen table when Rita came in. "Hi, hon, what's going on with you?" Sunny asked. Rita told her about Victor's coming in for a haircut and giving her a ride home when she couldn't get a hold of Lee; taking the wrong exit; and then finding her car at a strange apartment building.

"What do you think I should do?"

"I'm not saying anything. You know how I feel."

A phone rang. Rita picked up. There was only a dial tone. "Another hang-up," she said irritably. "This has to be deliberate, but who could it be?"

"I got a couple today, myself," Sunny said patting the seat next to her.

"It's all too much." Rita sank onto the couch beside her mom. Floyd jumped in her lap and rubbed his head on her shoulder. Her emotions were still on fire.

She snapped at Sunny. "Did you hear me? I said what do you think I should do about Lee? I think he might be cheating on me. I don't want to go through any drama."

Sunny's voice rose. "I've already told you, dump him. But . . . you're not sixteen, remember?" She hated doing this dance with Rita. "You'll have to figure it out. You're an adult."

"I know. I will. It's just not that easy."

"Yes it is. But I'm too tired to debate with you about Lee, so let's just go find him. Go get a heavier coat and grab mine. It looks like it's going to snow."

Gratitude washed over Rita. "Really? Oh, Mom, that's great."

"We'll find your car, if it's still there. Then we'll wait as long as it takes, and follow him. Lee doesn't know what my rental car looks like. Whatever he's doing there he's being a jerk," Sunny said. "Besides, I don't like anyone using or hurting my daughter."

CHAPTER TWENTY-FIVE

Rita gave her mom directions. Going back to the turnoff, Rita sat forward, looking out the window, explaining where the apartment building was where she last saw her car. Rita pointed as they drove up to the carport.

Sunny found an empty stall where they could watch Rita's Mazda. Sunny killed the engine and flicked off the headlights.

"Good. We're lucky he's still here. Mom, do you think it's possible that he is telling the truth?" She bowed her head and fidgeted with her hands. "Maybe he ran out of gas, or his friend is working on it."

"Stop making excuses for him. Wouldn't he have called you if that were the case? And why would his friend work on *your* car?"

With her bottom lip pushed out, Rita stammered, "I guess."

Sunny sighed. "Rita, honestly, what do you want me to say?"

It was getting dark as they watched the choreography of snowflakes disappearing on the black, slick street. The lights in the carport gave a winter glow to the neighborhood.

"I wish we knew what apartment he's in," said Sunny. "We've been here a half hour. It's getting cold."

"Look! There he is!" Rita shouted and wiggled in her seat. Lee walked out of a ground-floor apartment. She knew it was him, even from a distance. He wore his faded brown shirt, his khaki pants, and black jacket. His hair was a mess, like a scarecrow. Next to him was a tall woman. They appeared relaxed with each other, more than friendly.

"Who's that with him? Dang." Rita grabbed the door handle.

Sunny reached over and pushed her shoulder against the seat back. "Settle down. Wait."

Lee and the woman clung to each other as they walked to the car. Taller than Rita, the woman wore a navy pea coat and a dark beanie. Her long blonde hair poked out from under her cap and rested on her shoulders.

Rita's eyes were watery. "Oh, great. A tall blonde."

Lee opened the car door and got in behind the wheel, leaned over, and gave the woman a lengthy kiss. She got into the passenger seat beside him.

"That tells you all you need to know," said Sunny.

Rita felt her life crumble. Her eyes teared. "What a fool I've been. What the hell? And in *my* car, the bastard!" Rita let her tears go. "I'm going to kill him."

Sunny held Rita's arm. "Stay put. Let's follow him first. Find out all the details before you chop him into little pieces . . . or I kill him."

Lee backed out, then drove away from the apartment complex and tore across the street onto the freeway.

Sunny trailed behind. "I told you he wouldn't recognize us. Try to keep calm, okay?"

Rita pounded the dash with her fist. "I feel sick. I'm embarrassed, and pissed. Worse, he kisses another woman . . . in my car, for Christ's sake. And look how he's treating it! I love that car. It looks like he's headed to his apartment." She fell back in the seat, tears streaming.

Sunny trailed Lee, careful to stay a few cars behind. He drove off the freeway, down his road, and pulled into his carport. Sunny parked across the street. The spot gave them a good view of Lee's place.

"Mom, I'm going to go get my car." She wiped her face.

Already, Lee and the woman were entering his apartment, closing the door casually, as if this were nothing out of the ordinary.

"Rita? Wait!" But it was too late.

Rita opened the car door and bolted. "Don't worry, I won't start anything. After the way he's treated me, I just want to scare the crap out of him. He's nothing but a dog. I can't wait to see how surprised he's going to be." She slammed the door and ran across the street.

Rita bent her head, charging into the swirling snowflakes as she walked up and banged on the door of number 104. When she heard footsteps she moved out of the way of the peephole. When Lee opened the door and saw her standing there, his mouth dropped open.

Rita smiled and walked in, not waiting to be asked. "Hi," she said. She moved over to shake the hand of the pretty blonde, who had kicked off her shoes and made herself comfortable. *Whore.* "I'm Rita, and you are?"

Lee jumped in. "This is . . . um . . . my real estate agent, Cathy. Remember, I told you I was buying a condo? Wha . . . what are you doing here? I was going to bring your car back . . . uh." He glanced at the clock on the wall. "Uh, I guess I'm a little late. We were finishing up with the paperwork."

Rita looked around and saw no documents. "What paperwork? I guess you haven't had time to get to it. And you were going to bring my car back when . . . ? When you were flippin' good and ready." She smirked, delighted that she'd caught them outright. She could see how nervous she was making both of them. "What a pitiful liar you are," she told Lee.

Then she turned to the woman, who stared at her, mouth half-open. "You must have something he wants. Be careful, sweetie, he'll use you too. It's what he does best, next to lying."

Lee walked to her. "Wait, Rita, listen." He stretched his arm out as if to touch her.

She held her palm out to block him as she backed up a step. "No butthole, you listen. Give me my keys. I want out of this hellhole, and away from you and your lying-ass, user bullshit."

He reached in his pocket, pulled out her keys and handed them to her. She walked out and slammed the door.

Rita tromped in long, angry strides to the car and motioned for her mother to roll down the window. "What happened in there?" Sunny asked. "I was getting worried."

"I'm fine, called him a few names. Met her. Cathy. His 'real estate agent.' Wonder what else she's selling him?" Rita wiped at her eyes and looked at her mother.

"Or giving him . . ."

They smiled.

"I'll get my car and meet you at home."

Sunny nodded. "Be careful." She waited until Rita was in her car before she drove off.

Rita was so mad she couldn't think straight. She had to escape. Lee had messed with her car, pushed the driver's seat so far back she couldn't reach the gas pedal. She had to readjust everything: the car seat, the rearview mirror, the side mirror. What a mess. And really, all she wanted to do was get the hell out of there.

The lingering scent of another woman's perfume made her sick. Then she realized she had smelled it before, in the car when Lee picked her up. She felt like crying, but wouldn't. Not for him. She started the engine to drive straight home.

As she shifted to reverse and backed out, she almost ran into Lee and his "realtor." Slamming hard on the brake, she rolled down the window, ready to bite their heads off.

Lee begged, "Can you give us a ride back to her house? It's starting to snow, and Cathy needs to get home."

Rita laughed. "Call a taxi. This one's out of service." She rolled up the window, smiled sweetly, waved, and drove off. Her entire body shook. How could he be so cold-blooded?

As soon as she got home she told her mother what happened.

Sunny's eyes were on fire. Her face turned red.

"Is he nuts?" exclaimed Rita. "What a coldhearted asshole! That takes nerve! Well, he's out of my life. I don't feel as bad as I thought I would." Rita rubbed at her eyes again. "So why do I keep crying?"

Sunny sat with her head bent. "It'll pass. I know you're upset, but he wasn't the one for you. If someone loves you he'd never do that to you. Now, only your pride is hurt."

Rita sat across from her mother at the kitchen table. She looked into Sunny's face and could tell something had happened, something else, more than with Lee and his blonde. "What's wrong?" Rita put her hand on Sunny's arm. She knew Sunny had her own relationship problems.

"I walked past the mirror and saw the dark circles under my eyes. I'm tired of crying too. I love Barry, but I can't put up with the drinking. I don't know what to do about Gina and her 'suicide.' My face is a mess. I can't sleep. And crying does no good." She reached for a tissue on the coffee table.

"I'm sorry, Mom." Rita sniffled and gave her a hug. "Guess we're both crybabies."

Sunny stood and threw the tissue in the fireplace. She rubbed hard at her face. "God, I'm so sick of all of this. I need a break. You need a break. Why don't we forget about our problems for a while? Let's go to the Cal Neva and gamble a little. My treat."

Rita grinned. "Sounds good to me, especially the treat part."

"Oh, yeah." Sunny swatted her on the butt. "No more tissues for us. Let's take your car. You just drove. The engine should still be warm."

CHAPTER TWENTY-SIX

An hour later twilight fell in a purple haze as they walked into the casino. Both glanced at the outrageous carpet. Red-and-black swirls designed to be disorienting. The place was busy, thanks in part to tour buses from Canada and Washington. The odors of cigarettes and booze mixed with multiethnic restaurant smells.

Sunny glanced over at the slot machines. Bells and carnival music went off on the slots where tourists tried their luck. They passed by the tavern known to locals as The Long Bar.

"Rita, you know, this bar is the size of three bars strung together." Sunny was mesmerized by it.

Rita elbowed her mom and jerked her chin toward a man sitting there. "Look, there's Jesse."

A drink sat in front of him and there was a napkin on top of the beer glass at the next stool. "Someone's sitting beside him. Must've gone to the restroom."

He looked up and motioned to them. They strolled over to greet him. He stood and hugged them. Sunny felt her skin grow hot. She was uncomfortable with Jesse, and not for the first time. Sunny pointed to the slots against the wall. "I'm going to try the machines over there." She felt suffocated. She had to get away.

Rita smelled a familiar cheap fragrance and turned around. Eva, who was coming up behind them, pushed herself between Rita and Jesse. "What the hell is this? Why is she here?" asked the evil woman.

"What the hell does it look like?" Jesse hollered. "You don't get to say who I can talk to."

Eva grabbed her drink, spilling some of it on the long bar. She turned her nose up. "My friend's upstairs in the restaurant. I'll be in there." She stormed off.

"Man, she's something else." Rita pulled up a stool next to Jesse. She watched her mom out of the corner of her eye. Sunny was scanning all the machines, looking for that lucky one. Rita chuckled. Sunny picked the last one in the corner and climbed on the chair, eager as a little kid.

Jesse playfully punched Rita's arm. "Hey, where's the boyfriend?"

She felt her stomach tighten. "We're done. Through. Over and out."

"Great. He was a phony, anyway. You're too good for him."

Rita frowned and changed the subject. "Enough about him. How are you doing? How're the kids?"

"I'm doing okay. The boys are still with my mom. She has a lot of land for them to run around on, and the boys love all the horses, dogs, and cats. They still have nightmares about their mom. It's horrible for them. I go over every evening." He played with his napkin.

"I'm sorry, Jesse, for all of us." Rita wanted to focus on something else. "Why is Evil Eva always around?"

"She sticks to me like flypaper. I don't know what's wrong with her."

Rita smiled. "Eva's always been in love with you. Now she's obsessed."

"Believe me, the feeling's not mutual. It was over the minute I met Gina. Not that it was all that much in the first place. I have to give Eva hell all the time. She thinks she's in charge, and that's not going to fly. I don't know why she's at my house all the time. She's wearing me out talking to herself all the time and singing. She drives me nuts."

"She has a big problem with both my mom and me." Rita ordered a merlot. "I don't know why. We never did anything to her, but she's never liked us. Who can figure her out?"

"Eva's jealous. She knows Gina told you and Sunny everything, but never confided in her," he said. "She's one weird chick."

Bells went off across the crowded room. She touched his arm. "Look, my mom is jumping up and down and waving. It's her machine. Let's go see what she won."

"You go on. It's late. I'm heading out. Catch ya later." He gave her a hug. She watched him walk up the few steps and through the large glass double doors.

Rita felt bad for him and his boys, but she and her mom had loved Gina too. It was all too much to think about. She picked up her wine and hurried over to her mom.

The bells and music from the slot machine were loud enough to get the attention of all in the vicinity. Rita arrived just as the attendant paid her mother one thousand dollars in hundred-dollar bills. Sunny was so excited she hugged everyone around her.

Eva appeared from around the slot machine. Sneaky, like a snake.

"Where's Jesse?" Eva hissed. Eva and her friend were glaring at them. A cigarette dangled from the corner of the friend's mouth. She looked older than Eva, skinny, dark, a wrinkled face, short salt-and-pepper hair.

They reminded Sunny of high school bullies. Eva's large round glasses gave the impression of a cartoon turtle.

Rita pointed toward the front entrance as they made their exit, then turned her back on them. "Good riddance," she mumbled. Music and bells went off on other machines announcing other winners.

After Sunny tipped the change person, she put her winnings in the inside pocket of her jacket and zipped it up. She grabbed a seat at the small table. "I'd like a soda. Winning makes me thirsty. I want to arrange the money in my purse."

"I'll get you one." Rita set her glass on the table and moved over to the snack bar.

When Rita returned, Sunny was waving toward the gambling tables. "Who are you waving at?"

"My friend, Karen. She's the pit boss over the Twenty-One tables." The woman behind the tables was a tall, dark woman with a close-cut Afro. Karen had aged some but was still beautiful, her complexion flawless, big brown eyes, full lips.

"Karen and I used to work together, before your time. Back in the early sixties black people weren't allowed in the casinos. And neither were Indians."

"What! That's crazy."

"I know, but true. This town was something else. Back then, when the casinos were for whites only, a Chinese man bought a casino and brought busloads of minorities in from San Francisco and Oakland. The club had a big entertainment room for the celebrities he brought in."

"Glad it's not like that now."

"I'd go say hello, but bosses don't appreciate that."

She and Karen waved at each other. "I guess she's just a casino junkie." She laughed. "But . . . good for her. You ready to go?"

Mother and daughter went out the door arm in arm, their matching smiles announcing they were big winners.

"Can you believe it! A thousand dollars!" Rita squealed.

"I sure can!" Sunny shouted.

Rita laughed, glad to see her mom happy.

"Eva and her friend looked like they wanted to kick our asses," said Rita.

Sunny jutted her jaw out as they raced down the steps of the casino. "You mean *try* to kick our asses."

They giggled so hard they couldn't stop. Finally, nearly sick from laughing, they entered the parking garage.

The smiles on their faces disappeared when they saw a uniformed policeman and another man standing by Rita's car. "What's going on?" Rita asked. She immediately thought, Lee? Did he mess with my car?

The cop introduced himself as Officer Boyle, and the man next to him as Mr. Adams. The man tried to say something but was cut off by the cop.

"This your car?" the officer asked.

Rita's heart sped up. "Yes. What's wrong?"

The officer continued. "Somebody slashed your tires. Mr. Adams saw two people."

Rita looked at the men, knots in her stomach. Gathering herself together she bent down and checked out one tire. "What the . . . ? My new tires?"

Sunny circled around to the passenger side. "Damn. I can't believe these things keep happening. Is someone targeting us?" She stopped and looked at the trunk. "They keyed the trunk, Rita. Officer, did you see the trunk?"

"No. I didn't."

Sunny motioned for him to take a look. He walked to the back of the car. "That's really observant," he said.

"I've had some training," she answered. "I'm a fraud investigator in San Francisco."

Rita joined them at the back of her car. She shook her head, took in a deep breath, and stood up, looking throughout the parking lot for other possible witnesses. Mr. Adams was looking around also, obviously shaken. It was as if he was being protective of them. That was nice, for a change.

Mr. Adams had seen enough to call the cops. Rita wanted to talk to him. She joined the men at the front of the car.

Mr. Adams leaned toward Rita. "I saw them bending down. At first I thought they needed help. When I saw the one slashing at the tire, I yelled, and they got up and ran off."

"Male or female?" asked Rita, wondering if it could have been Eva and her friend.

Mr. Adams looked directly at them. "I'm sorry. They had jackets with hoods. I only saw them from the back. But when they took off I did notice that they were both slender. One was shorter than the other."

Sunny stared at the policeman whose buttons were pulling against the buttonholes. He removed his cap and ran his meaty fingers through his thin blond buzz cut.

He didn't look up as he pulled his notebook out of his shirt pocket and got busy writing. Suddenly he stopped and asked Rita, "Registration and license, ma'am?"

"What? Why? This is my car. I'm not going to claim a car with two slashed tires."

"I know, ma'am. Procedure."

Rita passed her mother on her way to the passenger side and got in. She opened her glove compartment and retrieved the documents, grabbing them, along with her license from her wallet. "Crap. This is a mess. What kind of jerks would do this and why? Eww, he called me 'ma'am.'"

Rita opened the door and walked by her mom. A small whirlwind of dust circled around the flat tire. Rita gave her documents to the officer.

"Do you have any idea who might have done this?" he asked.

Rita looked from the cop to her mother.

Moving to the back of the car, Sunny dropped to her knees. She was engrossed in the back tire. She didn't know if a voice emanated from the little whirlwind, or was it her instinct? She looked under the wheel and found a small pointed triangular silvery item. It looked like part of a bottle opener.

Sunny held it out to the cop. "Here. I found this under the tire, something to key a trunk with?"

The cop's eyebrows shot up and his mouth turned down in surprised admiration.

"That's my mom," Rita said. "One of the best fraud investigators ever."

Sunny spoke up. "Officer, I can understand one tire being an accident, or maybe mischief. But two tires and a keyed trunk indicate a targeted attack."

"You could be right, ma'am," he said.

"Yes, she's right," Rita said. "I have a good idea who could have done this. We've had some weird and terrible things happen to us these past few weeks. My mother's car was rammed from behind repeatedly when both of us were in it . . . on the highway. I get hang-ups, nearly nonstop."

The officer looked at them and gave Rita back her documents. "Did you call the police and file a report?

"No, we didn't. We're still not certain who's doing this. When the ramming happened it was dark and pouring down rain."

"Too bad they got away." Rita shook her head in disgust.

Sunny turned to Rita. "It sounds like Eva. She knows your car, and she and her friend were in the casino tonight."

"I'm sorry. Did you say you *think* you do know who's doing all of this? Or do you *know* you know? You can come into the station tomorrow and make out a harassment report. Might be hard to prove, but it will be on record." Officer Boyle asked, "For now, do you ladies have anyone who could come help you? A friend? Triple A?"

Rita spoke up. "Yes, I have Triple A. I live on Park Street, close to the police station. I have a spare tire in my trunk and another one in my garage. I just bought these two tires. They were brand-new. I kept one for a spare."

"Good thinking. Keeping a spare is smart," Mr. Adams said.

Officer Boyle looked at Rita. "Yes, you're lucky. Sorry. Well, I guess we're finished here. Maybe you could take a taxi back or call a friend."

"Let me drive you home," Mr. Adams said. "I wish I'd arrived earlier, maybe I could have prevented it. I can help you bring the other tire back."

"We appreciate what you did, Mr. Adams," said Sunny.

Rita nodded. "Yes. But we'll be fine."

"No, I insist. Look at what parking floor you're on here, and you can call Triple A when you're leaving your house. It'll take them a while."

"Well, I don't know. What do you think, Mom?"

Officer Boyle spoke before Sunny could answer. "I have Mr. Adams's name and address, if that's a concern."

"All right, thank you." Sunny and Rita followed Mr. Adams and got in his brown Mercedes, Rita in the front, Sunny, in the back. The car matched his clothes: brown slacks and a tan shirt with a brown suede Western jacket.

Mr. Adams was quiet on the drive and finally they pulled into the driveway. He kept the motor running and popped his trunk. Rita and Sunny got out and hurried to the garage.

"We'll get it," Rita called to him.

They rolled the tire out to the car. While Mr. Adams put it in his trunk, Sunny got back in and Rita ran into the house to call AAA.

Later, as they drove into Cal Neva's parking garage, AAA had not yet arrived. After a half hour, Mr. Adams said goodbye. As they thanked him the mechanic showed up. He replaced two tires, quick and easy, and was gone. Sunny was glad they'd called AAA. It made the night easier somehow, as did the cop and Mr. Adams.

It was all done in a matter of minutes, but they were left wondering who and why.

CHAPTER TWENTY-SEVEN

At home they discussed what had happened. Rita eyes flashed fire. She was livid. They both were.

"It's Eva. It has to be."

Sunny patted her knee. "You need to get some sleep. Worry won't help anything right now." Rita hugged her and headed for bed.

Sunny stayed on the couch. Rage flooded her. She felt like killing Eva for doing this. But she needed proof. She began to formulate a plan.

Although it was late Sunny wanted to call Barry to share her good news, and the bad news. She missed her best friend. She needed him now.

"Hello?" Barry sounded groggy.

"Hi, sorry if I woke you. I have some bad news and great news. Which do you want first?"

"I'll take the bad news first. That'll wake me up."

Sunny finished telling him about Rita's slashed tires and keyed trunk. She withheld the other things that had been happening. A little at a time.

"Damn! Well, at least the guy helped out. And he called the police. Both of you go down and sign a harassment statement. Whether or not they're ever caught you'll have it on record."

"We will. Now for the good news. I'm so excited! I couldn't wait. I won a thousand dollars!"

"Wow, great. I get half, right? Community property."

"No," she kidded. "I won it in Nevada, so it doesn't apply in California."

"Won't fly, babe. It's the same law in Nevada. I'm an officer of the court, remember?"

"Probation Department doesn't count."

They shared a happy, close moment. Her heart was full of longing for him. She loved his humor, needed his friendship. Regardless of how things were, she missed her husband.

"How's everything else going?"

"Rita and Lee broke up. She found out he's a cheating asshole." Sunny told him about Lee using Rita's car, the money, and about the so-called real estate agent.

"Good. There was something about him I didn't like . . . or trust. I'm glad she's rid of him. "

Sunny shook a cigarette loose from its pack and lit it. "What's going on with you?"

"If you're asking if I'm drinking, the answer is no. I've worked on the house, both inside and outside." He chuckled. "The broken window was from a baseball. I found it under the dresser."

"Good. Go back to sleep. I'll call you tomorrow."

"All right, you be careful. I love you."

"I know. Good night." She wanted to say I love you too, but couldn't. Not yet. They'd been through so much. She had no idea if their marriage was going to work out.

CHAPTER TWENTY-EIGHT

SUNDAY AFTERNOON

Rita had talked Sunny into getting her hair styled and her nails done. As they headed to the salon Sunny said, "I wish our shops in California were open on Sunday."

"Reno's a twenty-four seven town, not like other places."

Later, while Rita cut her hair, her mother said, "Getting the whole beauty treatment is a great way to relax. Thank you. It's what I needed."

The chime on the door rang. A woman bustled in, a stack of business cards in her hand. She walked right up to Rita and handed her one. *Madam Carmen—Psychic. Fortunes Read.* The woman's straight black hair was held at the nape with a large turquoise comb. "I'm from Guatemala," she said, her speech heavily accented. "I read fortunes my whole life. I like to read yours."

Rita looked at the card and handed it back. "You can put your business cards on the desk, but don't bother my customers."

Sunny sat straighter. "I'll let you tell my fortune."

"Ma'am?"

"Come back after the salon closes at five thirty," Sunny added.

"Okay. Thank you, ma'am."

Rita finished combing her mother's hair. "Do you think that's a good idea?"

"You know I'm always intrigued by fortune tellers. I have my own visions. So many strange things go on. I might be able to learn something. This could be interesting."

"Well, don't tell her a thing. Let her do the talking."

When Rita's employees left she tidied the salon, then pulled a manicure table over. They sat and waited.

At exactly five thirty Madam Carmen walked in, dressed in an ankle-length ebony dress. She wore a matching scarf with a black cape draped over her shoulders. A large black felt hat shaded part of her face. She sat opposite Sunny and produced a well-used deck of tarot cards wrapped in a silk scarf from an oversized tote bag. Piously peeling off the silk, then shuffling the cards, Madam Carmen asked Sunny to cut them into three stacks: one for the past; the second the present; and lastly, the future. Watching Sunny intently, she turned each one facedown on the table.

The fortune teller instructed, "Think who or what you want to ask cards about. I'll know."

Sunny nodded. *Did Gina kill herself? Why? What happened?*

Madam Carmen dipped her head in acknowledgment and began turning the cards over. "I see turmoil in your family, many things are there. You married, yes? Someone else interested in you. Be careful. Not good energy around you. Do not trust friends . . . jealous people around you." Madam Carmen studied them. Her eyebrows drew together in a wrinkled V as she studied the faded Death card. "Hmm, you have tragedy, yes?"

Rita sat up and took notice. Sunny turned and looked at her daughter, then back at the fortune teller. "Yes."

"Woman, close friend, she try to contact you . . . so you know truth. I see you have gift of spirits also. See, here in card."

Sunny looked at the cards but they had been used so much the images were faded. She leaned over the table and saw the king next to the emperor. "I see the emperor in the chair covered with a red cape, holding a specter and sword. The king sits on the throne covered with a patterned cloth."

"Emperor: father figure of cards," said Madam Carmen staring at it. "Something wrong. Needs fix. You can fix."

"Does it say anything else? Like how?"

"Many people in this circle. You know what your friend wants. Don't be fooled by outsiders. She want to help you find truth. She has journey to finish." Madam Carmen suddenly stopped and looked around. Her large dark eyes grew larger.

"Can you feel her spirit here?" Sunny rubbed her goose-bumpy arms.

"I finish. Time up, I go." With shaking hands the fortune teller gathered her tarot deck. She dropped some, looked around, and nervously picked them up. The rest she threw in her bag and rushed out the door before Rita and Sunny were even out of their chairs.

"Wait!" Sunny and Rita hollered in unison as the fortune teller shot like lightning down the sidewalk.

"What was that about?" Rita asked, combing her fingers through her hair as she glanced after the fortune teller as the salon door banged shut.

"I'm not sure."

SUNDAY EARLY EVENING

On the way home Sunny and Rita stopped at Juicy's for hamburgers. Rita stayed in the car and waited. Sunny was ordering when a man behind her murmured in her ear, "You still have your great high school figure."

She whipped around. About to tell him to mind his own business, she came face-to-face with Gerald, her ex-fiancé. She was shocked to see him. "You didn't know me in high school," Sunny said, dismissively, regretting even answering him.

They picked up their orders and stepped outside. "Doesn't matter. You look terrific."

"You probably shouldn't be saying that to me. You-know-who might get offended and blow a gasket. I know it's not my business, but why are you dating Eva?"

"Believe it or not, she's fun. Kooky."

"You mean cuckoo, don't you? Like wacko?" She smiled. Talking with him seemed odd, but easier now.

"She's not uptight, like somebody else I know."

Sunny's mouth gaped and her eyes widened as she pointed to herself. "Are you talking about me? I'm fun," she said and scrunched her eyes at him.

"Sure." He winked at her. "Can I call you while you're here?"

Sunny's anger rose. "No. I'm married. And I'm uptight, remember? You're with her. You stay on your own side of the street. Bye."

"There's no ring in my nose. I'll call you," he shouted after her.

Sunny hurried to the car, her face hot. "I won't be picking up."

"What happened?" asked Rita. "Isn't that Eva's boyfriend?"

Sunny slid onto the car seat and handed Rita the bags of food and large paper cups of soft drinks.

Staring straight ahead, she started the car. "Yeah. Ran into Gerald. He flirted with me, then insulted me. Said I'm uptight. Humph. End of story."

Gripping the wheel she pursed her lips, unwilling to answer any of Rita's questions about him.

On the ride home music filled the car. Sunny's mind was going in a hundred different directions. They were met at the door by Floyd's strong *mee-oww*. He weaved in and out of Rita's legs, begging for attention. After they finished their hamburgers and colas, Rita went to close the blinds.

"Mom, look outside. There's a car parked across the street. It looks like Jesse's. I noticed it when we came home. Someone's in it, smoking a cigarette. I can see the glow."

Sunny went to the window. "If it's Jesse, go out and tell him to come on in. It's starting to rain. I'm looking for the papers I found at his place."

Rita stood on the front porch and motioned to the driver. The engine started and the vehicle sped away. "Odd. Why would he leave?"

"Are you sure it was him?"

"Not really, but the car's the same make and model as his."

Sunny sat at the big oak table and finished the last of her cola. "This entire day has been strange. Starting with the gypsy, or whatever she was. The whole scene was eerie. At least now I know Gina really does want our help."

"What about that car?" Rita said, biting her nails. "Do you think it could be Eva? She seems to be everywhere and into everyone's business. And she bought herself the same car as Jesse's."

"Or it could simply be someone reading a map. Something might be going on, but I don't want to overreact. I want to be sure," Sunny said.

"Well, we didn't imagine almost getting run off the road. Or my tires being slashed. Eva's crazy enough to do it."

Sunny nodded. "She is crazy."

Moving down the hall, Rita announced, "I'm going to take a shower."

Finished with her shower, she came out, removed Floyd from the chair, then brushed cat hair off the cushion so she could sit next to her mom. "What's up?"

The ringing of the phone interrupted their conversation. Rita got up to answer. "If it's another hang-up I'm going to scream."

It wasn't. It was Jesse.

"Hi, Jesse," Rita said. "How're you doing? Did you come by earlier tonight?" She looked at her mom, shook her head and shrugged her shoulders.

"I'm relaxing, and Mom's looking for those papers she found at your house."

Sunny jumped up, almost knocking over the table. She shook her head and waved her hands in a panic.

"Uhh, never mind, it's not important. What's up?" She listened. "I don't know . . . Is Eva going to be there?"

Looking at her mom, she poked her fingers into her mouth, making a gagging motion. "I'll call you when I'm ready." Pausing, she went on. "Okay? Bye."

"Mom, what's going on with you? I thought Jesse knew you took those papers."

"No! No one does. Someone tore them up and threw them in Gina's wastebasket. We don't know yet why Gina killed herself, or if, who, or why. Until I figure it out I don't want anyone to know I'm looking into this. Not about my book or the papers or anything, especially Jesse. He could have something to do with this. Or he could tell Eva. She could have done it. Maybe even Victor. And who knows who else?"

Rita chewed on her bottom lip. "I'm sorry, Mom. I didn't think. I can't remember now if I said anything about this to Victor."

Sunny patted her daughter's hand. "It's okay, we'll figure this out. What did he want?"

"He wants me to come over and see if there is anything of Gina's we'd like to keep."

Sunny felt her heart sink. "Oh, that's nice of him, and awful, at the same time. Seems to me a little too quick. I don't want anything. It's too soon and too horrible." She thought for a moment. "But you know him. He'll probably just give her stuff away. That's also terrible."

"I can't handle taking her things right now," Rita said. "It's too hard on me. Plus, I don't want to be anywhere near Eva. But I don't want her to have Gina's things."

"Maybe I'll take the dream catcher earrings I made for her when she first came to live with us. She always wore them," said Sunny. "Now that I think about it, I'm sorry I didn't have them put on her to be buried in."

Rita took a step down the hall, turned around, walked back, and gave her mom a hug. "I'm tired; I'm going to go to bed."

"Me too, but, I want to finish writing in my notebook. Then I'll turn out the lights."

Sunny was asleep when she felt Gina's presence. She sensed her coldness and tried to hold her close. Gina's ghost form swayed back and forth. "Oh, Gina, I miss you. Why would you do such a horrible thing? Why?"

Gina gazed at her. *I need to be with my boys. I can't leave.* Suddenly Sunny felt Gina shake her shoulders and heard her piercing scream. *What happened to me? I can't find peace. Where are my boys?*

Sunny grabbed at Gina's hands, trying to hang on to her. Her spirit disappeared. "No! Gina. No!" she hollered. "Don't go!"

"Mom. Mom, wake up! Are you okay?" Rita shook her. "Wake up."

Sunny's eyes snapped open. She breathed hard as she looked at her daughter. "Damn, I had a dream about Gina again. She asked me what happened to her and where her boys are. I tried to hold her. I thought it was her shaking me until I woke up. She's still with us. But her spirit is unsettled."

Sunny watched her daughter leave the room and bring her a drink of water. They sat and talked about the dream, while Sunny's breathing returned to normal. Rita gave her a bear hug and lay with her mother, until they both fell asleep.

CHAPTER TWENTY-NINE

EARLIER IN THE EVENING

Jesse had made a quick run to the liquor store, grabbing his usual six-pack and a fifth of Old Crow, before he pulled into his driveway. His gaze was on the radio knob so he didn't notice the identical silver Mustang until he looked up, seconds later. "Shit!" he hollered, feeling his eyebrows pull together. Eva! In his house! He jumped out of the car, slammed the door, and took the stairs two at a time. His lips were set in a hard line. Boomer, his black lab, ran to him to be petted. Jesse was too mad and ignored him. He swung open the front door. "What the hell are you doing here?" She stood at the phone like a innocent bystander, but couldn't pull it off, as she covered the mouthpiece with her hand. She seemed surprised to see him, then embarrassed, as she slowly hung up.

"Wh-what are you doing here?" Her face turned red.

"What do you mean, what am I doing here? I live here! What the hell are you doing here? Who were you calling?"

"No one. I dropped by to pick up some of my clothes." She snatched up her small bag from the chair. As she passed Jesse, he grabbed her arm and swung her around.

"Leave my key on the table and get the hell out of here. Don't come back unless I invite you. Which ain't gonna happen." He turned on the porch light and shoved her out the door. Sniffing the air, he said, "Driving drunk again? I can smell it on you." She yanked her arm free.

"No."

"Bullshit, I know that smell." He pointed. "What'd you do to your front bumper? It's all dented." Eva squinted her eyes and gave him a dirty look.

"None of your business." She unlocked the car door, slid behind the wheel, and sped off.

"Next time, call first," he shouted after her. He picked up a small rock and threw it at the dust behind her moving car. "Damn crazy woman, sneaky bitch, always slithering around, and talking to herself or her cat. Drives me crazy." He walked back into his house accompanied by Boomer. In his kitchen, he put the beer in the refrigerator, save one, popped the top, and took a swig, trying to forget about how Eva infuriated him. In his recliner, sipping his beer, his mind began to relax. The boys could stay at his mom's for a while, but then what would he do? Then he wondered about Rita's comment to him over the phone about finding some papers. "She sounded sexy." He smiled. "What papers is she talking about?" Boomer licked his hand.

CHAPTER THIRTY

Driving along the wet street, Eva smiled and turned up the radio. One of her favorites, "Me and Mrs. Jones" by Billy Paul, came on and she sang her version. "Me and Mr. Jesse."

"I think I'll go by Rita's one more time. Last time she came out on the porch and almost caught me." She laughed and continued singing until she parked across from Rita's house and cut the engine.

"Darn, they closed their blinds. Shit. I wish I could see inside. There's only a little glow. I wonder if they're talking about me. I bet they are. Good." She tapped her fingers on the steering wheel. "Humph. Well, if I can't see anything I don't want to just sit here."

The light sprinkle changed into big drops. Splatters smeared the dust on her windshield. The rain picked up and hammered the roof and hood. As she turned the key to leave, she saw a small drenched dog whose thick fur hung like a heavy blanket. "I can't stand seeing the poor defenseless creature in the rain. I've always been a sucker for animals." Eva opened the door. "Come here, little guy. You're all wet. Bet you're cold."

The soaked terrier scurried over. She scooped him up and set him on the passenger seat. "Phew, you smell like a wet dog." She laughed. "Oh, you are a wet dog." She turned on the heater, aiming a blast of warm air at the dog. She grabbed an old sweater from the back seat to dry him. "There, how's that, little guy?"

He trembled in her arms like an infant. She'd thought about having a baby once, but once was all it was. Plus, no one ever wanted to have kids with her. Maybe Jesse'd want to start a second family? She decided to be satisfied with her cat.

Lost in thought, she glanced through the windshield. *Good, the rain's stopped, just a black cloud passing over.* The dog whimpered and squirmed. She opened the door so he could jump out and watched him run toward a block of houses.

Eva started the car, turned on the radio, and sang to the music as she drove home. Now she smelled like a wet dog. It made her laugh. "Life can be good for me," she mused. "I just have to take care of one more detail. Then the future I've always wanted will come true."

Entering her house, Eva mumbled, "Gina's gone. Now I have to get Rita out of the picture. Then I'll have Jesse all to myself."

She started straightening the living room, picking up socks and shoes, arranging pillows on the couch. She'd never been very neat. She wondered if Jesse would care about that when they were together, but didn't really care if he did. She had first dibs on him, way back when.

"I've loved him forever," she declared, stooping to pick up a fast food wrapper. "I always thought Jesse and I would get married. Hell, I didn't even know Gina existed. Ended up, she's my half sister. Same mother, different fathers. Who cares? Big deal. I was fine on my own since I was eight, with my foster family." She looked at her cat. "Isn't that right, Pandora?"

Satisfied with the room, she threw her coat toward the couch. It landed on the floor.

She looked around her small place. It was tidy now, well, if she didn't count the cobwebs or the water stain on the ceiling, or the slippers under the couch. "Jesse belongs here with me. I should have had the big house, not Gina. He should have married me. Now we can fix things." Her gaze moved in the direction of her living room and bedroom. Two bookcases with scarves hanging over them blocked her bed. She tilted her head toward the little hall to the bathroom and the pink kitchen.

"God, this place is tiny. Well, it'd be cozy if Jesse lived here. There's enough room when Gerald stays over. He's sexy, and fun. I've known him a long time. But he's not Jesse." She thought she could smell Gerald's cologne. The smell made her wrinkle her nose. It wasn't the smell she wanted. She focused on Jesse.

"I'll invite Jesse over for dinner. After all, he has to eat," she said as she looked in the fridge and checked the freezer. "Wow, nothing but beer and ice cubes. Guess that means a trip to the store."

She picked her coat off the floor and walked out to the car. The streetlight showed dents in her front bumper. "Ha, Jesse thought I smashed my bumper because I was drunk. Oh no, honey. I was stone sober."

She chuckled to herself.

"Humph. Let's see. I'll serve Indian stew with fry bread. That should get him over here. He won't stay mad. I know how to butter him up."

In the store Eva picked up a pound of hamburger, green and yellow vegetables, and tomato sauce. In the cooler she eyed a twelve-pack and giggled, as if she'd just run into an old friend. "Eeee, can't ever have too much beer."

While paying for her groceries, she stared at the back of a thin woman with waist-length black hair. As Eva walked past the counter she tried not to stare but couldn't help it. *Is it who I think it is? Sunny? What's she doing here?* Hatred rose from her gut. She clenched her fingers on her grocery basket. "Bitch. I hate her and her whore daughter!" Her words tumbled out loudly. The woman in front of her turned and frowned at her. Eva moved around her. On closer scrutiny it was a stranger. Eva blinked, wondering how she had made such a silly mistake. Then she forgave herself. *Oh, it's not her. Just as well, what would I have done anyway? I can't punch her out in the supermarket.*

Interrupting her thoughts, the clerk asked, "Miss. Miss, are you okay? Do you want to sit? Your face is bright red. Can I get you something?"

"No, no, I'm fine. I just need a moment."

"That'll be fifteen dollars and twelve cents."

Eva paid with cash and grabbed her groceries before the clerk could make change and hurried out. Gripping the keys at the bottom of her purse, she felt upset for no good reason.

Gratefully, she sank behind the steering wheel, safe but breathing hard. "Boy, those two women sure can get my heart racing. Why do they do this to me? I hate them. They can go to hell, for all I care. They never liked me anyway." Eva wiped tears of frustration from her eyes.

After a few minutes, feeling better, she turned on the ignition and drove toward her tiny house, humming and singing her favorite country song, "Somebody Needs to Leave," by Reba McEntire.

At home she set the groceries on the kitchen counter and checked the clock. It was too late to call Jesse. Or cook dinner. She opened the refrigerator and laughed. "I'll just have a liquid dinner tonight." She pictured herself in bed with Jesse. She'd be a good wife for him. After finishing off the six-pack she called it a night.

MONDAY MORNING

Eva woke up early, excited about her big plans to have Jesse over for dinner. She turned on her radio and sang while she mixed up flour and water for fry bread. Patting the dough like tortillas, she dropped them into the pan as the oil snapped and crackled. Then she plated and stacked them to save for dinner.

Taking out the ingredients for her Indian stew she heaved the big kettle onto the stove and chopped and fried the hamburger, all the time singing.

"I should be a singer. I feel like I'm in a Disney movie. Some day my prince will come, and be mine, all mine. What do you think, Pandora? You always listen to me."

Later in the afternoon she called Jesse. "Hi. Want to come over for dinner? I made Indian stew and fry bread. And I have plenty of ice cold beer."

"No. I can't."

She hadn't expected his refusal. It shook her up. "But I cooked all day for you."

"What? What do you mean for me? Don't be doing shit like that. I told you before, I run my own life."

"I know, I know." She tried the guilt routine. "I'm just disappointed. Can I at least ask where you're going to eat?"

"It's none of your business, but I'm having dinner with my mom and the boys."

She saw herself in the mirror as she faked a smile. "Oh. Can I tag along?"

"No!"

"Oh, okay." Eva felt her world collapsing.

"I might take a run by Rita's."

She gripped the receiver so hard she thought it would break. Tears welled up.

"Well, then, I guess that's . . . all right. Goodbye." She was having a good cry and was ready to trash the fry bread and stew when the phone rang. *Oh good! He changed his mind!* Excited, she raced to answer, but it wasn't the voice she hoped to hear.

"Hi, baby. What's going on?" It was Gerald. "I was thinking about you. I thought maybe you went back to work."

Eva swallowed hard and answered slowly, "Nah, they gave me two weeks family leave for my sister's death, and I intend to take full advantage."

"Yeah, you should."

"You know, I've given the Social Security office fifteen years of my life. Shoot, I should retire." . . . *and take care of Jesse.*

"I thought maybe we could go out to dinner."

Good old Gerald, always there when I need him. "Why not come over here? I made Indian stew and fry bread. I have plenty of beer. Besides, it's too cold to go out."

"Okay, I'll be there after work. See ya."

"Great." She took her time hanging up. Tears blinded her. "Yeah . . . bye." She railed internally, wondering why couldn't it be Jesse instead? Gerald was okay, but she was crazy in love with Jesse. She felt kind of bad using Gerald, but it wasn't her fault he paid attention to her. Plus, she deserved it.

Gerald showed up handsome, dressed in black slacks with a charcoal-gray shirt under a black V-neck sweater that showed off his turquoise bolo tie. His temples matched the shirt. He smiled. "I'm glad to see you."

Eva thought she'd better paste on a believable smile. "Ditto."

"It smells great in here." He took a deep breath and gave her a big hug.

After the Indian stew and a six-pack, Gerald asked, "How 'bout I stay the night?"

Her head dropped down. "Sure."

Lying in bed watching him undress, she couldn't help comparing and wishing it were Jesse. She turned her face to the ceiling, her thoughts elsewhere. She'd close her eyes and pretend. She was good at pretending. But when she and Jesse were married it'd be for real.

CHAPTER THIRTY-ONE

TUESDAY MORNING

As Rita was rushing out to work, she picked up the ringing telephone. "Hello, hold on a moment. Mom, for you."

"Who is it?"

Rita shrugged, handed her the receiver, and blew her a kiss as she raced out the door.

"Hello?"

"Hi, Sunny, it's Gerald. You remember, your ex-fiancé?"

"Funny. What d'you want?"

"Since I saw you the other day I've thought about you. You look great. I thought we could have a drink or get cup of coffee."

"Who was it I introduced you to?"

"Your husband. I know, but Eva said you guys are having problems. I thought maybe you could use a good listener."

"What does Eva know?!" Sunny clenched her hands. "If I were having any problems, it'd be my business. You should concentrate on your girlfriend. Worry about her, not me."

"I don't know why Eva even wants me around. All she talks about is Jesse this and Jesse that."

"Well, too bad. Like I said, she's your problem."

"Are you mad at me about something?" he asked.

"Why?"

"Maybe it's your attitude?"

"Not mine," she said.

"What happened between us anyway? We haven't seen each other in years, but the last time I ran into you at the casino, I thought we were at least on speaking terms. Anyway, you look great."

"Save the compliments for Eva."

His voice softened. "Why did we break up anyway?"

"You didn't want children. Ever. You wanted to be Mr. Party Man. Don't you remember our conversation?"

"Twenty-some-odd years ago? I don't think so. Enlighten me."

"You told me, 'No kids no way.' You didn't want to bring any into the world."

His voice was low. "Make's for a small world. I was dumb."

"Not funny. I'm lucky. I have a good husband, and he's a great father to our daughter."

"If you say so. I guess it turned out all right. By the way, your daughter's beautiful. I'd ask her out, but I'm old enough to be her father. How old is she anyway?"

Sunny sucked in a sharp breath. "It doesn't matter."

"Be nice. So, does this mean you won't meet me for a drink?"

Sunny felt her stomach turn over. She could barely speak. "What do you think?"

Laughing, he said, "If you change your mind, I'm in the book. Under Listener."

Or Shithead. "Goodbye, Gerald." She stood ramrod straight for a few seconds, dropped the receiver into its cradle, and rubbed her sweaty palms along the outsides of her thighs. She never thought she'd run into him again. But worse, he'd noticed Rita. She didn't want him to know the truth about her. She had too much on her mind right then.

Was this the right time to tell Rita that Jerry was her biological father? She'd have to think about it. Gerald would have to be told. Barry too. She'd held on to this secret for twenty-three years. How were they going to feel about her? She felt like she'd OD'd on frustration. Floyd, draped over the couch back, purred. She went over to him.

"I guess you can't help me with anything, can you, Floyd, ole cat?"

Damn, why did Gerald have to call? She needed to concentrate on Gina and the mysteries surrounding her death. She didn't want to think about him or the possibility of him asking questions about Rita. She closed her eyes and rubbed her forehead. It was all too painful.

The phone rang, startling her. "Crap." When she answered, she heard nothing but a dial tone. "This is getting ridiculous. Who could be doing this?" Gerald? She hoped he was too mature for that. It must be Eva. Sunny decided she'd done enough thinking for now. Unless someone confessed, there was no way to prove who it was.

That didn't stop her from thinking it had to be Eva.

CHAPTER THIRTY-TWO

Needing to do laundry, Sunny headed for the bedroom and opened the closet door to grab her jeans. She searched the pockets, turning them inside out. As her hands fumbled, something crinkled beneath her fingertips. She took it out and saw the tissue containing the pink papers. "There you are."

Her hands began to tingle. Initially she felt drawn to them only because they were in Gina's house. But now her senses were exploding.

For some reason a rush of adrenaline had her feeling strange, as saliva filled her mouth. She felt shaken as she looked at her hands and was surprised they were steady. Leaving one strand of hair to twist around her finger, she pushed the rest from her face and retied it in a tight bun.

Carefully she opened the tissue. She had kept the torn bits of paper she'd found to herself. It was up to her to put them together. She felt that they were important. It could be a letter the boys wrote to their mother. Gina had said they wrote her all the time. Or maybe it was something else. So many things were going on right now. It could be anything.

She didn't know what she'd find by arranging the different shapes. She thought it could be a grocery list, until the skin on her neck started to prickle. Her gut feelings were jump-started.

Moving to the kitchen table she started to work on the papers. She spread them out, found her purse, and took out the tweezers. Some were small, others only slightly bigger. The scraps were hard to maneuver on the table. "This isn't going to work."

Returning to the laundry room, she found a square cardboard pizza box that she flattened. Scrounging around, she found a tape dispenser in one of the drawers.

Tools in hand, she returned to the kitchen and began to move the pieces around on the cardboard, trying to make sense of the handwriting on each piece.

Gently, she laid them out one by one, like a jigsaw puzzle, smoothing them with her fingertips. In search of . . . she didn't know what. She had a strange feeling: a direction to take, and she desperately needed the distraction they provided to get her mind off her internal pain. She focused hard, determined to make the pieces connect. There were no easy answers.

The cat jumped on her lap. She placed him on the floor.

One piece had the letters *oy*. What could they mean? Sunny worked on it for a while. They were so small she could barely make out what was on them. Progress seemed impossible. "Oh, Gina, please come help me, please. Help me to know what I have here," she muttered.

Finally she began to make some progress. The note or letter or whatever it was started to come together, the letter *I*, and there were two *ing*'s, an *a*. She didn't know if these were parts of the letter Gina had left. Why would they be in the trash? She pulled out a strand of her long hair and chewed the end, trying to think of all the possibilities. Sunny took out her notebook in which she'd recorded conversations overheard from people who were at the party. She included Gina's argument, overheard by Gerald, and the words Gina's spirit had whispered in the wind.

Sunny took a page from her notebook and wrote what Gina had told Victor was in the note to Jesse. She tried to come up with letters that made sense. She managed to get some words: *and* and *the*. Then she moved the scraps of papers around, trying to line up the edges, like on a puzzle. The combinations were endless. Tired, rubbing her aching shoulders, she decided to stop. *This is going to take longer than I imagined.* She put everything away in the hall closet, careful not to disturb anything on the cardboard.

She relaxed for a while. Her neck and fingers began to tingle and her hands felt shaky. Contemplating what to do, she went back to the closet and reached in for the board, compelled to work with the crumpled paper.

She spent most of the morning fitting small pieces together. "This is a tedious job. Why am I doing this? It could be a waste of time." Finally, those placed next to each other became clearer. She saw what she had so far, *vor*, *ta*, *ke*, and *the*. Now excited, she said, "What have I found? This has to be part of a letter, and it's certainly not a grocery list. Is it from Gina, or her boys? I haven't a clue what it means yet but I'm going to find out."

Trying to come up with more words, she scattered them. She felt someone standing over her right shoulder. She turned around, but no one was there. "Oh, Gina, I hope it's you." Sunny continued trying different combinations of the tiny scraps to form words. She'd been at it for hours and was exhausted.

The door opened and Rita hurried in. "Hi, I left the key to the supply room in my bedroom. I'll only be a minute."

"Sure, fine," Sunny said absently. Then she felt her stomach roll. Again she felt like someone was behind her. Once again she checked, thinking maybe Rita had come out of her bedroom. No one was there.

As she put her hands on the papers she felt a force guiding her hands. "I feel like I'm on a Ouija board," she said.

Her hand went to the papers spelling *ett ing*. She had found those letters before but didn't have a clue what they meant. Now things began to make more sense. She had the letters *vor ce* and *b oys*. The feeling of someone's presence behind her was gone. Sunny smiled. "Thank you, Gina."

She closed her eyes. Startled, she heard Floyd jump onto the table and start to purr. "Shoo." She waved him off. He jumped off the cardboard and the table, taking a few shreds with him.

"Darn cat!" Sunny yelled and stood. "I'm gonna strangle you." She looked down at the pieces Floyd had walked over. The tiny bits of paper that clung to his paws now stuck to the carpet. Floyd stared at her, then jumped back onto the table. She picked up papers from the floor, looked at the table, and saw the letters *d* and *i*. She glanced around the room and whispered, "Gina?" She stared into Floyd's eyes, then put her hand over her mouth. Was it Gina? She placed those two letters back on the board. Next to the other letters she recognized the word *divorce*. It seemed to appear like magic . . . or an omen. Gina?

Rita came into the kitchen. "What's going on? What's the matter?"

Sunny put them on the table and pushed the cardboard over to her. "Look at this! Floyd moved these pieces around, and these were stuck on his paws."

Rita stared at the word. "Divorce! Was Gina planning to divorce Jesse? What other words do you have? Mom, this is important. Gina had to have written this."

Sunny looked at her. "Remember when Victor came the first time and he told us what Gina said she wrote? Well, I jotted it down in my notebook, so I wrote it out again and now it makes more sense."

Rita kept looking at the table. "I hope now it will all come together. Before I leave, do you want me to help you? I'm good with puzzles. I can tape things into place."

Sunny leaned over the table. "Thanks, but I feel like I need to do this myself."

"I think you're right about things not adding up," Rita said as she dragged the chair over to the table. Stretching her legs straight out in front of her, she chewed on her bottom lip.

Sunny took a deep breath. "I found these words *take* and *gett* and another *ing* on the pieces. This isn't making any sense. I wonder if this could be a practice letter Gina wrote before she . . . well, you know. I'm trying to connect these letters and words, but it's hard. I don't have the answers yet."

"I can see it's not a list. I think it is her letter, but why would it be shoved in a wastebasket?" asked Rita.

Sunny rolled her shoulders up and down. "I'm tired. I need to stop for now. But let's go to the store and get some soda. The sugar will help pick me up."

After paying for the soda, chips, and dish soap they were ready to leave, when they passed tribal police deputy Joe Brown. He was tall, with thin eyes and a gray mustache. Sunny stopped. She had the bag of groceries in her hands. *Now or never.*

Reaching deep for her courage she approached him so he couldn't walk past her without shoving her out of the way.

"Deputy Brown. Why did you drop Gina Wilson's suicide case?"

Agitated he answered, "Because it was suicide. There was a note. End of story."

"Did you investigate?" she fired back.

He looked sheepish, and his face turned a soft shade of pink. He shouted at her, "We did our job."

"Not in this case. It wasn't suicide." Sunny switched the grocery bag to her hip and stormed out. Rita was right behind her.

In the car Sunny turned to Rita. "See I told you they don't listen unless the evidence is sitting in front of them. Hopefully, I'll find some evidence so I can make Deputy Brown eat his words.

Sitting at the table and drinking her soda, Rita finger-combed her hair. "I wonder what it is. Did the boys write it? Or was Jesse writing to another woman? Why would Gina write a suicide note and throw it away? Would anyone do that? None of this makes sense."

"There are too many possibilities. I found the word *take*. Some of these only have one letter on them. It's hard arranging them to know how to mix them up or what order to put them in. Besides, maybe parts are missing."

"Don't worry. You'll work it out." Rita stood and leaned over to give her mom a hug. "Mom, sorry. This is all so hard . . . and sad. Maybe these are clues. If you need help later . . ."

"Soon it will start coming together. I just feel, no, I know, that the answers are in those bits of paper. If it's incriminating I'll go to the police and the BIA. Putting all this together is stressful, and I have to be correct on everything. I have to be able to back it up and prove everything I say."

"You'll figure it out. You've always been good at solving problems. Catch you later."

Sunny exhaled and read a few of the letters in the note. She watched Floyd and wondered if Gina had anything to do with him and those pieces. He started licking himself. Maybe not, and she giggled. She picked up the cardboard square to set the small parts on the cardboard and smoothed the end of the tiny shreds again and again. After a while she put together a word: *b-o-y-s*.

"Hot damn. It reads *boys*." She jumped out of her chair. "Is it possible?"

She stared at the board. There it was: *take, boys, divorce*, and *gett*. She was stunned. She looked around like she expected someone to help her.

Shaking, she went into the other room.

CHAPTER THIRTY-THREE

Sunny called her friend. "Barb, can you come over right away? I need to talk to you. It's important." Barb was her best friend in the world at that moment.

"Fire up Mr. Coffee," said Barb. "I'm on my way."

Sunny put on a pot of coffee, set the table, and got out a carrot cake, all the while thinking about the paper and words she had managed to put together. But letters, or words, for that matter, could be put in different combinations and form or imply different things. Did she even have the right ones? And if she did, what did they mean?

There was a knock and Barbara entered and draped her Donna Karan jacket on the back of the chair before she sat.

"Okay, what's going on? You sounded strange. Look at you. Are you all right? We've been friends too long. I know when something's going on."

Sunny started at the beginning, first with the torn papers she'd found at Gina's house, the hang-ups, and the ramming of her rental car, and her tires slashed. She ended with Gerald's unexpected and unwelcome call.

Agitated, Sunny retrieved the cardboard box with the taped shreds of paper. She showed Barbara the torn ones she'd put together.

"Look." She pointed. "I also found *divorce* and *g-e-t-t*. But I could have put the letters together wrong. What do you think?"

"It must be something. You do have a lot of different letters. You have several *a*'s and *ing*'s. It's tough to know."

"Yes, but it feels right. I matched the jagged edges, and I wrote down what Victor told me Gina said she wrote in the note for Jesse. She said she was going to take the boys and get a divorce."

"Look, if you took one of these *ing*'s and put it with *g-e-t-t*, you see you have *getting*."

"Wow, that's *take, boys, getting*, and *divorce*. Damn, girl, what have I found? It practically says the whole thing."

Barbara's mouth turned up in a half-smile. "Intriguing," she said and stroked her chin. "You have a genuine mystery here."

"I'm serious, Barb. Why would somebody tear these papers up so small? I don't think Gina did a practice letter before she killed herself. Do you?"

Barbara's smile disappeared. "You sound like you aren't convinced Gina killed herself."

Sunny shook her head. "I don't know what to believe. Now that I have the words, I know Jesse would go apeshit if Gina said she was divorcing him. You know how he is. He never mentioned divorce, or taking the boys, in Gina's letter. We have two different stories. I have to be sure, really sure. I don't want to jump to conclusions."

Barbara eyed the scraps, with words out of order, the ones Sunny had put together. "You have a lot to put together. The evidence has to be flawless."

Sunny put her coffee down and pushed back her chair. "Have more cake while I reheat your coffee."

Again, Barbara looked at the layout. "Why put them in a wastebasket if you were trying to hide them? If what you say is true, why not throw them in the garbage or dumpster? Or burn them? Why take a chance of someone finding them?"

Barbara and Sunny studied the papers. "Hmmm."

All the same, Barb had put a voice to Sunny's thoughts. Barbara glanced at the table. "Maybe someone threw them away in a hurry and forgot to go back and take them out."

"Or they were drunk," said Sunny. "And I just happened to be in the bathroom when I discovered the papers. People were going in and out of there all day."

She held the box of Marlboros out to Barbara, shook one out for her, and then took a cigarette for herself. Sunny wondered that she'd come so far both with and without smoke or cigarettes in her life. How long would it take to stop? How long this time?

She was exhausted, stressed, and also scared. Puffing on a cigarette right now was the least of her worries, and yet, as the smoke curled up and around her, she couldn't help but think about the traditions of smoke and ceremonies throughout her childhood. Smoke was comfort, and spirit healing, and peace. It represented safety and guidance.

Sunny knew she would eventually need to win the battle to quit smoking. Her health was important, but right now she needed the crutch. She knew she would do it, but couldn't even think about that until she solved Gina's mystery and helped Gina's spirit find peace and move on.

While she sat smoking, Barbara read the notebook that Sunny had kept, with all the comings and goings.

Finally, Sunny said, "I have to get my hands on the letter Gina left for Jesse."

Barbara continued holding her cigarette in one hand while reading. She tapped her long ash into the ashtray. "Sounds like a good idea, if they have it. But I don't know if the police or BIA will show it to you. I guess we could assume Eva is the one who hit your car, and is also doing the hang-ups."

"Agreed. I'm talking to her first, and it won't be pretty. Then I'll go talk to the others who were at the party."

"Be careful. Eva is three kinds of crazy."

Sunny nodded and laughed.

Barbara held the book with both hands and gave it back to Sunny. "Now, let's get back to Gerald."

"I don't know what to do. Rita and Barry know her biological dad is named Jerry, but I don't think they've made the connection, and I don't know how to explain it to them. Especially Gerald."

"What! Are you kidding? You never told him about Rita?"

"No! Remember, when I told him I might be pregnant? He went off the deep end. By the time I found out for sure, we'd broken up and he'd left town. So I didn't mention it. I've seen him a few times over the years, but never with Rita. It was a quick hello, blah, blah, and goodbye."

"Good God, Sunny! What were you thinking? I just assumed you told him years ago. What are you going to do now?"

"It's why I called you. I've kept this secret way too long. You're the therapist. What will it do to Rita and Barry when I tell them?"

"Piss 'em off."

"Not funny, Barb. I'm worried. I told you what Gerald said when he noticed Rita. He'd ask her out if he wasn't old enough to be her dad."

"Yuck. Let's take one thing at a time. There's no hurry about Gerald. You've waited this long, you can wait awhile longer. I agree with you. Go talk to Eva. Check with everyone at the party. You know who they are. Go to the police and see if you can take a look at Gina's letter to Jesse. Didn't you say the cops took the letter Gina left? Or does Jesse have it?"

"Jesse said the police took it."

"Don't tell him or anyone else you have those papers." Barbara stood and put on her jacket. "I'm sorry. I have an appointment with a client this afternoon. Let me know what happens. You should tell Rita and Barry before this blows up in your face. And please, please be careful."

Sunny walked her to the door. "Thanks for coming. I'll keep you informed."

Barbara buttoned her coat. "Be careful when you talk to Jesse. You never know how someone will react. And you know he's got some violent tendencies."

CHAPTER THIRTY-FOUR

Back at her salon, Rita finished with her customer, made change, collected a tip, and was sweeping the floor when the broom bumped into two shiny black shoes. "Oh, I'm sorry . . ."

Surprised, she looked up and peered into green almond-shaped eyes. The heat rose in her face. "Hi, Victor. What's up?"

He cocked his head to the side, his shoulder-length hair swinging loose. "I worked near here today and thought maybe if you aren't busy we could have lunch."

"Sure, give me a minute to finish up."

She could barely put the broom away and unbutton her smock, her hands were so shaky.

They chose Joe's Diner, the closest burger joint. Rita glanced around at the shiny gray tiles that scaled the walls. The employees' red shirts matched the red chairs.

"Gina and I used to come here a lot," she said as they waited at the counter for their order. She felt her heart contract, thinking about Gina. Rita looked around. The place hadn't changed, although she knew she had. She felt older now. Years older, which didn't make her feel any better. She dropped her eyes. "I remember those happy conversations, especially the last time Gina and I ate here."

They sat in a booth by the front door. Victor watched her while he took a bite out of his hamburger, and then his eyes focused on the little gray circles in the Formica table.

"Yeah, Gina liked this place. She used to meet me here when I worked this area."

"Can you believe I started to call Gina this morning to ask if she wanted to go to lunch?" Rita said with a catch in her voice. "Then I remembered . . ." Her voice trailed off. "She comes to me in my dreams, but I can't talk to her like my mother can. It's so hard." She blinked back tears.

"For me too. My divorce was final and Gina was going to move in. But she changed her mind. She told me she wanted to live by herself, with just the boys. I only wanted to make life easier for her. I don't know what changed her mind. I can't forget that we were angry the last time we talked."

"That has to be rough," said Rita.

"It is."

"Do you have any kids?"

"No. My wife is pregnant," he said, gritting his teeth. "But not by me."

"I'm sorry." She looked at his bow-shaped mouth and cleft chin. *No wonder Gina was ready to leave Jesse. I just ended a relationship. I'm not jumping into another one.* Somehow it felt disrespectful to Gina.

"No need. I've learned to deal with it. How about you? How's the boyfriend?"

"Out of the picture." She shook her head and changed the subject. "What tribe are you?"

"Sioux, South Dakota. Why?"

"I'd heard that South Dakota Indians have green eyes."

The corners of his mouth turned up. "Just some of us." They shared a laugh.

Smiling, Rita asked, "Do you enjoy your job?"

He picked up a napkin and wiped his mouth. "Not really. I wanted to go to law school. To be a lawyer for my people. But, you know how life doesn't always work out the way we want."

"What happened?"

"Reality set in. Got married, needed a job. Sierra Power was hiring." He shrugged. "What about you?"

"Me too. Wanted to be a lawyer, that is. Ever since I was young, I would go to the courtroom with my dad. But like you say, things change. My godmother died and left me the salon. So here I am. Ended up in cosmetology school instead."

While they talked, someone's car alarm went off in the parking lot. A young boy walked past, balancing a heavy tray of food. He tried hard to control it, but his arms gave out. The cokes, fries, and hamburgers tumbled onto the floor.

Victor jumped up to help the boy clean up the mess. The young customer stood and thanked him. "Darn," the kid said. "That was all money."

Victor put his arm around the boy's shoulder and led him back to the counter. "Don't worry, here's a ten. Try again." The boy thanked him.

Victor returned and asked, "Now, where were we?"

"That's so nice of you." She took a napkin and was wiping her pants where the boy's coke had splashed on her. She thought about the fact that Lee would have never done what Victor did.

"Did you end up going to college?" she asked.

"Yes."

Her face felt hot. "Sorry about all the questions. Guess I get it from my parents."

"Well, I went to South Dakota State U. Made the dean's list." He brushed his nails back and forth across his chest. "Are you ready for this? We were known as the Jackrabbits."

Rita gave a loud laugh. "Are you sure you weren't in the Nevada desert?"

That gave both of them a good chuckle.

"How about you, did you go to college?"

"I started at Nevada University, here in Reno. I was so-so in school. I took a Native American history class. It was interesting. Take for example we didn't get citizenship until 1924. Utah was the last state to allow Indians to vote, and that was 1958. Can you believe that mess? Even though women got the vote in 1920."

"I know. Do you know it's only been a short while that we have the right for our religious ceremonies, and grounds, and Indian child welfare? I'm considering starting night classes in prelaw."

Rita pounded lightly on the table. "What's stopping us from doing what we always wanted to do?"

He laughed."Maybe that mustard on your chin."

"Oh." She grinned.

They ate their lunch in silence, each lost in thought. Finally, it was time to go. They got up. Victor said, "I'll do the dishes," as he loaded the tray, threw their trash in the bin, and walked to the car.

Victor pulled into her salon's parking lot. He'd been quiet for some time, and then his voice seemed to boom in the car. "Do you like to hike?"

"I do, but I haven't gone for a while. It wasn't Lee's thing."

"Would you like to go to Windy Lake? We could hike the back ridge. It's a pretty easy climb."

"Like a date?" Embarrassed at blurting that out, she felt the heat flush her cheeks, and sweat break out on her forehead. She felt like a teenager with her first crush.

"Not really," he said, and gave a casual shrug. "Just friends hanging out. It might do us both some good. Besides, I like talking to you about Gina. Fresh air helps clear out the cobwebs. I'll call you."

When he smiled thrills ran down her spine. She got out of the truck, thanked him for lunch, and watched him drive away. Nervous and a bit flustered she hugged her arms to her chest, whispering, "My God, what's happening to me? I'm jumping to conclusions. How embarrassing." *He said it was something to do, nothing else. I'm the one reading more into it. He likes to talk to me . . . about Gina. It's about friendship, nothing more. I'm not ready to get involved. Friends are fine . . . for now.*

Still smiling, she strolled into the salon and busied herself cleaning around her station. Before she knew it, it was closing time. Rita counted the cash in the register, and said good night to her employees as they walked out the door. She locked up and headed home, still surprised at how much Victor had affected her. But she brushed it off. They were both involved with Gina, that's all it was.

TUESDAY EVENING

Rita entered her house, threw her keys on the counter, and spotted a long white box on the hall table. Sunny sat at the kitchen table doing her nails. "What's this?" Rita slid the box toward Sunny.

Sunny looked up. "It came for you this morning. Doesn't say who sent it. Probably has a card inside."

"Hmm, I hope it's not from Lee." She lifted the lid and pulled back the green tissue. "Oh, crap, what's this?" She threw the contents on the floor.

"What's wrong?"

"Someone sent me dead black roses."

"Why would a florist have dead roses? And black, at that?" Sunny pushed her chair back and stood to look at the contents of the box with Rita.

Rita studied the box. "It's from the specialty florist on South Virginia Street. I heard they sell gross things for a bad breakup or a gag gift."

"Maybe it's from your loser boyfriend."

"I don't think so. I can't imagine him spending the money . . . or doing something like this."

"Who else would do that?"

Rita's eyes were misty. She was so sick of everything. Gina's death, the driver who rammed their car. Lee being such a jerk, et cetera. "I have no idea. I'm worried, Mom. Why are all these things happening to us?"

Sunny blew hard on her freshly polished nails. "I intend to find out. This is too much."

Rita picked up the roses, put them back in the box, and closed the lid. She carried them out to the backyard and dumped them in the garbage can, closing it with a bang. "Tomorrow I'll call the florist and find out who sent them."

"Good idea. I'm going outside. I've felt restless all afternoon. It's a full moon, and I want to see if I can connect with Gina. The wind is up. Maybe I can hear her whispers. That's when the whispers are strongest."

Rita nodded. "Take a jacket. It's cold. Be careful."

Sunny sat on a big rock at the edge of the driveway and called out to the moon and the wind. She was worried, thinking about everything that was happening and needing Gina's help. *What if I'm way off base here? Maybe Gina did get so upset she committed suicide. How would I know?*

She raised her face toward the black sky shadowed by clouds dancing back into the full round moon's light. She spoke to the Great Spirit. "Grandfather Spirit, is Gina with you? Can you hear me, Gina? I thought I heard you whisper in the wind. I miss you. I am so confused. Please help me. Tell me where to look. Stay with me and guide me. I am so sorry for our argument. I hope I didn't cause you to do this horrible thing."

Sunny sat with her eyes closed and her head hung on her chest. Then she felt an easy shaking of her shoulders and opened her eyes.

"Mom, are you asleep? You've been out in the cold for a while."

"No. I guess I was in a trance. I tried hard to reach out to Gina. I felt her pulling me toward a woman, or it could be a man? Maybe it's two of them, I can't tell. She whispered to me that she's with me and will help me. I thought she said something about leaving her boys." Sunny sighed. "It does take a lot out of me."

Exhaustion overtook her. She couldn't make herself think anymore. Sunny stood and stretched. "I'm going to bed."

They walked arm in arm into the house.

CHAPTER THIRTY-FIVE

WEDNESDAY MORNING

Rita gave the florist her name and address over the phone. The woman was gone for a few seconds, then came back on again. "Yes, they were delivered yesterday in the morning at ten thirty. It was sent by . . . oh, she paid cash and didn't sign the receipt." Her voice sounded flustered.

"She? It was a woman? Could you tell me what she looked like?" Rita asked, praying she could get more information, trying to stay calm as she asked questions.

"Yes, let me think. She had black hair and big round glasses. We weren't busy, and I remember because she grinned and giggled, like something was funny. Like she was playing a joke on someone."

Rita thanked her, hung up, and went out on the porch where her mom was bundled up with coffee and a cigarette.

"Mom, the florist said a woman sent the roses. Dark hair, big glasses. It has to be Eva. Boy, has she earned her name: Evil Eva."

Leaning her head back, cigarette in hand, Sunny blew smoke into the air. "Probably. This is all so complicated. I mean, what is Gina trying to tell me?"

"Mom, it's freezing. Put out your nasty cigarette and come inside."

Rita hurried inside and lit a fire in the woodstove as Sunny came in and refilled her coffee cup. Both sat, relaxing their feet, sharing the ottoman.

Rita pondered before asking, "Mom, why can't I see or hear Gina? I don't have the feelings of intuition and spiritual knowing the way you do."

"Yes, you do. It's not that you don't have gifts but that you ignore them. Remember? Gina came to you in your dreams. Instead of denying your talents, you need to develop them. I've always had mine, like your grandma and auntie. But knowing about them isn't enough; you have to hone them, to follow where they lead you."

Sunny remembered that when she was a child images would come to her, either in a dream or in her thoughts. She hated when that happened, the images scared her. She was too young to know what they meant. Her mother told her not to share this knowledge with others because they might think she was a witch. The memory of her mother holding that ridiculous belief made her smile. She loved her mother and did as she was told. So she never talked about her images, except to her mother.

Sunny blew on her coffee. Deep in thought about her family's past, she spoke up to bring herself back to reality and center her spirit inside Rita's house. "I'm having strange feelings about all of this. Maybe Gina is trying to get my attention. I don't know what to think. There are endless possibilities."

Rita grabbed her cat, placed him on her lap, and put her feet back on the ottoman. "What would be her reason to kill herself? Was she depressed or mad? Did she want revenge? Was she drunk?"

"No, I can't see her doing that, but something was odd. There was a hole in the television screen. Something happened. Barry told me Gina threw an ashtray at it and made the hole."

"Did Barbara have any suggestions? She must have some training in this type of situation, or have gone through similar things with her patients. What're you going to do?"

Sunny thought, Yes, Barb had suggestions. She hadn't forgotten that she needed to speak to Rita about her biological father. She just couldn't do it right now. Guilt assailed her, and now she'd have to release it. She'd talk to her when things quieted down.

"Slow down. I have to think this through. I have people I want to talk to. Barb suggested I go see Eva. So I'll start with her, if she'll talk to me, and find out what she knows about the party."

Rita turned her mouth to the side and scrunched up her eyes. "That's going to be hard. She's so sneaky. And it's obvious she has issues with both of us. She can't be trusted."

"I might as well try. She was around everything and everyone. She must be involved with the weird things going on with us. I also made a list of people I think were at the party."

Sunny called Eva, who answered immediately. "Hi, it's Sunny. Don't hang up."

"What d'you want?" Eva sounded suspicious.

"I want to talk to you about Gina and the crank calls we've been getting."

"Tell it to the phone company. Do I look like Nevada Bell?"

"By the way, why did you almost run us down the other night?" asked Sunny.

There was a pause. "Stay away from me." *Click.*

"I thought you didn't know who it was," said Rita.

"I don't. I accused her to see what she'd do. It's an old investigator trick. Act like you know more than you do." Sunny kept calling Eva. She tried three more times. Each time Eva hung up on her without a word.

"Damn it, she keeps hanging up."

Rita grinned. "It's her trademark."

"I'll go over to her place. At least I know she's home."

"Want me to go with you?"

Sunny smiled. "No thanks. One of us showing up is bad enough. She'd really freak if both of us went. I have to be careful. I don't know what she's capable of."

"I have a pretty good idea. Maybe I should go with you."

Sunny smiled. "No. I'm trained to handle people like her, remember?"

Before Rita could follow her, Sunny fetched her coat and left. She hurried so she could catch Eva at home. "Maybe I can surprise her, throw her off guard," she mumbled.

CHAPTER THIRTY-SIX

Eva's house was a short distance away on Kettle Lane. Sunny drove to the end of the dirt-and-gravel driveway. Dust flew everywhere. She came to an abrupt stop in front of the wooden porch. Eva came down the stairs and stopped in front of her Mercedes, her hair pulled back into a short ponytail, wearing black sweat pants and a gray sweatshirt and carrying a gym bag. When she saw Sunny, she pivoted, ran back inside, and slammed the door. Sunny jumped out of the car, scrambled up the steps, and banged on the door.

"Eva, this is stupid. Open the damn door!"

"Go away! I'll call the cops."

"And tell them what? How you rammed my car? How you call us at all hours and hang up? We know you sent Rita the black roses. You were positively ID'd."

"That's not illegal. I'm calling the cops."

Sunny paced back and forth, patting her arms. "Yeah, you go ahead and call them. I want to talk to them myself."

"You can't prove anything."

"Open up, Eva. It's freezing out here."

"Good, I hope you freeze to death. Then you'll be out of my way."

"Let me in or I'll call the cops myself."

Eva opened the door a small crack. "I'm not interested in anything you have to say."

"Just let me in. What are you scared of?"

Eva threw the door open. "I'm not scared of nothing, 'specially you and that daughter of yours."

Sunny walked in. Eva made a huffing sound. "Did you hear me ask you in?"

Sunny breezed past her. "Did you hear me ask to come in?"

She kept going and entered the living room. It was the first time she had been inside Eva's house. Sparsely furnished but mostly clean. A big black cat with yellow eyes was curled on the sofa. Sunny positioned herself between the door and Eva. She didn't want to take any chances.

Eva squinted her eyes. "Why can't you and your daughter leave me and Jesse alone?"

Sunny's mouth flew open and her eyes widened. "You and Jesse? What are you talking about? There is no 'you and Jesse.' It's not our fault Jesse doesn't want to be with you, can't you understand? He married your sister. It's got nothing to do with us."

Eva's voice cracked. "He was mine . . . until Gina came along. He's the only one I ever loved."

Sunny noted the pained look on Eva's face. She should have thought before speaking. It was obvious she'd cut Eva deeply. *Even though we don't like each other we're both women and can relate to the pain of young love.*

"Sorry, I didn't mean it the way it sounded. Of course you love him, and you were with him first. That was a long time ago. You have to remember—" Sunny lowered her voice. "—he married Gina because he was in love with her. Rita and I have no part in it."

Eva's eyes filmed and her chin puckered. "He wants Rita." Eva's cat slithered through her legs, then circled round and did it again. "And you are always meddling. Stay away from me, both of you."

"Look, Eva, Rita doesn't want Jesse. He was her good friend's husband, so they were all three friends. Nothing more. She'd never betray Gina." Sunny hoped she was right. "You did a lot of damage by spreading lies that they were having an affair."

"It wasn't a lie. I followed them."

"You mean you stalked them, sneaking around, spying. And what did you ever see? Anything incriminating? No, because it never happened. Rita and Jesse were friends, not lovers."

"You don't know," sobbed Eva. "You don't know." She bent to pick up her cat and nuzzle him.

"Nice cat." Sunny changed the subject. "What's his name?"

"Pandora."

"Good name." Sunny scratched the cat under the chin, then rested her hand on Eva's shoulder. "You need to let it go, Eva. Otherwise, you'll be miserable the rest of your life."

Eva pushed Sunny away and wiped the sleeve of her sweatshirt across her wet cheeks. "Just . . . go. Get the hell out of here!"

As she pulled the front door open Sunny turned to Eva. "And what about Gerald? Are you being fair to him? Letting him think you care about him."

Her head snapped up. "Get out of here! Don't worry about Gerald. Mind your own business, meddling bitch. Leave me the hell alone."

Sunny had enough and scooted out the door. Eva slammed it shut behind her. Sunny felt a little shaky and stood for a moment. "Well, that went well. Eva's back to her old evil self."

The morning felt like a bust. Wrinkling her eyebrows, she headed back to Rita's. She couldn't figure Eva out. She needed to forget Jesse and continue her friendship with Gerald. Never happen. It would mean that Eva was mentally stable and Sunny didn't think she ever would be. She was surprised that Gerald really didn't know Eva. He just thought she was fun.

Rita was still home when Sunny pulled in. "Well, how'd it go?" Rita asked.

"Not good." Sunny threw her car keys on the table. "Maybe I'm too hard on her. She is desperately in love with Jesse. Every breath she takes is with Jesse in mind. To see him with Gina every day must have been torture. Why would anyone put themselves through that every day. Eva wanted to *be* Gina, then and now. She wants Jesse! It's going to drive her over the edge."

Rita poured hot chocolate into two cups. "Why are you siding with Eva now? It was her choice to hang out with Jesse and Gina and suffer, watching them together. She's an adult." Rita handed the steaming cup to her mother.

"I know. I surprised myself. I actually felt sorry for her. We have our differences, but right then, I couldn't help it."

Sunny nodded at Rita's obvious confusion. "If she's obsessed with Jesse, why is she with Gerald?" asked Rita.

Sunny was just as shocked for her sudden empathy for Eva's lonely and lost solution. "Better than nobody, I guess. Gerald knows how she is, so she's his problem now. He'll have to handle it himself."

"That's it? Nothing else happened?"

Sunny smiled. "Well, she has a big black cat. 'Pandora.'"

Rita smiled back. "Hence her nickname. Evil Eva."

"Oh yeah, she said it's you that Jesse wants. That's why she hates you so much."

"What a crock o' shit! He played around a lot, and I guess he flirted with me some, but I never took it seriously. I don't think he did either," said Rita. "But I guess Eva did."

Sunny took out her notebook and listed all the events as they'd happened at Eva's house. She was aware that Eva hadn't denied doing all the things she'd accused her of. "I want to talk to everyone at the party, including Jesse." Sunny was back in investigator mode.

"Do you think someone else gave Gina a reason to shoot herself?" Rita said.

"I'm still not completely convinced she did. I'll see, after I've talked to everyone. You know how it is with me. The side of my neck gets hot when I'm around certain people. It's hard to tell why. I have suspicions about different things, but I want to be sure before I say anything." Sunny searched in her purse. "Do you have Madam Carmen's card? I can't find mine."

"I think so." Rita rummaged in her handbag. "Here. Are you sure you want to see her again?"

Sunny took the card. "I'm positive. I need to know if Gina is with me. Also, I hope she can help me understand why she killed herself, if she did. Or, if it was something else. And what exactly happened to her." Sunny hurried to the hall table and dialed Madam Carmen's number.

Rita whispered, "Tell her you'll meet her at the salon."

Sunny talked to the fortune teller for a moment. "How about five thirty, at the beauty salon? . . . Good, see you then."

WEDNESDAY EVENING

They were a half hour early for their meeting with Madam Carmen. The employees had left. An eerie feeling permeated the place. Twisted images of streetlights shadow-danced around the inside walls. Rita stepped in and flipped the light switch, chasing away the shadows.

"I'll put the coffee on. It's cold out there," said Rita. "I don't remember March being this cold."

She was pouring coffee when the door opened and Madam Carmen walked in, wearing a long licorice-colored dress under a black wool cape. A lilac plastic comb held her hair up. Around her neck, a plum-and-turquoise knitted scarf hung almost to her ankles. Her kerchief was so colorful, she reminded Sunny of a peacock. Her large felt hat covered half of her Guatemalan face.

"Hello." Sunny stood, shook her hand, and motioned for her to sit.

Rita moved the manicuring table between them and hung Madam Carmen's cape on the wall peg.

"*Hola*," said Madam Carmen as she sat on the black stool.

Rita brought in the coffee and handed her mom and the fortune teller each a piping hot mug.

Madam Carmen held it in both hands and let the steam flow over her face. She gulped the whole cup and returned it to a surprised Rita.

She took her tarot cards out of a large cloth bag, unwrapped the silk scarf enfolding them, and laid them in front of Sunny. "Cut them into thirds, like last time. Who you ask about?"

Sunny had planned to ask simple questions and to stay composed, but she was in too much pain about her friend. She blurted out, "I want to know about Gina. What can you tell me about her death?"

Madam Carmen shuffled the cards and looked harder into Sunny's eyes. "She comes to you. Many times, you talk to her. She hear you. *Mira. Mira las cartas.*"

Sunny looked where Madam Carmen pointed, but didn't know how to interpret the mystical cards.

"Look, they say it. Gina say she with you. You feel her? Many times, right there—" she pointed "—over your right shoulder. When you love a person, and they love you, they be with you behind your right shoulder. If you no love, you have nothing."

Sunny put her head down and whispered, "She knew I loved her. But when we had our argument . . . I thought she would hate me and stay away."

She shook her head. "*Argumento no es importante.*"

Sunny looked at the cards, then at the fortune teller. "I'm so confused. Why would she kill herself? What would cause her to do something like that?"

Madam Carmen cleared her throat. "She talk to you. *¡Escucha!* She tell you, *She no leave boys.* Listen! Yes? She tell you, *she no kill self.*"

Sunny and Rita gasped. "Oh my God! Who would do that? What happened?"

"See, the cards. They show; you have what you need."

Sunny kept her head down. "Maybe it's in the papers I found. I have to be right before I can do anything. It can't be a guess."

"You learn more. Be careful. Many not-good people there. *Muy Malo.* Danger! *¡El peligroso!* She gone now. She be back. She protect you and want to help you."

The fortune teller stood, the reading obviously over. Sunny paid Madam Carmen, who wrapped the cards in silk and repacked them in her large bag. Before she left the salon, Madam Carmen said, "Please be careful, very careful. Gina tried to tell you that you are in danger."

She pushed open the door and left. She made Sunny think of a sorcerer moving along the damp street, entering and then being swallowed up by fog.

Sunny and Rita looked at each other with raised eyebrows. Rita laughed. "Is it my imagination or did she just speak perfect English?"

Sunny smiled. "Yes, she sure did. Is she conning us? Now I don't know if we should believe everything, or is it all bullshit? All of this is so confusing. That surprised me."

Rita nodded. "What should we believe? Do you follow your instincts or not?"

Sunny shrugged one shoulder. "I don't know. I believe with my heart, but with my head it's a different story."

Rita turned out the lights, leaving only the streetlights through the windows to dance in the shadows.

"Let's go get a pizza and go home, Mom. I'll buy."

Sunny shivered. She was spent, worn to the bone, scared of the unexplained. She also felt in some way she was letting Gina down. She wasn't able to help any more tonight. "Sounds good. Then we can talk."

Sunny took the flat square box and cokes into the living room and plopped the pizza down on the large maple coffee table. She scooped up a piece of pizza. Folding it, one of the pepperoni slices dropped. "Everything Madam Carmen said comes back to 'danger.'"

"If we can believe her." Rita started a fire and turned on the table lamp to give a soft glow. Sunny was tired and wanted to relax. She ate slowly. She tried to digest not only the food, but also what they had learned.

Sunny thought about the hang-ups and their car being rammed by a mystery driver, possibly Eva. Who else? She also wondered if she should believe the fortune teller. "She's said the same thing before. Now I will be careful. But who can I trust?"

"We have to know if or why Gina killed herself." Rita sucked on the straw in her coke. "We do have to be careful now."

"There is no 'we'. It's me. You're to stay completely out of this. Understand?"

Rita tapped her foot and nodded. "Can't I at least go with you to see what the people at Gina's party have to say? It's not such a hot idea for you to go alone either."

"Well, maybe you could go with me to talk to Patty and Mike Fielding. I know they were there. Then we'll go over to Frank Allen's. He's the one who called the police after the boys found her. I'll see them before I meet with Jesse."

"Good. I'll go put on a sweater. Be ready in a sec."

"But they're the only ones you can go see with me," Sunny shouted after her, flopping her half-eaten pizza back in its box. She'd lost her appetite.

Sunny had her coat on. Rita hurried after her.

"I called Patty while you were changing and explained a little of what I wanted. She was fine with us coming over at this hour."

"Mom, it's only seven fifteen."

"Well, it feels later to me."

CHAPTER THIRTY-SEVEN

They traveled back to the reservation and across Fourth Street to the Fieldings' house. It looked like the rest of the houses in the neighborhood—beige with brown shutters. A small yard with aged chain-link fencing to hold in kids and animals.

The night air was cold and damp. They found the stairs, thanks to the porch light. The television was blaring *Punky Brewster*. She knocked hard. "I hope someone can hear me." She knocked a little harder.

This time the door was opened. Patty stood looking down at Sunny and Rita. She was a large woman, attractive, with short black hair and dark tanned skin. "Haw-uh." She invited them in, turned off the TV, and shooed her two little girls into their room, telling them "Put your pajamas on."

"Sorry. Please sit down," Patty offered. "I'll be with you as soon as I put the girls to bed. Mike had an emergency at work. The power's off somewhere."

"Did he used to work with Gina?" asked Rita.

Patty stopped and glanced at them. "We both did."

"Mommy?" The call came again from the girls' bedroom.

Patty hustled around the small room. "There's coffee on the counter. Please help yourselves. I'll only be a minute."

Sunny and Rita looked around the living room. They sat together on a brown overstuffed sofa. The matching chair across the room faced the television. On both sides were small shelves holding beautiful black-and-turquoise Indian pottery. On the small coffee table, an ashtray filled with cigarette butts gave off the scent of stale tobacco. Next to it stood a jar of peppermint candy. Rita pointed to the large painting, on the other wall, showing three tipis with fire glowing through the skins of their walls. A blue mist surrounded the entire area, making an intriguing picture.

Patty returned. "Before we start, could I get you anything? Something to eat?"

Together they answered, "No thanks."

"We ate right before we came," said Sunny.

"What is it you want to know?" Patty asked, sitting in the chair opposite the sofa, "I don't know how helpful I'll be. We'd already left the party when this terrible thing happened."

Sunny took out her trusty notebook, ready to write. "Just tell me what went on at the party. Whatever you remember."

Patty rubbed her forehead. "At first, nothing much. We sat around drinking, acting Indian, like we do, cutting each other down and telling crazy stories. We were laughing and carrying on, while Eva kept bugging Gina about how she can't drink like her big sister. At first Gina didn't care, but Eva kept bugging her to drink up. So Gina finally did."

"Did Gina get mad?" asked Rita.

"Was Jesse there?" asked Sunny.

"Yes, to both questions. Jesse told Eva to knock it off, and then Gina and Jesse got into an argument."

Sunny continued making notes. "About what?"

Patty watched Sunny as she wrote. "Jesse wanted her to quit drinking. She told him to mind his own business. I think there was more to it 'cause Gina said, 'Why are you interested *now* in what I do?' She got up and went toward her bedroom and Jesse followed. In the meantime, Eva's boyfriend told her to knock it off and she got pissed. There seemed to be tension among all of them. By this time, Mike and I were buzzing and decided to go home. When arguments start, fights always follow. We know when to get the heck out."

"You said something about 'more to it.' What do you think it was?" asked Sunny.

Patty linked her fingers together. "I don't really know, just the way they acted toward each other. I felt they'd had a big argument earlier. And the way she said 'now.' Like it meant something."

"So that's when you both left? That's all you saw?"

"Yeah, sorry. Wish I could help you more. It was a terrible thing."

"Yes, it was. If you think of anything, please get a hold of me," Sunny said.

Patty scrunched up her face, as if straining to recall anything else, but then shrugged. "Sorry." Sunny got up and Rita followed. Sunny put her notebook back in her purse. Patty walked them to the door. "Good to see you, Sunny. Haven't seen you in ages. You're still looking good."

"You too. Thanks for seeing us this late."

Rita rolled her eyes. Sunny felt withered and ancient, as if she'd been up all night, losing a battle she could never win. Not a quitter—good or bad—she wasn't about to give up on Gina.

Driving back to Rita's they discussed what Patty told them. Sunny spoke up. "I don't know if it's anything new or the same as what we heard before. I wish I knew what Gina and Jesse's fight was about."

Rita said compassionately, "You have others to interview; maybe you'll learn something else from them."

Sunny felt distracted; she was thinking about what Madam Carmen said. "Ah-huh. Madam Carmen said danger is all around. She said I could be in danger, and maybe you too."

"You could. We all could. But can we trust Madam Carmen? We still don't know who to trust. We just have to keep on keepin' on. Who do we see next?"

"I told you, there's no 'we.' I'm going to call and see if I can talk to Frank Allen."

"You already said I could go there with you."

"What about the salon?"

"I'll work around your schedule. That's the advantage of being the owner."

"All right, but that's all. And please keep quiet. Not like you did at Patty's."

Rita playfully saluted. "Aye, aye, Captain."

Sunny smiled. "I gave birth to a smart-ass."

When they got home Rita checked the answering machine. "One from Victor, one from Barry, and four hang-ups."

Reminded of the warning from Madam Carmen, Sunny called Barry, but there was no answer. "Maybe he went to sleep early and turned the ringtone down," she said to Rita, but her thoughts went elsewhere. She silently prayed, Please don't let him be drinking. Drinking would surely ruin their marriage. It was possible that it was already too late.

After Rita turned in for the night, Sunny was unable to sleep. She was too anxious about their talk with Madam Carmen. She was also thinking about Gina. Also not getting a hold of Barry bothered her. *Should I call him again?* No, it's late. He would think she was checking on him, which is what she would be doing. She mumbled into her pillow, "Well, he's an adult. I don't need to babysit him. I wonder if Rita's right, maybe I don't give him a chance."

She made a mental note to call him the next day when he got off work. She rolled over, hoping to shut off her mind. However, after another ten minutes of tossing and turning, she switched on the table lamp and settled for rereading her notes.

CHAPTER THIRTY-EIGHT

THURSDAY MORNING

Sunny called the Allen home and made an appointment with Frank's wife, Helen. Sunny would go to their house at noon when Frank would be there.

Rita stepped into the living room and handed her mom a cup of coffee. "Remember, you said I could go with you to Frank's?"

"Yes, I remember. I need to talk to Frank and he won't be there 'til noon. What about the shop? Are you able to get away?"

"Yes." She hugged her mother goodbye. "I'll work 'til eleven, then meet you here."

Sunny nodded. "Okay." She set her unfinished coffee on the end table. As she paced nervously around the room, the facts of Gina's death rolled around in her mind. She felt like her brain was going to explode. *Gina, why do I feel so helpless and unsure? Help me to know what's going on.* She couldn't keep from wondering why Gina didn't tell them what was happening to her. *Come to me, please. Help me understand.*

Sunny caught her image in the mirror as she put on a sky-blue sweater and dark blue jeans with black high-heeled boots. "Yeah." She liked how she looked.

Rita's car pulled up; she rushed inside and headed to her bedroom to change. "I'll be ready in a minute," she said, then hurried out dressed in a scoop-neck black sweater.

Sunny liked how it showed off Rita's silver-chained diamond *R* initial that Barry bought for her when he married Sunny. Rita's hair was tucked under her black knit hat, revealing the triangle birthmark beneath her right earlobe.

Sunny was surprised but said nothing. Rita seldom wore her hair up, self-conscious as she was of her birthmark.

Grabbing her notebook and pen she stuck them in her purse. "Okay, let's go. Remember, just listen. I'll do the talking."

CHAPTER THIRTY-NINE

Sunny and Rita drove the six miles across town to the reservation. As they passed Gina and Jesse's house, both turned their heads. Rita pointed through the window. "Jesse's car's not in the driveway."

"Good, I don't want to run into him until I'm ready."

She parked in front of the Allen home. The house was yellow with brown shutters, like all the other cookie-cutter homes in the rez. A waist-high chain-link fence made its way around the front yard where a yellow lab lay half-asleep. As they approached, he jumped up, barked, and lunged at the fence. They hesitated at the gate until Frank stepped out onto the porch. "Haw-uh," he said to Sunny and Rita. He turned to his dog. "Gunner, knock it off."

Gunner went back to his spot and lay down, growling to himself. They entered the yard, keeping him in sight, and climbed up the few steps to the porch. Both echoed, "Haw-uh."

Frank stood in the middle of the open door. "Gunner's all bark and no bite." Laughing, he said, "No teeth."

Frank was the color of someone left out in the sun too long. He always smiled, even with a missing front tooth. He tried to cover his bald spot by parting his hair on one side and combing it over the top, which only drew more attention to it. He led them into the house where his wife was busy making fry bread.

Helen came out from the kitchen. "Good. You're just in time." She wiped her hands on her apron. Her black hair was piled on top of her head, with a few strands loose along her hairline. "We're having Indian tacos. Would you like one?"

"Oh, I didn't mean to interrupt your lunch," said Sunny. She hesitated. "But I'd love one."

"Me too, if you have enough," echoed Rita.

"There's plenty," Frank said. "My buddy from work is coming by, so Helen made enough to feed a tribe." He chuckled.

Sunny followed Frank into the cozy kitchen. She smelled the hot grease. "Well, this shouldn't take long," she said. "You don't have to talk to me if you don't want to. I'm here as Gina's friend. I just have a few questions."

"I want to help as much as I can. Heck, you're from the rez. You're family," he said. "We loved Gina. I care about Jesse too, but sometimes I want to kick his ass 'til I knock the Indian out of him."

"Things aren't adding up for me." Sunny looked from his face to his wife's. "Why would Gina kill herself? Did she ever say anything for you to think that?"

"No, we never had a clue. It was sickening, what happened," he said. "We've been upset ever since."

"Terrible, terrible," said Helen. "Those poor boys . . . what they went through."

Frank sat at the kitchen table with Sunny and Rita. "Many a time when Gina came over, her eyes were bruised black-and-blue. We heard screaming when Jesse was drunk and acting crazy. He don't know, but I called the cops plenty."

Helen added, "The last time I saw Gina alive she had a cut lip, and the skin under her eye matched her purple sweater. I could tell Jesse beat on her all the time. Made me sick to my stomach."

Sunny kept writing. "What's 'all the time'?"

"Enough that the kids were scared to go home when Jesse was drinking," said Frank.

Helen chimed in. "They stayed at our house a lot."

Frank helped his wife put the platter of tacos on the table. "We didn't hear anything unusual that day. I heard music and laughter and people were outside, coming and going," he said. He crowded the table with plates of fry bread, meat, tomatoes, and the rest of the makings, with plenty of bottles of hot sauce.

"We're used to it, so we didn't pay attention," Helen added, dishing up the Indian tacos. Then she paused. "Now I wish we had."

"You weren't invited to the party?" asked Sunny.

"Yeah. But we're older, and we know what can happen when everyone gets to drinking. Arguments start and, before you know it, fights break out. 'Course we've never seen anything this bad," said Helen.

"I told the cops and BIA. It was something awful, the little kids running over here, screaming and crying. Helen and my girls kept the boys here, while I ran over to their house . . ."

Helen interrupted with her eyes wet. "It was terrible for those boys."

Frank continued. ". . . no one was there. Gina was on the couch. Blood all over, I thought I was going to lose my lunch. Horrible, horrible. I called the tribal police. Helen called Jesse's mom. She said he was down at Louis's. I raced down there and we all ran back to the house." Frank grimaced, closing his eyes as if it all was too much to remember.

Sunny felt sick too. Frank and Helen were good people, and she was forcing them to relive the immediate aftermath of Gina's death. She wondered briefly if she should keep questioning them. Was it too hard on them? She was startled by a knock at the door. Frank stood. "That's my buddy, Jerry. He comes by now and then for lunch. Likes Helen's home cooking."

Frank ambled to the door and stepped aside to let Jerry in. "You've both met my friend Jerry, haven't you?"

Sunny's mouth fell open. She dropped her pen.

Gerald smiled at Rita as he shook her hand. "Yeah, we met at Gina's. Good to see you ladies again." He studied Rita for a moment and looked at Sunny. "I knew Sunny when we were teenagers. How're you doing?"

She had a hard time finding her voice. "Fine . . . thanks." He was the last person she wanted to see. Rita stared at him and then at her mother. Gerald's eyes widened as they focused on Rita's birthmark, then stared hard at Sunny.

Totally unnerved, Sunny fumbled, putting her notebook and pen in her purse. She craved air and light. She needed to be anywhere but here. "I'm sorry. I just remembered I have another appointment. Sorry."

"Here, take a couple of these tacos with you." Helen bundled two large tacos in plastic wrap.

"Thanks for the information . . . and the tacos. Come on, Rita, let's go." Sunny was nearly at the door.

"Nice to see you again." Rita followed her mother out.

Looking over her shoulder at Gerald, Sunny saw that her daughter had noticed the triangle birthmark below Gerald's ear. They said goodbye to the Allens. Rita looked confused.

When they reached the car, Rita looked at her mother. "What the heck was that all about? You don't have another appointment. Why are you so addlepated? Is it because of Gerald? You've run into him before. Did he try to hit on you? Is that why he makes you nervous?"

They got in the car and sat for a moment. Sunny sat holding the keys in her lap. "Thinking and talking earlier about Gina overwhelmed me. I felt like leaving."

"Did you notice Gerald has a birthmark below his ear, like mine? I thought only people related had the same birthmarks. How odd is that?" Rita stopped and took a deep breath. "Is there something you want to tell me?"

"No."

Sunny tried twice to put the key in the ignition with her trembling hands. She was confused with the things that had just happened. How would she handle this? How would she explain it to Rita? She'd waited too long. She'd really screwed things up. She turned the corner and pulled over in front of an empty lot.

Rita jerked off her seat belt and turned to look at her mother. "What the heck is going on with you? You act like you never had a guy flirt with you before. He knows you're married. He talked to Dad at Gina's."

"It's complicated."

"How can flirting be complicated? Oh God, Mom, did you go out with him?"

"Of course not. All right, all right. The reason Gerald has the same birthmark as yours is . . . ah . . . uhmm . . ."

Rita gasped. Her hands flew to cover her mouth. Her face blanched. "Oh no, I just got it. Jerry. Is he the same Jerry who is my father?"

"Yes . . . but listen."

"Mom, why didn't you tell me? You knew when we saw him at Gina's. You've seen him all over the place . . . and you never said a word!"

"It just didn't seem the right time to tell you. It never seemed like the right time. If it's any consolation, Barry doesn't know either."

"My God! What were you thinking . . . not saying anything to us? Dad stood talking to him at Gina's and didn't know who he was. That's so wrong! Dad's going to be pissed, and I don't blame him." Her eyes filled with tears.

"Mmm . . . well . . . one more thing. I might as well tell you. Gerald doesn't know either."

"What! How long did you think you could keep this a secret? Another twenty-two years? I can't believe you! I can't breathe in here." Rita opened the car door.

Sunny's eyes widened. "What are you doing?"

"I'm going to get some air. Maybe walk home."

"You are not. It's freezing out. Get your butt in here."

After standing outside a minute, tears frozen to her cheeks, she got back in the car.

"All right, I didn't handle this whole thing very well. I'm sorry," said Sunny.

Staring at her mother, Rita said, "Sorry is just a word to make the other person feel better. Why didn't you tell me?"

Sunny's stomach churned. Afraid and panicky, she gripped the steering wheel. Her hands shook. "Well, you know now. First you were too small. I did tell you his name was Jerry. But at the time I didn't know where he was. Then I thought I'd wait 'til you were older. Somehow the time got away from me."

"Yeah, like twenty-two years. There's no excuse."

"I can understand you being upset. I did what I thought was best for us. I know you're mad. You have a right to be."

Rita chewed on her bottom lip. "Heck yeah, I'm mad! What do you expect?"

Looking down at her hands, Sunny folded them. "I hope it doesn't change anything with us."

"This Gerald, or Jerry, is a stranger. I don't know if I even want to know him. I hope he doesn't want to be my father. Eeeuuuch."

"Let's cross that bridge when we come to it. He may repeat his disappearing act and we won't have to worry about it."

Rita turned in her seat and stared out the window, stewing in her anger. "I can't believe you did this to me, Mom! I feel stupid, humiliated. Like, I'm so dumb. I should have figured it out sooner. But how could I? You didn't share anything with me. And I never laid eyes on him 'til today."

"You never asked," Sunny said quietly. "I guess I figured it was best to leave well enough alone."

"Like, if it ain't broke, don't fix it?"

"That's one way to put it."

"That's a cop-out, Mom. You should have told me." Rita's cheeks were wet, her breathing labored.

Sunny started the car. "I never meant to hurt you. Everything I ever did was for you. I gave you all my love, all my everything, to make up for not having a father."

"I don't know if that's possible, Mom."

The phone was ringing as they walked into the house. Rita snatched it up as Sunny listened. "Hello . . . Yes, I'm fine . . . Yes, maybe we could get together soon . . . She's right here. Mom, it's for you." Rita flung the receiver at her and stomped out.

Sunny steeled herself. "Hello?"

"What the hell is going on?" Gerald's voice was gruff. "You see me and you leave? What the hell!"

"Just stay away from me."

"I'm coming over there now."

"No." She spoke as forcefully as she could. "That's not a good idea."

"I couldn't care less. She's my kid, isn't she? I saw the birthmark, Sunny. I saw it plain as day. You tell me if I'm wrong. She's my kid."

She didn't answer.

"Tell my daughter I'm on my way." *Click.*

She called out to Rita, "Gerald is on his way over." The phone had gone dead.

At the first knock Sunny went to the door, dreading this face-to-face meeting. She stopped just inside and exhaled breath she didn't know she'd been holding. Gerald stood on the porch, feet planted wide, hands on hips, elbows sticking out like grasshopper legs. He glared at her as the veins in his neck pulsed. He looked like he wanted to punch somebody—and that somebody was Sunny. In response, she stared him down.

"Can I come in?"

Without a word she stepped back. He stormed into the house like a one-man SWAT team.

Rita had returned from her room and stood, awkward and uncomfortable in her own home, as if she were a stranger in a strange land, driven by curiosity.

Sunny led them into the kitchen and indicated the table and chairs. "Would anyone like to sit down?" She pulled out a chair and sank onto it, more to still her trembling legs than anything.

Gerald remained standing, facing Sunny like a kid itching for a fight. Rita sat across from her mother, taking it all in.

"Well, I guess it's now or never: Rita, meet your father." Sunny did her best to keep the quiver out of her voice. "Gerald, meet your daughter."

"What the hell, Sunny? That's all you've got to say? Just 'Gerald, meet your daughter'?!" he began, eyes accusing, voice demanding. "Explain it, Sunny. I'm curious where you get off keeping something like this to yourself."

That was the wrong thing to say. Sunny exploded. "And I'm curious where you get off barging in here and acting like I owe you something. Boy, have you got that backwards. I'm the one, if you remember, who got left holding the bag while you took off, footloose and fancy-free. So you figure out who owes who. I hope you brought your checkbook, 'cause there's a helluva lot of back child support due, if it gets down to who owes who."

Gerald's jaw dropped. It was obvious he'd come expecting an apology, like he was the wronged party—the only wronged party.

Sunny plunged ahead. "You want an explanation, I'll give you an explanation. In case you forgot, it takes two to tango. If you were so damn sure you didn't want a baby why didn't you use a condom? Why didn't you abstain? But no, you knock me up and then, rather than suffer any of the consequences—and there were consequences—you take off like a grizzly bear's on your tail. No forwarding address. No 'Let me know if you ever need anything.' No 'Give me twenty-three years to change my mind.' No nothing."

Gerald gulped and sank into a chair at the table, staring at Sunny.

Sunny glared at him, her voice more strident with each word. "You might want to think about . . ."

Rita looked like a goldfish—her eyes wide and mouth open—as she glanced back and forth, back and forth. She stood up. "Um, maybe I should go somewhere and let you two talk."

Sunny stopped and exhaled, her heart pounding and her eyes frenzied. She fought to regain control. "I'm sorry, honey. Gerald and I can finish this later . . . or not. Sit down. I don't want you to go anywhere." She took a breath and exhaled with resignation before going on. "Please, sit down."

Rita did, looking uncomfortable, sneaking glances at Gerald.

"I guess I was off base," admitted Gerald. "It seems like your mom's got a lot to say to me, Rita. And I probably deserve it. But now's not the right time." His eyes demanded consent from Sunny whose chest rose and fell before she dipped her head in assent. He turned back to Rita. "It was a big shock just now over at Frank's. When I saw my birthmark on your neck and it dawned on me . . . Well, you could'a knocked me over with a feather."

Rita said, "Yeah, me too."

Gerald continued. "After I thought about it a minute or two, I got mad. I thought to myself, I should have known. Why didn't I know? 'Cause nobody told me. I have a kid, a grown-up kid, and nobody ever told me. Then I started thinking about all the people who had to know, but didn't tell me, and I got mad at everybody."

Sunny interrupted. "Nobody knew, Jerry. Only my mom and Barb."

Gerald continued as if she hadn't spoken. "Anyhow, by the time I got over here I'd boiled it all down to you, and I was hot under the collar. It's a lot easier to blame you than myself. Sorry, Sunny. Maybe someday we can sort it all out and forgive each other, okay? It's obvious you're a good mom. Our daughter is amazing."

Sunny flinched at his reference to "our daughter." Rita blushed and grinned.

He took a deep breath and locked eyes with Rita. "I'm not the same stupid asshole kid I was then. I want to know you, Rita. I'll be proud to know you . . . and I hope you'll want to know me." His hand reached toward hers.

Rita nodded, allowing the hand of the stranger who happened to be her father to rest on hers, but just momentarily. Then she gently pulled back.

He went on. "Maybe we can get together soon, just you and me?"

Rita shook her head as if overwhelmed. "God, this is so hard. It's a lot to take in all at once. I *have* a dad, Gerald. A really good dad, and I love him a lot. Before we go any further I want you to know that. All I ever knew about my biological dad was that his name was Jerry."

He looked at Sunny. "You mean she didn't know either?"

Sunny replied, "I told you, Barb—you remember Barb—and my mom were the only ones who knew."

"Wow." Gerald turned to her. "That's heavy." He stood and made his way to the door. "Dinner tomorrow, Rita?"

"Okay. Call me with the particulars."

"Sunny, I guess we need to talk. Sometime in the next few days, okay?"

After Gerald left, Rita zinged her mother with sarcasm. "Well, that went well. Now do you understand why I'm so mad? You saw how furious Gerald was 'cause he didn't know something he should have known. It's just as important—maybe more—for me. I should have known all about him all these years. And vice versa."

"You're probably right, but he just disappeared. Besides, he rejected both of us so thoroughly that I just put him out of my mind and didn't even try to track him down. I should have realized what it meant to you . . . but I was so hurt and so mad I didn't."

"Right, it's all about you. Now what about Dad? You owe him the truth."

"I don't know where to begin."

Rita crossed the room to pick up the telephone and handed it to her. "Start here."

Sunny dialed Barry at his office. It rang and rang. She was ready to hang up when he answered, "Hello?"

"Hi. I thought I'd missed you."

"I was on my way out. Had last-minute catching up to do. I'm glad you called. What's up?"

"Well, there's something I need to tell you."

"What? You sound serious." He coughed his smoker's cough. "You and Rita okay?"

"Well . . . ahh . . ."

Rita crossed her arms in front and mouthed, *Tell him.*

"Well, you know I've been asking questions of people at the party. I was at Frank Allen's house when Gerald came over."

"Did he make a pass at you?"

"No, no. He noticed Rita's birthmark on her neck."

"Yeah?"

"Let me finish. A . . . uh . . . well, you know that Rita's father's name is Jerry?"

"Right. So?"

"Anyway, he has the same birthmark."

"Okay, again I ask you, what's this leading to? Oh man, wait. Gerald—Jerry—right? What the hell? I stood there at Gina's place talking to him. I bet everyone at the rez knows. I must've looked like a fool." He paused to let it sink in. "You could'a told me that at the motel. You could'a just said, 'Oh, by the way, Gerald—my ex—that's Rita's father.' What else haven't you told me?"

Sunny sniffed. "Wait, nobody thought you were a fool because . . . ah . . . uh . . . nobody knew. Even Gerald didn't know 'til today."

"You never told him? What the hell . . . ? You seem to have a bad habit of not telling people important things."

The phone went dead. Sunny stood holding the receiver. "He hung up on me. He's never done that before."

"Can you blame him?" asked Rita.

Sunny stabbed at the buttons, trying to reconnect. No answer. She tried again, still no answer.

Rita grimaced and put on her coat. "I can't take this right now. I'm going to the salon." She slammed the door on her way out.

Sunny sat at the kitchen table feeling a little sick and more than a little angry, but she couldn't figure out who she was mad at: herself, or Gerald, or Rita, or Barry. Or all of the above? "Why does everyone blame me? I have to make them understand, or I might lose both Rita and my husband. My friend was right. Barb said they'd be pissed. Well, guess what, so am I."

While Rita was at the salon the next day, Gerald called Sunny. "Can I come over? Rita's at work, isn't she? I'm taking the afternoon off so we can talk . . . if you're free, that is."

Quite a bit more subdued than he'd been when he arrived the day before, he was invited in and seemed willing to hear her out.

Sunny started the conversation. "I never realized how angry I've been at you all these years. Way back then, when I told you I might be pregnant, you went ballistic. You said, 'You better not be.' You said you didn't want any kids, 'now or ever.' You swore at me. I thought you were going to slug me. You even said, 'Well, don't worry, you can get rid of it.' Don't you remember? We had a big fight, and then we broke up."

"No. I don't remember that but I'll take your word for it. I wasn't too bright or mature back then."

Sunny went on. "Later on, when I found out for sure that I was pregnant, it was too late. You were long gone . . . from my life, and from Reno."

"People change, you know," he said. "You should have told me. I might have stepped up to the plate. You cheated me out of years of knowing her, seeing her grow up. Cheated her too."

"I was really upset. You weren't interested in a pregnant girlfriend. You were a party animal to the core—no grown-up responsibilities for you. Or you'd have made me get an abortion, and I wasn't about to do that. Abortion was illegal . . . and potentially deadly . . . in 1963. Sorry, but you weren't worth it."

She took a deep breath. "Besides, you'd already gone and I didn't even know where to start looking for you."

"Hey, we're both from the rez. Somebody could'a told you. Somebody would'a known where I was, sooner or later."

Sunny just nodded. She'd probably always been aware of that possibility, but hadn't wanted to consider it. She was getting mad all over again.

She got in his face; her voice escalated. "How come you shouldn't be judged . . . 'cause you were young and stupid. Try to remember, please, I was the same age as you. We were both teenagers, but I was supposed to act like a wise, mature adult. I was supposed to do everything right. The old double standard is alive and well."

He sighed. "I guess we both made mistakes. What can I say? I was an idiot. I'm sorry."

"We both have to do what we can to make it up to Rita. I didn't realize how unfair it was to her."

"Hey, you got a beer or something?"

Sunny went to the fridge and came back with a couple of sodas, checked the cupboard for glasses and came up empty, took two clean glasses from the top rack of the dishwasher, and poured.

"Well, enough of the blame game. I really want to know how you managed all those years as a single mom. Can't have been easy."

"You got that right. But I had my mom, thank God. After Rita was born my mother took care of her so I could go to college."

CHAPTER FORTY

Rita was still upset with her mom, but the phone was ringing off the hook at her salon. She needed to get it together and act professional. "Good afternoon. Rita's Hair Happening." She was shaking all over. She hoped the caller couldn't tell it in her voice.

"Hi. How're you doing?"

She was surprised to hear Victor's voice. "I've been better. What's up with you?" Any other time she'd have been happy to hear his voice, but today was different. She just met her real dad. And she learned she'd been lied to her whole life.

"I have the rest of the afternoon off. I thought maybe we could drive out to Windy Lake. There's still a few hours of daylight. Besides it sounds like you could use some fresh air."

"Uhh . . . I don't know. I might not be the best company."

"Sure you will. Fresh air and hiking clears your mind. You'll feel better. I can come by in about ten minutes. What d'you say?"

"Oh, why not? It might help my mood."

"Good. See you in a few."

Rita scooted her chair back from the desk and rushed to the supply room where she kept an old pair of boots. She also grabbed her purse and searched for her lipstick. "Oh, dang. Why didn't I pay more attention to my makeup today?" she said to the mirror.

A couple of employees were at the table in the break room.

"Why so nervous?" asked one of her hairstylists. "You never had a date before?"

"Do something with your hair," said a second one.

"Who is this guy?"

"Just a friend. We have people and things in common."

"Mmm . . ." The girls giggled knowingly.

Rita rushed to the reception desk to wait for Victor, feeling like a schoolgirl. Considering what she'd just been through she needed air and space and sunlight, not more stress over Gerald and Barry. And her mom.

Fifteen minutes later, Victor walked in and Rita stood to meet him. "Are you going to cut my hair?" He grinned.

"No, why?"

"You have your smock on."

Rita's face grew warm; she knew her cheeks were rosy. She hung up her lab coat and grabbed her jacket. Her heart was racing.

Windy Lake was a twenty-minute drive from her salon. The sun had played hide-and-seek with the clouds all morning. Now it dismissed the clouds and took over the sky.

As they rode along she noticed the black shiny upholstery and the new-truck smell. The rock station was playing Pink Floyd, one of Rita's favorites.

They passed the giant corral filled with wild mustangs. Victor pointed to the right of the road. "This is where Mustang Annie started saving the horses. They'd be in the mountains starving if it wasn't for her."

Rita was quiet. While driving, Victor turned to her with a half-smile. "How're you doing?"

She met him with silence, and shrugged. Her mind was going full speed about the secret her mother had kept. She told Rita the name of her real father—his nickname, anyway. Why not introduce them? Or just let her know at Gina's that Gerald was her dad? It really hurt. So many emotions were flowing through her. *I should have stayed at work.*

Finally, Victor asked, "Is there anything I can help with?"

"No, it's personal."

"Isn't everything?"

That made her snicker and she started to feel more comfortable. "I guess you're right."

"Sure, you share with me and I'll share with you."

"Sort of, like you show me yours and I'll show you mine?" Her eyes grew wide and she put her hands over her mouth, feeling the heat rise in her face. "Oh man, did I just say that?"

"Whoa, what kind of guy do you think I am?" He laughed. "Is bright red your natural color?"

Rita started laughing from pure embarrassment and Victor joined in, breaking the tension.

The cattle guard at Windy Lake's entrance rattled as they drove over it. At the side of the road were two long spears crisscrossed near their tops. From the tips of the arrows hung a sign, "You are now entering Indian Country."

Rita sighed. "This lake always amazes me. Nothing but blue water as far as you can see, to the left and right. Especially the huge natural stone pyramid in the middle. I don't know how it was formed, but there it stands. Such beautiful colors."

"Imagine, back in the Old West, riding out in the desert. As the pioneers came up over the hill, they'd see this giant lake. I bet they thought it was a mirage."

Rita nodded. "Some call it Superstition Lake. A lot of stories come from there. People who fish out in the middle of the lake are told by the old-timers not to get out of the boat and swim because of the undertows, but they usually don't listen. Then their bodies are found almost a hundred miles away."

"Wow. We're not going fishing or swimming." He drove around part of the lake, up a winding dirt road, and over a hill before stopping.

"Let's get out here. We can hike across the hill and down the other side, okay?"

"Sure, looks fine," Rita answered. More comfortable now she was glad she'd come. She loved being out in the open and close to nature. A hard breeze made sand and dust swirl around her and up her nostrils. Rita scratched her nose. "How are you feeling without Gina?"

"Still bothers me. Actually makes me mad. I don't know why she changed her mind. Gina and I argued all afternoon. I hate thinking about how everything ended." He made a fist.

Rita looked at the ground. "Were you in love with her a long time?"

"I wasn't in love with her. And she wasn't in love with me. I felt sorry for her and the boys. I thought I could help them get out of their bad situation. I have a big house, plenty of room. That way she could take her time to look for a place." His voice rose.

While speaking about Gina, Rita thought she noticed tones of anger and disappointment in his voice. They discussed the ways both had loved her. She wondered if Victor had what her mother called a Knight in Shining Armor syndrome—wondered if he just needed to rescue people. She didn't know if that was a good or bad thing.

Rita walked along lost in thought, when her foot slipped on a large sandy rock. Victor's hand stretched out to grasp hers as she began to slide down the hill but fell short. Small rocks in front of her raised a cloud of dust. Fumbling for a foothold, her fingers outstretched toward him, she clawed at the air. She extended her arms toward him to break her fall. She headed down the hill, collecting sticker weeds, dirt, rocks, all sliding down, creating dust. Stepping closer, almost within reach, his feet slid downward as small rocks rolled beneath his boots. He struggled to right himself. He lunged to grab her around the waist, but missed. Her arms flailed in the air. He bent over and tried to catch her and managed to grab her wrists and pull her up.

All of a sudden, she was upset. "I'm so embarrassed, what a klutz."

"Are you all right? Are you hurt? I was trying to grab hold of you. Sorry. I tried to keep you from falling. Didn't want you hurting yourself."

They continued hiking around the hill, making their way back to the car. "Look at how beautiful the shadows are, starting to fall on the mountaintops." Moving down the last muddy hill, Rita lost her footing again; her legs went out from under her. Her arms flailed in the air. Victor reached out to catch her at the same time she tried to grab hold of him. Both tumbled and fell in the mud. They landed on their stomachs, facing each other, so close they could feel each other's breath. They locked eyes, then looked away.

"Oh." She felt so awkward. "I sure am clumsy." She smiled.

Victor brushed back the hair from her face. Moving closer he touched her lips with one finger, then moved it slowly down across her chin, his eyes never leaving hers.

Spellbound by his green eyes, Rita sat motionless, goose bumps prickling her arms.

He looked at a hawk overhead, breaking the spell, and stood up abruptly, then grabbed her arms and pulled her up. "We'd better go, we're losing daylight. It's getting cold, especially since we're wet and muddy."

Rita wondered if the hawk was one they'd seen at Gina's funeral.

The last remains of sunlight dipped below the mountain line as they walked back to the car in silence, hand in hand. At the touch of his hand Rita shivered slightly wondering what had happened back there? Had there been electricity between them, or was it just her imagination?

"Here, I have a couple of towels in the back of my truck, to wipe off with. We're not too bad." He dabbed at her cheeks with the towel. Driving back toward town, he asked, "Hungry? Jack's is up ahead."

"Sounds good."

He pulled into the parking lot at Jack's Restaurant and helped Rita out of the truck. They were seated right away. It was Thursday night and the place wasn't crowded, which was unusual. Jack's was known for good food, and a lot of it. An older restaurant with worn booths of green-and-yellow vinyl, it had a warm, cozy feel. They could hear the clatter of pots and pans and the bell for waitresses to pick up their orders. Waitresses wore traditional black pants and white shirts. The smell of French fries made Rita hungrier. Jack's had employed the same waitresses for years. An older woman who brought two glasses of water, took their order, and disappeared.

"The heat feels good." Rita rubbed her hands together.

"Yeah. You seemed to be somewhere else today, Rita," Victor said. "I'm sorry if you didn't enjoy the hike."

"No, I did, really. It helped to take my mind off things for a while. I'm sorry. It's . . . I do have something else on my mind."

"Can I help? I'm a good listener."

"Well, I don't know if it'll help, but I guess it can't hurt. It's about Gerald. You know who he is, don't you?"

"The guy who's going out with Eva?"

They went silent as the waitress brought their cheeseburgers, fries, and colas. Rita gestured with a fry as she talked. "Yeah. As if dating Eva weren't bad enough, what makes it worse . . . uh . . . I just found out . . ." she swallowed hard and placed the remainder of her French fry on the rim of her plate. "Well, I just figured out that Gerald is my biological father."

Victor had started to take a bite of hamburger but stopped with it in midair. "No shit. How'd you figure it out?"

"Well, I always knew my real father's name was Jerry. We went over to Frank Allen's house 'cause my mom wants to know about the party, and what they knew about Gina. Gerald works with Frank and he came over for lunch. He and my mother went steady when they were young and she lived here in Reno. But they broke up before I was born. She married Barry, and he adopted me when I was little. He's a great dad and I love him. He has my heart."

"So, how'd you find out?" he repeated.

"I saw the birthmark on his neck. It's identical to mine, and in the same place."

"Wow. You got all that?"

"Yeah, just because of my neck."

"Oh, I saw your birthmark the other day when you had your hair pushed behind your ear. It's different, a perfect triangle. I like it. It's weird, both of you having the same one."

"Yeah. So when I asked my mom if he's my dad, she got all upset but admitted it. Listen to this, then he came over to my house and confronted her. Turns out, he didn't know either."

"Wow! That's some heavy shit. What did your mom say?"

"She had a lot to say. Suppressed anger, I guess. When I was young all she ever told me was his name was Jerry, and she didn't know where he lived. So the story goes. When she thought she might be pregnant, she told him and he threw a fit. Said he didn't want any kids, ever. They broke up and he took off for parts unknown, and later, when she found out for sure she was pregnant she never told him."

"It put your mom in a hard place."

"Yeah, I guess. I've never seen her so upset. She read him the riot act."

"Sounds like you should call and see how she is. Talk to her. She did what she could, you know, and you already have a great dad. You're lucky; you have two dads. I didn't even have one. Mine cut out when I was born. He didn't want my mom or me."

"Like Jerry, I guess. I'm sorry. Was it hard on you?" she asked.

"I'm fine. As a kid I didn't notice. It was hard on my mom, though. In a way, I understand your mom's decision. He said he never wanted children, so she was protecting you."

Rita thought about that. "Will you excuse me? I'm going to look for a pay phone."

Victor smiled at her. "Good." He went to work on his hamburger.

Rita hurried down the hall to find a pay phone. She spotted it outside the restrooms, pulled some change from her purse, and dropped it in the coin slot. She dialed her home number, but hung up on the first ring. *Mom's used to hang-ups. She won't think anything of it.* "I don't know if I want to call her right now," she whispered. When the coins clinked into the coin drop she slid them out with two fingers and pushed them into her jeans pocket.

Victor had paid the check and was waiting by the door. "Everything all right?"

"Yeah, fine."

He drove Rita back to the salon. As she started to get out, he touched her arm. "Thank you for today. I had a good time. Hope you'll feel better. And . . . uh . . . take it easy on your mom, okay?"

"It was nice. Thanks. And I do feel better." But she was still ticked off at her mom.

He got out of the truck and came round to open her door. They studied each other a moment and then, as he took her hand to help her out, she blushed and dropped her eyes.

At her car they hugged before saying goodbye.

On her drive home, she thought about her situation with her mother and what she should do. She couldn't change the past but she could get to know Jerry—Gerald. She didn't even know what to call him . . . Dad? . . . No, she didn't think she could do that. Barry was Dad. What would she say to Sunny?

THURSDAY EVENING

Sunny called Barry, both at work and at home, but he didn't answer. She was on the couch petting Floyd when Rita walked in. Sunny watched her daughter pass by en route to her room without speaking.

Sunny laid her head in her arms on the table and let the tears run down her cheeks. Her body shook as she sobbed.

A few minutes later Rita touched her shoulder. "Mom? I don't know what to say or how I feel toward you right now. I'm still mixed up. I feel a little betrayed. Well, a lot betrayed. I don't like seeing you hurt, but we're all hurt."

Sunny reached for the tissues. "I knew in my heart that Gerald wouldn't be there for us."

"I thought about what you said. Gerald told you he never wanted kids. You protected me from being hurt and gave me nothing but love. You're a great mom and my best friend. This is going to take some time. I'm in a hard place right now."

Rita helped her mom up and gave her a rigid hug.

"I guess I'll have dinner with Jerry—Gerald—tomorrow and see what happens. I love you, Mom, and I don't want this to come between us. You'll have to give me some time."

Sunny was surprised. "The way you talked to Gerald showed me a mature side of you. I'm sorry too, and I love you. I promise I won't interfere." I hope Barry forgives me.

The phone rang and Sunny snatched it. Maybe it was Barry. All she heard was the buzz of the dial tone. She tossed it down. "Damn it, I'm sick of this."

It rang right away again. This time Rita answered it. "What!" she yelled in frustration. This time it was Victor.

"Oh. Sorry. Did you just call?"

"No, this is my first time. I wanted to see how you're doing and thank you for today. I guess I caught you at a bad time."

"I'm much better. Thanks. It was just what I needed. It's the hang-ups we keep getting. It's been too much."

"I'm sorry; that's a pain."

"Didn't mean to holler at you."

"How about going again on Saturday? We can drive to Hidden Valley and hike up the mountain that overlooks the city."

"Well, I don't know. Saturday is my busiest day. I also have to make sure my employees have all their supplies for the following week. I'll have to let you know." She ended the call.

Rita whirled around and faced her mother. Her voice was excited, her face all smiles. "Do I have something to tell you!"

Again, another ring, and Sunny started for it, but Rita grabbed it. Sunny waited, watching, hoping it was Barry.

"Hello? Hi, Gerald," Rita looked at Sunny. "Good, tomorrow night at Harrah's Steak House." Rita rubbed the back of her neck. "Okay, I'll meet you there. Six-thirty . . . All right, see you then."

"I guess I can tell what that was about. You're going to dinner with Gerald."

"Yes, but more important, I want to tell you about today." The tea kettle whistled on the stove. Rita reached for two mugs and poured the boiling water. She put in two tea bags and continued. "Victor called me at work. He wants me to go hiking with him again. We went to Windy Lake today and hiked for a few hours. Listen to this; I kept falling down a hill."

"What are you talking about?"

"We had a conversation about Gina and how she wouldn't move in with him. He wanted to help her get away from Jesse. She decided not to, though. To live with just the boys. I slipped, and he made a grab for me. I felt like such a klutz, not only once, but twice."

Sunny leaned in close. "Wha . . . what did he say?"

"He kept trying to grab me. It was my own clumsiness. Plus, I was still upset from this afternoon."

"He kept trying to grab you? Sounds like a teenager." She laughed, then turned serious. "Be careful, you could hurt yourself in those hills."

"Listen, right after I fell the first time, I slipped again and he caught me and we both fell."

"What's going on with you two?"

"When he's close I feel nervous."

Sunny shrugged and sipped her tea. "Sounds like attraction to me."

"Mom! No, we're getting to know each other. We have Gina in common. That's all."

"Sure. And those drop-dead good looks of his don't hurt." Sunny half smiled.

So did Rita. "By the way, they weren't lovers; just good friends."

Her mother's eyebrows shot up. "Oh?"

"Yeah. He just wanted to help her get out of her bad marriage. He felt bad for her and her boys." Rita finished her tea and stood. "I'm worn out. 'Night." She hugged her mother and went to her room.

Sunny rose and picked up the receiver to call Barry again, but still there was no answer. She felt numb.

CHAPTER FORTY-ONE

At six o'clock, after a long day of paperwork and that disturbing call from Sunny, Barry locked his office door. On his way out of the building, he spotted his friend Ed. "Hey, how about a beer at The Corner?"

"Sure, but I can't stay too late. My ole lady is putting the screws to me. I don't want to deal with her when she's pissed off."

They shared a knowing chuckle and walked along the marble floors that echoed their footsteps in the Hall of Justice. Barry pushed the gold-plated double glass doors open and they took the stairs two at a time. The Corner Bar was what the name implied: a small, semidark place at the corner, where lawyers, judges, and courthouse and social services employees hung out.

Initially, Barry and Ed ordered their usual—Coors. Then Barry changed his to a gin and tonic, double lime.

Ed turned and looked at him. "Whoa, buddy, what's been eating you today? I heard you barking at your assistant. You've been grumpy as an ole alley cat."

"Sorry. Just personal, I have to work out something."

"Well, if I can help . . ."

"Thanks."

Each had a couple more. Then Ed stood. "I better go before the ole lady sends out the troops." He patted Barry's shoulder and left.

While Barry sat nursing his third gin and tonic he noticed the woman a couple of stools down staring at him. He raised his glass in acknowledgment.

She picked up hers and scooted down to the stool vacated by Ed. "Hi. I know this sounds like a pick-up line, but you look familiar."

"I come here a lot."

"No, I don't come here often. I usually go to the Bar Grand at Market and Van Ness, with the gals from work. Do you know it?"

"Yeah. Sure," he said.

"My name's Lisa. You?"

"Barry. You work around here?"

"I'm a fraud investigator with Social Services."

"Really? So is my wife. Do you know Sunny Davis?"

"Sure." Lisa snapped her fingers. "That's where I've seen you. Your picture is on her desk."

Barry smirked. "Small world."

"I heard what happened to her friend. What was her name?"

"Gina."

"Sorry. Is Sunny home yet?"

"No. When we got there, things didn't seem right."

"You went too?"

"Yeah."

"Is that why you look so sad and distracted?"

He held up his glass. "Another?"

"Sure, if you're having one."

After a couple more gin and tonics things started to loosen up between them.

She put her hand on his arm, slurring her words. "You have somm . . . hard bi . . . ceps. You work out a lot?"

Barry pulled away and ordered another round. He smiled. "Nahh," he lied. "Not really. Jus' natural."

"You must be lone . . . ly by now. I can fix that. How about we go somm . . . where else?"

Barry watched her and lit a cigarette. "You live around here?"

"Surr . . . Taxi can take us there in a hot minute. Come on. What do ya say?"

"Let's go."

He knew he shouldn't, but he was so mad at Sunny. If she lied about Gerald, what else was she lying about? He put on his blue parka, the one Sunny hated, and asked the bartender, whose frown telegraphed disapproval, to call them a taxi. He helped Lisa with her coat and held her arm. They staggered out to the curb as the taxi pulled up. Lisa got in and Barry reached in his pocket and pulled out a twenty.

He held the door open and looked at the seat next to her. Shaking his head, he took a step back and mumbled, "Sorry, I can't."

She reached for his arm. "What? We're going to my place. What's wrong?"

"I'm already in the doghouse. I need to fix the problem, not make it worse. Here's money for the taxi."

"Shove it. I don't want your damn money." She tapped the taxi driver on the shoulder. "Get the hell away from me."

Barry went back into the bar and ordered a beer.

The bartender pressed his lips tight and shook his head. "This is your last one. I'm cuttin' you off."

"Okay." He thought again about how angry he was at Sunny, and how he'd never lost control before. He'd almost gone home with that woman. That scared the crap out of him. It would destroy his marriage.

Shit, I'm drunk.

He wasn't too drunk to know they needed to talk this thing out, but should he tell Sunny about tonight? *If Lisa blabs I'm screwed.*

He put his half-full beer on the bar with a tip and walked out into the night.

CHAPTER FORTY-TWO

LATE THURSDAY NIGHT

Sunny sat at the table trying to put the shredded papers together. Once again she was going to try to get a hold of Barry. To her surprise, he answered immediately.

"Hello-o."

Sunny knew all too well, by the slurred greeting, where he'd been, and decided to delay a heavy conversation. "Can we talk tomorrow?"

"Grrr . . . eat. Now's not a good time."

"I see that. All right. Call you tomorrow."

Barry slurred. "I was a good boy. Ha ha."

"Barry? What the hell does that mean?"

No response.

"He's passed out. I gave him a reason to drink. But that doesn't make it okay." Disappointed and pissed, she placed the receiver in its cradle.

She'd been sure he'd go out drinking. Every time they had a problem he went straight for the bottle. She doodled on her tablet. Maybe a separation or a divorce would be the right thing. But she loved him. Maybe this time she really had hurt him, but she refused to take all the blame.

FRIDAY MORNING

Sunny was in the kitchen, fixing bacon and French toast when Rita came in and hugged her mother. It felt to Sunny like things were back to normal. She wasn't used to Rita being mad at her.

Rita poured herself a coffee. "Bacon and coffee; a good way to wake up." She picked up Floyd, got his dish, and fed him.

Sunny smiled and couldn't help asking, "Are you excited about your dinner tonight with Gerald?" She placed Rita's breakfast in front of her.

"Not excited. More nervous and curious. I want to call Dad and talk to him first."

Me too, thought Sunny.

"You know, remember I told you Victor and Gina weren't in love, more like friends and confidants. He was trying to help her. I keep thinking about that." Finished with her breakfast Rita put her dishes in the dishwasher.

"Mmm . . . What does that mean to you?" She looked at Rita.

Rita grabbed her purse and blew a kiss at her mom. She smiled, shook her head, and left.

CHAPTER FORTY-THREE

Sunny was busy getting together everything she needed to once again go over what had happened at Jesse and Gina's party: her notebook and the piece of cardboard with bits of paper attached. She pondered over her notebook first. Everything she could think of was already there: Jesse's story; Victor's explanation; and Patty's, Frank's, and Helen's versions.

The papers wrapped in the tissue caught her eye. It didn't make sense to her why these would be torn up and tossed in a wastebasket where anyone could find them. Of course, they wouldn't have caught her eye if she hadn't bumped it with her knee, knocking them out.

She also noted the hang-ups, the car-ramming, Rita's tire-slashing, the dead roses. She felt sure Eva was responsible, but needed solid evidence. What else had Eva done? So many things had happened in the past few days that they'd forgotten to go to the police station to file a harassment report. She'd have to remind Rita.

The phone rang, startling Sunny. "Hello." It was Rita. "Hi, I was just thinking of you. We never filled out the police report."

Rita's voice sounded rushed to Sunny. "Mom—I had a break in."

Sunny took a breath, then plopped down in the chair. "What? When? Are you all right?"

"Yes. They came in through the bathroom window. I guess it was left unlocked."

"I thought it was mandatory every night to check all the windows. What was vandalized? Was anything taken?"

"They made a mess, no money taken. They spilled two bottles of hair color and tipped over chairs and knocked brushes and combs on the floor. Nothing damaged, just messy."

Sunny dug in her purse for a cigarette but came up empty. "Good. Easy cleanup. Can I come down and help you?"

"No. The police are almost done."

"That was quick. Make sure you fill out a report and tell them about all the other things."

"I will," said Rita.

"Okay, honey. Call if you need me, and please be careful."

She hung up, thinking about Madam Carmen's warning. They'd been lucky, so far. No one had been hurt.

Sunny went and showered. Then out to the kitchen table, to write and finish with the papers. She thought she knew what she had. But the evidence had to be clear-cut. Her findings had to be correct and convincing She kept busy as the hours dwindled away.

Rita came in and threw her purse and coat on the chair, then plopped down with her legs stretched out. "Wow, what a day."

She proceeded to tell her mom about what had happened at the salon, including the tipped-over chairs. "Even the brushes and combs were thrown on the floor. There's a tiny crack in the display case. We got it all cleaned up but it took us over an hour. I'm bushed."

"Sounds like someone had a temper tantrum."

Rita shrugged and forced a grin.

"You look exhausted. Are you going to be able to go to dinner with Gerald?"

"Yeah, I have a couple hours. I'll go rest and take a shower. I'll be fine."

Sunny was watching the six o'clock news when Rita emerged from her room dressed in black Levi's, a red turtleneck, and black boots.

"I don't know what time I'll be back." Rita struggled into her coat. "I called Dad. He said to tell you he loves you, but needs some time to digest everything. His problem isn't with Gerald, it's with you. Keeping it a secret from him after you saw Gerald, knowing Dad had talked to him. He's upset. You made him feel like he's not important."

"I'll call him." Sunny rose from her chair.

"No! No, Mom. Give him some room. He's hurt. I'm leaving to meet Gerald now. Promise me you won't call Dad."

"Okay, I won't." But I'm hurting too.

Rita smiled, blew her a kiss and went out the door.

Sunny started for the phone. The door opened and Rita popped back in.

"I knew you wouldn't listen. He said he'd call you. Do you want to make him madder? Do I have to unplug the phone and take it with me? Stop acting like a kid."

"You're right. Go have a nice time." Anxious and grumpy, Sunny settled in to watch *The Golden Girls*. She dozed off on the couch, visions of Barry moving away from her, his arms stretched out to her, mixed with fog. Startled, she woke.

The eleven o'clock news was almost over when Rita walked in.

Sunny rubbed her eyes. "That was a long dinner. How'd it go? Did you have a nice time?" She tried to act casual but was dying to know all the details. She imagined she'd been a major topic of their dinner talk.

Rita nodded. "We had dinner then went to his place. It was small, nice, and cozy. He showed me a photo album—pictures of his mother and father. Felt funny seeing my blood grandparents for the first time." She showed a picture of them to Sunny. "Oh, he took a picture of me to send to them."

"How does this make you feel?" Sunny had never thought about Gerald's parents. "I never met his parents. His dad's job transferred him to Wyoming. Gerald stayed with his aunt to finish his senior year at Reed High. I met her, though. I think she's passed on."

She wondered how to fix the situation between all parties, or could she? All these years she'd never considered Rita's other grandparents. Again she felt a hot coal of anxiety in the pit of her stomach. In survival mode, just trying to make it through each day, she hadn't thought of a lot of things.

"They live in DuPont, a small town in Washington."

"Have you thought about seeing them?"

"Yeah, he asked me if I'd like to go with him and meet them. I told him yes, I think so. First, I want to talk to Dad, though. Gerald understands. He liked Dad and said you and I were lucky."

"I think so too."

"It's been a long day, Mom. I'm going to bed. Got a busy day tomorrow."

CHAPTER FORTY-FOUR

SATURDAY MORNING

After breakfast and cleaning the kitchen, Rita left early for work. Sunny stepped out on the porch to pick up the newspaper. Cold crisp air. Patches of packed snow glistened against the curbs and trees. She read the announcement of her friend, Karen Washington, celebrating her twentieth year as casino manager. They'd worked together when Sunny was twenty-one. Now she wished she'd stayed until Karen's break to talk to her rather than just waving across the huge casino the night she won at the slots.

Maybe a walk would clear her head. So many things were happening. Were she and Rita actually in danger? She should ask Gina. But what if she'd lost contact? Sunny desperately needed her. The walk would be a good idea. Maybe Gina would come to her in the wind. She remembered her friend, Karen, and retrieved her address book from her purse. Although she hoped to hear from Gina, seeing her friend from the old days would be good too. Karen could always make her laugh, and right now that's what she needed. She found her new number and called her, explained why she was in town, and confided the awful things that had happened to her and Rita. They agreed to meet at the intersection of Second and Bally Streets.

Sunny put on her knit cap and gloves. It was so cold she could see her breath. She walked past the neighborhood houses and motels and listened for Gina's whisper in the wind.

Have you abandoned me? I need you to help me understand what happened to you.

Sunny saw Karen turn the corner and hurried toward her. They smiled and embraced.

"So good to see you. It's been too long," Karen put her arm around Sunny's shoulder. "How are Rita and your husband?"

"They're fine. How about you? I saw your announcement in the paper. Congratulations. Couldn't get out of those casinos, I see."

"I'm a casino junkie." She smiled. "In fact, they just called me in to work. Do you mind if we cut our walk short?"

"No, not at all."

"I'm so sorry. I saw Gina's obituary in the paper. Such a terrible thing. She was so young."

"I'm trying to figure it out. I can't believe she'd kill herself." Sunny didn't comment further.

As they walked and talked, a woman walking toward them clutched her purse and crossed the street.

Karen pointed at the woman. "Did you see that? I want to holler, "Lady, this is 1985. I'm black, and I'm the manager of a casino I couldn't even step inside in the sixties."

"Maybe it's me," said Sunny. As they walked, they reminisced.

Karen said, "Remember when we went to the lunch counter at Woolworth's, and you were shocked because the waitress wouldn't serve us? And you didn't know why. Did you know that Reno used to be known as The Mississippi of the West?"

"Not The Biggest Little City in the World?"

"Yeah, that too."

Sunny looked down Virginia Street at all the casinos, keeping her ears open, listening for Gina.

"Odd, how things have changed. When I see how buildings are now, it's like I look through them and see them the way they were when I was young," said Sunny.

"Me too. I feel sad. Of course, things are much better. Not great, but better. Forget this. Let's go get a cup of coffee before I have to go to work."

They giggled like schoolgirls. Sunny put her arm around her friend as they walked to the coffee shop.

After coffee, Karen went to work.

Sunny remained at the table having a second cup. The signs across the street sparkled against the sun. She took the sketch pad from her purse and began to draw. The image that emerged was a tree with dead limbs and a diaphanous woman beside it, the wind blowing her hair into its branches. *Talk to me, Gina, please!* She put her pad back and started out into the crisp air.

Sunny took her time on her walk thinking about Gina and the bits of papers she'd found.

Gina, can you sense me? Limbs from the tree moved back and forth, the wind picked up dust and swirled below the fire hydrant, and around the bushes in the planter boxes. "Is that you, Gina?" She stopped, stood still, cocked her head, and listened.

Sunny. I'm with you.

"Oh, Gina, I thought you were gone." Sunny's eyes filled with tears. "Tell me what happened. I need to know. Why did you kill yourself? Was it because of our argument?

Help me.

"What did you write in that note to Jesse?" Sunny got an image of pink paper, Gina's handwriting across the page. She tried to read the words. "Gina, what did you write?"

Scared. Help me.

Sunny was getting tired. She could see the sun shining through Gina's sheer shape. "Scared? Why? Were you scared moving in with Victor?"

Help me . . . find peace. Tired. So tired. The wind whipped up. *Sunny, my boys.*

"They're fine. Gina, tell me about the note? You have to try. Think! What did you write to Jesse?"

The wind stopped. So did Gina's frail voice. Sunny tried to call her back, but she was gone. "Damn, I was so close. *This otherworldly communication takes a lot out of me.* "Was that all?" Sunny asked out loud. A woman walking by frowned and picked up her pace.

Sunny was worried. Maybe Gina didn't write that note. She took the shortcut back to Rita's. The weather had turned colder as it often did late in the day in March. As she walked, she thought about when she and Gerald broke up before she found out she was pregnant, Sunny had been scared half to death. *I did what was necessary for our survival.*

Sunny walked up the driveway as Rita drove in smiling and waving.

When they entered the house, Sunny said, "Looks like you're in a good mood. What's going on?"

Rita hung their coats in the closet. "I am good." She continued to smile. "Went for a hike with Victor, and later we parked on top of Hidden Valley Hill, and talked forever. Oh yeah, I called Dad this morning. We had a long talk. It was nice."

"Sounds like you're talked out. Did he say anything about me?"

"Yes, he's cooled down now. But he still wants to be the one to make the call."

Sunny stared out the window. "I don't want to lose my husband."

"You won't. He loves you. We talked about Gerald and his parents."

"I know your dad. He won't care if you get to know your grandparents. I'm not sure how he'll feel about you and Gerald, though."

"I assured him that I love him so much. No one or nothing can change that. He's so wonderful. He told me I'm a lucky girl to have two men who love me. See how awesome he is? Gerald called me at work. We're going to have dinner again next week. Probably not Harrah's Steak House though. Maybe someplace more affordable."

Sunny smiled at her daughter. "That's nice. Good for you both. I didn't tell you, I talked to Gina today on my walk. I heard her through the wind. She can't remember what happened to her. She just remembered writing the part of the letter she left. I tried asking her more, but then she was gone."

"What're you going to do?"

"I am going to put the cardboard in the trunk of my car so the pages don't come loose. I think I have enough to take to the police Monday. And I want to try to talk to Gina again."

"Feels like a roller coaster ride. We never know what's happening next."

"I worry too. I wish your Dad would call me. This waiting is so hard. Maybe he's punishing me. He knows I don't have any patience."

"Mom, do you mind if I go to a movie with Victor?"

"You don't have to ask. It's your house, and you're an adult. Sounds like you have three men, not just two."

Rita giggled. "That'd be nice."

"Go on. Have a good time. I have plenty to do here. I'll call Barbara to catch up on all the gossip . . . and I've got a good book. The new Stephen King thriller—*Skeleton Crew*. Don't worry."

"Okay, but only call Barb, no one else!"

After Rita left, Sunny tried to bring in Gina's spirit but nothing came through. She called Barbara. They talked about everything and how close Gina had come to talking about the note.

When they hung up Sunny was tempted to call her husband, then thought better of it. Rita had made her promise . . .

CHAPTER FORTY-FIVE

Sunny sat before the hearth reading when she heard a knock on the front door. She uncurled her legs, threw off the lap robe, and went to answer it.

"Barry!" She stared openmouthed.

"Well, can I come in?"

"Yes, of course." She laughed and swung the door wide, her arms wider. He pulled her close.

"I was sitting here waiting for you to call me."

"I had a lot of thinking to do. I thought about everything. I figured the best thing was to come and talk it out in person."

She took his hand and sat on the couch. He looked as nervous as she felt.

"Where's Rita?"

"At the movies, with Victor. She's been out with him a few times."

"I hope she doesn't rush into anything this time."

"Quit stalling and tell me why you didn't tell me you were coming." She covered her mouth with her hands. "Sorry, that sounded harsh."

"Because we need to talk. I've done a lot of thinking about us."

She looked at him, then watched the cars out the window. Her stomach was clutching with fear. "First," she said, "let me apologize. You were right. I should have said something when we saw Gerald. I wasn't trying to keep anything from you. To tell the truth, I never thought I'd see him again and I was shocked he was there. It kind of threw me into a panic and I didn't react right. I didn't want Rita to know. That was wrong."

"Or . . . Gerald," he said. "All these years and the man didn't know he was a father."

"I see how it looks, but in my mind it felt right."

He scrunched up his face and shook his head. "Not telling me was a lie . . . by omission. You were sneaky. That's what upset me. I thought I knew you. I thought we promised to tell each other everything."

Sunny gulped and replied, "Just to clear the record, I wasn't being sneaky. There was nothing sneaky about it. I was just getting on with my life . . . and Rita's. I put Gerald aside and shazam!—he didn't exist anymore. That's why I didn't tell you."

Tears fell. *Does he want a divorce? Is that why he came, to talk it out in person?*

Barry spoke. "I thought about everything you said. You and he were young. When he said he never wanted kids you believed him."

She turned and faced him, angry she was so misunderstood. "Yes, I believed him. What was I supposed to do? He was adamant. Vehement. No ifs, ands or buts about it. He was over-the-top clear about not wanting a baby. And his baby was already growing in my belly. So I put him out of my mind. If that makes me sneaky, or vile, or hateful, well, I'm sorry. I'll try to make it up to everyone, but I am not the terrible person you all seem to think I am."

Barry put his arms around his wife and held her tight. "Nobody thinks you're a terrible person, babe. But you kind of dug yourself into a hole all those years ago. Made some bad choices—but at this point it doesn't matter. Hell, everybody makes bad choices sometimes. What matters is that Rita needs to know Gerald, and vice versa. I'm comfortable knowing she loves me. I just wish you'd told me."

She shrugged. "So does Gerald. Wish I'd told him, that is."

"It must've come as a shock." He ran his tongue over his lips. "Let's sit down. I'm not finished. I have something to tell you . . . and you're not going to like it."

Sunny stood, her arms crisscrossing her chest, her breathing stopped, sure he was about to tell her he wanted a divorce.

Barry sat on the couch, motioning for her to sit beside him. Floyd jumped into her lap. She lowered her head and stroked his soft fur. She looked at Barry and whispered, "What?"

"I'm not making any excuses for anything I did."

Something he did? Like what!

"It started when you told me about Gerald. I was flabbergasted. I couldn't believe you held back information like that." He flung his arms in the air. "Like I was nothing. It hurt."

"No. I never meant to hurt you."

"Let me finish. I was mad. Of course I went to The Corner. Only this time I met someone."

Sunny gasped. Her hands flew to her throat. Fear gripped her heart.

"We sat; we talked and drank. Believe it or not, this is the first time I've ever done that."

"What else happened?" Her voice was hoarse. Her chest felt empty.

"Let me get to it. I'm mad and ashamed of myself."

"My God, Barry, what did you do?" A tear slid down her cheek. Her hands shook.

He took a hold of them. "We had too much to drink. I walked her to the taxi. She wanted me to go to her place. I'm not proud of it, but I almost did. Then I thought about us. Don't cry, Sunny. Listen to me."

Tears flowed. She walked over and picked up a few tissues. In disbelief she turned her back to him, but saw his reflection in the wall mirror.

Barry walked up behind her and held her close. "Babe, will you please let me finish? I didn't do anything. I turned down all her offers. I saw what could happen."

Eyes wide, Sunny looked up at him. "All her offers?"

"Sunny, please come here. Let me tell the rest. I've given this a lot of thought."

He's found someone else. He didn't cheat on me but he wanted to.

She sat next to him. Her heart beat so fast she couldn't speak as he grabbed her hands and played with her fingers.

"What happened scared me. She called me and wanted to have lunch, or a drink after work."

"You gave her your number?"

"No. Ahh . . . you work with her."

"What!" Sunny jumped up, hands on hips, mouth agape. "Who?"

"Lisa somebody, I don't know her last name."

"Loose-Legs Lisa? That's what we call her at the office. No wonder." She got up and paced.

"Yes, I think that's her name . . . the Lisa part, not the other."

"Not funny. I am not in the mood."

"Listen to me. Calm down and hear what I have to say. Come over here and sit with me." He reached for her hand. "I keep trying to tell you something. Please listen. Stop interrupting. My family means more to me than anything else. This whole incident scared me. It made me realize what

I have, and what I want. I want my family. I love you and I made my decision. If you'll help me, I want to quit drinking."

She looked deep into his face. "I love you too." She wanted to see what kind of feelings she got from him.

He held her close and kissed her. She reciprocated.

"I'll do what I can to help you. I'd fire Lisa if I could." She smiled. "Too bad she works in the other building now. But lucky for her."

He looked her in the eyes. "I want us to work on our marriage together."

"I do too," she said. "We have a good marriage. I know we can work on it. I feel lucky we love each other." Sunny felt like dancing. She kept a smile on her face, happy he wanted to stop drinking. She wasn't naive enough to just take his word for everything. This would take work.

Floyd hopped onto Barry's lap and purred like a diesel engine, which made them burst out laughing. She discussed with him going to the police on Monday. Feeling relaxed, they were quiet.

Barry started talking, "You know, you kept all those things that happened to you and Rita to yourself. Remember when we promised to tell each other everything? No secrets, remember? I need you to talk to me, and to stop thinking I'll go to a bar every time there's a problem. I need to get a grip on myself. I can do that."

"Well, we get a second chance. But it doesn't just *poof* and go away. It's something we have to work on."

"I know you're right. But you need to trust me to be able to cope with the tough stuff."

She moved closer to him. "I know. I'll try." He put his arm around her.

"Hey, I'm out of cigarettes. Come with me to the store."

She went to the closet for their coats. He came up behind her and grabbed her around the waist. He picked her up and kissed her over and over.

"We better go before I do something else."

"That's okay too." Playfully, she pushed him toward the front door.

CHAPTER FORTY-SIX

Victor walked Rita to her front door. "Thanks for the movie." She stood on her toes to plant a peck on his cheek. "And the popcorn."

"No . . . thank you." Victor smiled at her. "This was fun. Maybe we can do it again."

She nodded and turned to put the key in the door when she heard a rustling in the bushes beside the porch. Probably the neighbor's cat.

As she turned around to tell Victor good night, he slipped his arm around her and kissed the top of her forehead, then brought his lips down and kissed the end of her nose. With his finger he slowly outlined her lips, before he ran down her throat, and quickly kissed her cheek. "Good night," he whispered. That was unexpected. He made her tingle all over.

"G . . . g-good night," she murmured, and he drove off into the night.

She had turned to go in when someone stood up out of the bushes. Goose bumps rose on her arms. "Jesse! What on earth are you doing hiding in my bushes?"

He jumped up on the porch. "I watched you with that creep," he slurred. "First Gina, and now you." Whiskey vapors rose from him.

She opened the door to go in. He grabbed at her, caught her blouse by the shoulder and, stumbling to the side, ripped it. Rita slapped him. "Hey, stop it. You're drunk."

A car rumbled to the curb. Victor's GMC pulled up. He turned off the ignition, ran up the stairs, grabbed Jesse by his shoulders, and swung him around. They started throwing punches. Victor hit him in the jaw and Jesse countered with a fist to the stomach, then threw a punch that missed and went to the side of Victor's head. They regrouped and attacked again. Victor shoved Jesse, who landed on his back.

"Stop it, Jesse. Victor. Stop, you two," Rita shouted.

Jesse hollered, "I just wanted to talk to you about this creep." He coughed and wiped his face. "I lost my wife to him. I don't want to lose you too." Victor nailed him. Jesse fell and Victor leapt on him. Huffing and grunting, they rolled on the concrete porch. Blows kept going.

Rita screamed at Jesse, "You never had me. We're only friends. Nothing else. Now get out of here." She bent to push him off Victor but wasn't strong enough.

Just then, Sunny and Barry drove up the driveway. The car screeched to a stop and they jumped out. "Stop it, both of you!" Sunny ran up the steps, trying to grab at either one of them. "Stop it, I said, or I'll turn the hose on you."

Barry bounded up the stairs behind Sunny. With the strength of a wrestler he pulled Jesse by the back of his shirt and tossed him off the porch.

Jesse got up, shook his head, and brushed off his pants. He turned to Victor and smirked. With the bottom of his shirt he wiped the blood off his nose and face, rolling his eyes. He turned tail and staggered off.

Rita hugged Barry. "Dad, I'm so glad to see you!"

"What the hell?" he asked, looking at the two guys. Rita explained what happened.

"Looks like we arrived in just in time," he said. He shook Victor's hand and Victor winced. Barry looked closer at Victor's scraped, bloody knuckles.

"Come inside and wash up," Sunny said.

"No thanks, I'm fine. Jesse was too drunk to get a good punch in."

"Well, thank you," said Sunny, placing a hand on his shoulder. "You're her knight in shining armor."

"What made you come back?" asked Rita.

"You left your scarf in my truck. I looked back and saw Jesse on the porch, grabbing at you."

Barry and Sunny walked into the house, leaving Rita and Victor outside.

Rita said, "I'm lucky you came back when you did."

Sunny could hear Rita and gave Barry a nudge. "I think this relationship is going further than she thinks." She smiled and they moved to the couch.

"What the hell is going on here anyway? Were Jesse and Victor fighting over Rita?" Barry settled into the cushion while Sunny got sodas.

"I don't know," she said.

He popped the can. "They aren't teenagers. These are grown men, for God's sake."

Rita came in and plopped onto the recliner. "Victor left. Glad he didn't get hurt. Man, that was crazy. I don't know what got into Jesse."

The phone interrupted. "I'll take it in my room. You two probably want to talk," Rita said, raking a strand of hair off her forehead. She glanced at her torn shirt. "Damn. This was my best blouse."

"Wow, I'm glad I came when I did. What if Rita'd been hurt? Jesse's crazy, especially when he's fueled by booze. He better slow down or it'll catch up to him. I'm glad I've made my decision to quit," he said.

"Me too." She raised her soda can to touch his in a toast. "Rita was right. We do need to talk. You need to know everything that has gone on."

"C'mon, let's talk in bed." He took Sunny's hand and led her into the bedroom.

Sunny smiled and looked at Barry, who turned to face her, resting on one elbow. She put a cover over her legs and caught Barry up on everything, including the car-ramming and Madam Carmen and her last conversation with Gina.

Barry's eyebrows drew together. "You both could have been hurt. In fact, you may still be in danger. Before I left I warned you to be careful. Why didn't you tell me all of this when it happened?"

"I didn't want to worry you."

"No, you thought I'd run to the bar. Admit it. Hiding things won't work. We have to work together." He took her hand.

"Maybe. I feel this is a new beginning for both of us." She held his hand tight. "You know, I never missed drinking after I quit. I never think about it at all. If you're serious about giving it up, then I'm going to give up my cigarettes. Again. They stink now, anyway." She smiled and wondered if this was all true would it last? All her worries were about the drinking. Should she reconsider everything and believe him? He'd have to still prove it.

Later, they joined Rita at the kitchen table. She brought them coffee and chocolate cake. "Dad, I'll say it again. I'm so glad you're here."

He smiled and took a big bite of cake. "Me too."

"You make me feel safe," Rita added.

"I'd think that Victor guy does that for you too," said Barry.

Sunny nodded. "Your dad and I had a long talk. He wants to give up drinking, so I'm giving up smoking."

Rita jumped from her chair and ran around the table to give him a big hug. "That's wonderful. I am proud of you."

"My family is more important than the alcohol." He returned the hug.

Rita moved Floyd out of the way. "I know, let's go out tomorrow night and celebrate. We all need it."

Sunny drank the last of her coffee. "And deserve it."

"Oh, I almost forgot, Jesse called and apologized for ripping my blouse."

Sunny put her cup down. "Well, he should. He was way out of line."

"Somehow Eva came up in the conversation and he said he thought she'd been drinking and driving because her front bumper on the car was all banged up. She has to be the one who hit us."

Barry grabbed juice from the fridge. "Sounds like it," he said.

"That does it! I'm going to the police Monday morning. I put the piece of cardboard I taped the papers on in my car. I'll gather up everything else I have in my notebook to show them."

"Do you want to go now? I can go with you," Barry asked.

"No, I'll wait 'til Monday. The tribal police chief doesn't work weekends unless there's a crisis."

"Okay, Monday."

SUNDAY MORNING

It was a lazy morning for the Davises. Sunny smiled as Barry wolfed down his pancakes and Rita read the Sunday paper. This was her family; this was what she wanted.

Suddenly Rita gasped. "Look at this. Here! This picture." She laid the paper on the table and jabbed at it with her finger. The picture showed Lee, Rita's ex-boyfriend. He'd been arrested for embezzling from the casino where he worked. He and his girlfriend, Cathy, had been under surveillance for a few weeks. "Thank God I got away from him. I never had a clue. He was always borrowing money from me . . . and the casino, I guess. No doubt that's how he bought his condo."

"Amen to that," said Sunny.

Barry folded the paper. "It's been a while, but they might check back to when it started and question you. You might have to testify. Let's hope not."

"I can't believe it." Rita bit her bottom lip. "What else is going to happen?"

Barry folded up the sports section. "It'll be fine."

Over breakfast, Barry suggested they go to Rita's salon and help her clean up whatever was left from the break-in. Rita had decided she'd close the shop this Sunday and give her stylists a holiday.

First, Sunny needed to take the rental car back. Barry would follow her. After she paid and left the Hertz office, she got in their car and gave Barry a kiss.

They went back to Rita's house. Rita was in her room changing into sweats. Sunny got hers and Barry's sweatshirts and Levi's. They were ready to go to work at the salon.

Sunny got a pail with cleaning solution and headed to the bathroom to clean the windowsill. This latest event frightened her. She thought about how Rita could have been hurt. This was too much. She didn't know how much more they could take. Someone was trying to scare the bejeezus out of them, but who, and why? Unfortunately, whoever it was was succeeding.

The police had left black fingerprint dust all over the window and ledge. While the window was open, a breeze came up. Surprised, Sunny drew in a breath. "Gina, is that you? I need you."

I'm with you. I want to help you.

Then all was quiet. The wind had stopped.

Sunny opened the window wider, leaning to look outside. "Gina . . ."

In the meantime, Barry and Rita took plastic buckets from the cupboard and poured bleach and water into them. Barry got a mop and Rita used sponges to clean the hair color off the floor. As he mopped Barry asked Rita, "The police took a report, right? Damn, something weird is going on here and it's getting too dangerous."

Rita finished sponging off the counters and cabinets. "Yeah, they were very nice. I also informed them of the other stuff that's happened to me and Mom. So the report has been done."

Sunny had finished cleaning the black dust and walked into the supply room. "It's lucky they broke bottles of the light colors; that's easier to clean than the dark dyes."

Barry wrung out the mop. "I think we're finished here. We did a good job, kiddo." He put an arm around Rita. "Now that it's all done, let's go home and change clothes. We can go for a nice dinner at Chez Françoise. It's close to the house. Your mom's treat." He winked at Sunny.

CHAPTER FORTY-SEVEN

Barry opened the carved wood door with etched glass in its upper half. Sunny and Rita walked in with him and waited for him to give the maître d' their name. Looking at her husband and daughter, Sunny was happy to be with her family, especially tonight after working together at Rita's salon. They'd dressed up, Barry in his black pants, gray-and-white striped shirt with his silver eagle bolo tie and gray suit jacket; Rita wore her long black skirt and black sweater with a long white sweater vest; Sunny felt relaxed and comfortable in her brown midi and white sweater. She looked around the restaurant, while following the movements of the maître d'. She liked the flagstone fireplace burning piñon logs in the dining room's center. It cast a warm glow and a woodsy aroma. The decor was black-and-white and silver—cozy yet classy. They were shown to their seats and given menus.

"Nice," Barry said.

The waiter, a cute kid with flashing eyes and a Colgate smile, took their drink orders. He couldn't stop looking at Rita.

Rita whispered to Barry, "Will it bother you if I have a glass of wine?"

"Of course not," he answered. "I never liked wine." They laughed.

Sunny smiled and Barry ordered iced tea. She wondered how long his sobriety would last. Could he do it? She had. Of course, she hadn't drunk like he did . . . or had she?

Rita spoke. "Dad, are you fine with me going to dinner next week with Gerald?"

"Sure, it's no problem. Besides, you'll get a free meal." He chuckled.

"Your dad is in his jokester mood tonight."

When their order came the waiter flirted like an Italian with Rita. Sunny wondered if that was part of his training to wait tables at Chez Françoise.

Passing out the meals, the waiter's elbow knocked over her glass of merlot; the dark red wine shot across the table onto Sunny's white sweater.

The young waiter turned redder than the spilled wine. He rushed off, more upset than she, and returned with a towel. She dabbed and blotted the stain, which didn't help. Sunny felt sorry for him. "Don't worry. I'll just go home and change. We're nearby."

The owner/chef hurried over and apologized, using hand and shoulder gestures. "*Excusez-moi, madame.* We will pick up *l'addition*—um, ze check—for ze *dîner de famille.*" He was as French as the *escargots à la bourguignonne* on his menu.

"Thank you. I have to go get this wine out before it sets in."

"*Certainement.* And we weel pay also for ze dry cleaning."

Barry rose. "I'll drive you, hon."

"No. Sit down. Stay here with Rita and keep her company. It won't take long. Give me your keys. I'll be back in a jiffy."

"Are you sure, Mom? We could all go."

"It's fine. I'll change and be right back."

Ten minutes later when Sunny pulled into the driveway the porch was dark. "I thought we left the light on." Rushing up the front steps, she was surprised to see Floyd outside by the front door. Fear streaked up her back. How did he get out? Why did he get out? He's a house cat—hates the outdoors.

"What are you doing out here?" She stooped down and picked him up. He purred in her arms. "I bet you're cold." She turned to look behind her and rubbed the scruff of his neck. Floyd jumped down while Sunny fumbled with her key. As she opened the door he rushed inside.

She followed right behind the cat. The inside was dark too. She was positive she'd left a lamp on. The one by Rita's recliner. Fear hammered her heart.

She flipped the wall switch beside the front door. Nothing. Goose bumps rose on her arms. The power must have gone out. But that wouldn't explain Floyd being outside . . .

A familiar yet out-of-place fragrance hung in the air. Stumbling to the side table, her foot caught on something. She reached for the lamp and turned the knob. Again, nothing. Her hand moved to the light socket. Empty. Terror whipped through her. Her legs felt like lead. Her mind went in a hundred directions at once.

She shuffled over to the wall so she could get behind the chair, and pressed her back against the flat surface. Standing still, holding her breath, listening for any noise, she tried to regain her calm. She heard nothing until the refrigerator clicked on, startling her. She gasped and jumped. That proved that the power was on.

She pushed her back against the wall and listened. Was that breathing she heard? Was it hers? Was her mind playing tricks? Could there be a rational explanation? *What's that? It is breathing. Someone's in the house.* Sweat ran from her neck down her back. She strained to listen. The sound of breathing was faint, but the out-of-place fragrance intensified. Floyd hissed. Now her eyes were getting used to the dark and she was able to see inside the room from the streetlight.

Her mind went wild. She had to get to the front door. She held her breath and inched in that direction. Sweat dripped down the side of her face. Her bra was soaked. She didn't have to listen anymore. Someone was definitely here. Was it one person, or two? What was that smell? It seemed familiar. Perfume? After shave? She couldn't think straight. Was she surrounded? What did they want? Her brain was racing.

She held her breath and made her way toward the open front door. Before she could reach it, someone slammed her to the floor, knocking the breath out of her. She lay gasping for breath as the intruder ran through the kitchen and out the back door.

Sunny attempted to push herself up when a gust of wind whirled around her legs, giving her the boost she needed.

I'm here.

Gina! The back door banged against the kitchen wall as Sunny ran out the front and stumbled off the porch. A patrol car was parked at the corner, under the streetlight. Scared shitless, she took off running down the sidewalk and banged on the cop's car window. The patrolman got out and looked at her over its roof.

"What's going on?" He leaned forward and peered at her. "Don't I know you?" It was Officer Boyle.

"Yes," she wheezed. "My daughter's slashed tires, at the casino, remember? Officer, I just went home to change my sweater." She stood taller and pointed at the red wine stain and continued talking, breathless and hurried. "Someone was in the house. I heard breathing, the lights had been turned off. And the cat, who never goes outside, was on the front porch when I got there. Must have been tossed out by whoever was in the house. I heard him . . . her . . . them . . . run out the back door, after I got knocked down. I don't know if it was one, or more." Her throat was dry. She could hardly talk.

"All right, calm down. Get in and I'll go take a look." He radioed for backup.

The officer made a U-turn and parked behind the rental car in the driveway. "Stay in the car. We don't know what we'll find. I'll let you know when it's clear."

A few minutes later, two patrol cars with flashing red-and-blue lights screeched to a halt out front.

While she waited in the car Rita and Barry drove up and stopped at the curb. They jumped out and ran to the patrol car in the drive.

Sunny stepped out. "Stay outside. The police are in there. They'll let us know when it's safe."

"Lord's sake, Mom. Are you all right?"

"What happened?" Barry asked. "When you didn't come back right away we got worried." He grabbed her in his arms.

"I came home to change and the lights were out. I know we left some on. Someone was in the house. When I tried to get out the front door I was knocked down. They went out through the kitchen."

Rita's eyes widened as she looked at her. "I was scared when we saw the cop cars here. Glad it's not anything worse." Tears ran down her cheeks.

Barry took out his handkerchief and wiped her face.

"Are you hurt?" Barry whispered to Sunny.

"No, but I could have been. But listen." Sunny pushed her hair from her face. "Gina was there. When I was down on the floor, Gina came. She said she was with me."

Flashlight beams swung back and forth in the dark house.

"I thought, Is this what's going to happen to me? Is this how I'm to going to die? They'll find me with wine on my sweater."

"I'm glad you're okay, but after that remark—" Barry grinned, glancing at the stains on her sweater "—I think maybe you're in shock."

"Now I know Gina didn't kill herself. I believe I have enough evidence for them to question the person I think did this."

"What do you mean?" Barry asked. Both his and Rita's eyes were on Sunny.

"I mean. Someone killed her. It's clear now. That's what she meant by 'I wouldn't leave my boys.'"

Barry said, "You're going to need facts. Hard evidence."

"I'll get it. I have my intuition right now, and the papers. But the fact that someone broke into Rita's house and tried to hurt me makes me more certain than ever. I'm going to put my faith in Gina. She'll help."

Rita hugged her.

Barry turned to Sunny. "This has gotten ugly."

The front door opened and Officer Boyle came out. The other officers returned to their cars and drove away.

"I don't think this is a random burglary. You may have surprised the burglar. It looks like they were looking for something. Drawers were pulled out and papers are all over the floor. Of course, you'll have to go through the house and see if anything's missing. Are you having bad luck, or do you have something someone wants?"

He faced Barry. "And you are?"

"Her husband." Nodding down at Sunny, he put his arm around her waist. "I came up from San Francisco, where we live. Hopefully, we'll be able to get to the bottom of this."

Sunny wondered if that were possible. Now she was alarmed. She didn't want anything to happen to any of them.

"Is it all right if we go in the house?" asked Barry.

"You and your daughter can. I need Mrs. Davis here for a few minutes. Won't take long." Officer Boyle added, "You'll need a couple of light bulbs. It's unusual that they took out the lights. Very thorough."

Rita and Barry thanked the officer. Rita hugged her mother fiercely. Barry kissed Sunny.

"Mrs. Davis, let's sit in the car, out of the cold." He pointed Sunny to the passenger side.

"I need to take a statement from you, to file a report. So please tell me, the best you can, exactly what happened. We know how they got in. The back door was jimmied . . . the lock forced."

Sunny sat in the car; her sweat had evaporated. Now she was shivering. *Is she always with me, or does she come and go?* Sunny had never talked to any spirit before as she had Gina. *When she said, "I wouldn't leave my boys," she was telling me she didn't kill herself.* Gina couldn't journey on until they found out who killed her.

"Mrs. Davis, did you hear me? Are you all right?"

"Yes, sorry. This is such a shock."

He nodded. He took the pertinent information and asked her to check to see if anything was missing. He explained how to fill out the form and told her return it to the police station ASAP.

"Thank you, Officer." Sunny got out of the patrol car and started for the house, then turned and came back. She leaned into the car window. "Oh, Officer? Did you smell anything, like aftershave or perfume, when you were in there?"

"The other officer said he did, but he thought it belonged to you ladies. Mrs. Davis, please be careful." A light came on inside. "Guess they found the light bulbs."

Sunny stepped up onto the porch and went inside. Papers were scattered on the floor, drawers pulled out of the tables. It was a mess.

Barry had started a fire in the fireplace. Rita'd made coffee. Sunny collapsed on the couch, her eyes closed. She was exhausted.

Barry sat beside her. He took her hand in his and caressed her fingers. "Shit, Sunny, what would I do if something happened to you?"

Rita came in with steaming mugs on a tray. "It was so scary. What do they want? Who's doing this?"

"I'll tell you, I was terrified. I could hear them breathing. You know, I thought I smelled a familiar odor, like aftershave or perfume, but not one that belongs in this house. I also know I have to get those papers I found at Jesse's to the police and show them what I've put together, and then tell them what I suspect. I can't say Gina told me she didn't kill herself. They'll think I'm psycho. Rita, why don't you smudge the rooms again?"

"Good idea, I'll ask Victor if he'll come and help me."

"We're going tomorrow to file a report. Then we'll go to the tribal police," Barry said.

"I feel bad. She's told me before about never leaving her boys. I didn't listen. I didn't put it together. It doesn't make sense, if she wouldn't leave her boys she wouldn't kill herself, right? I've wasted a lot of valuable time, damn it! I want to talk to Jesse before we go to the police."

"Do you think that's smart?"

"I don't know, but I have to."

"I'm going with you."

"Fine. Let's see what he has to say about Eva."

CHAPTER FORTY-EIGHT

MONDAY MORNING

Sunny and Barry drove toward Jesse's house in comfortable silence. She glanced at him as he drove. It was nice having him with her. It would be wonderful if he'd only stick to his word and not drink. She could even handle him having a beer at home. It was the going-out drinking that got to her.

Barry startled her when he spoke. "Rita seemed a little nervous about going to work this morning."

She nodded. "This whole thing has everyone on edge. I have to find out the truth, just for our sanity."

"Well, let's make this quick, and go on to the police."

They parked in Jesse's driveway, stepped onto the porch, and knocked. Jesse opened the door and stepped back, jerking his head in surprise. He squinted at them through a black eye, and smelled hungover.

He moved out of the way and invited them in. He covered a yawn with one hand. "What are you two doing here so early this morning?"

They followed him into the kitchen.

"Hey, if you're here because of the other night, I'm sorry about that. I called Rita and apologized. That was real stupid of me."

Barry nodded. "I can't argue with that. And sorry isn't good enough. You need to get your shit together, buddy. And quit the boozin'."

Sunny grinned at him, then spoke up. "We're here because I need more information about a few things. I want to know where Eva was during the party. When was the last time you saw her?"

Jesse exhaled, looking around the kitchen before he answered. He picked up a pack of cigarettes and offered one to Barry, then to Sunny, who declined. Barry accepted and took out his lighter.

Jesse continued. "She came here yesterday afternoon, drunk as a skunk. Her car's bumper was smashed—like her. Said she scared the shit outta someone with it. Thought it was funny. She put her arms around me, trying to hug me." He grimaced and shuddered. "She asked if I remembered how it was between us. Before Gina. She said it could be the same now. I told her, 'Never in a hundred years.' I had to kick her out. She was talking nonsense."

"What kind of nonsense?"

He spoke slowly. "She's trying to run someone out of town. She wants to help me . . . like she did already with some papers." He frowned and shook his head.

"Do you know what she meant?" Sunny saw Jesse's jaw tighten and twitch.

He gulped, jiggling his Adam's apple. "Nah, just Eva's crazy talk."

Barry watched him. "Yeah, she's crazy like an eagle."

"I just wanted her out of here. I always have to tell her, 'Get out.' Hey, what's this I hear about Gerald being Rita's dad? Man, that's some shit. Wow, who knew?" He looked at Barry. "Did you know that?"

Barry fidgeted in his chair and chewed on his lower lip. Sunny's eyes told him she was sorry. "Yeah . . . I knew." He wasn't giving Jesse anything more.

"When I left the party, everyone was still here, I think. Hey, man, sorry. I gotta use the head."

"Well, thanks anyway. We'll just let ourselves out," Barry said.

As they walked past the laundry room Sunny stopped dead in her tracks. She lifted her head and sniffed. There was that odor. The same one she'd smelled in Rita's house last night. She sniffed again. "Yes, it is." She looked for where it was coming from. On the floor, next to the washing machine, was Jesse's plaid flannel shirt. She grabbed it and held it to her nose, then stuck it in her purse.

Barry grabbed her arm. "What are you doing? You can't take someone's clothes."

"Shh. Hurry up. Let's go."

Back in the car, Barry asked, "What's with the shirt?"

Sunny explained. "That's what I smelled last night, when the burglar was in the house. I'm going to see if the officer remembers this smell. Now I know why it was familiar. It's Eva's cheap-ass perfume."

"Then, after, we'll go to the tribal police," said Barry.

She nodded. "Now I'm nervous. I know Eva had a lot to do with the things that happened to us, and maybe even Gina's death. She was drenched in that perfume. Wears it all the time. She even got it all over Jesse's shirt when she was hugging him up."

"Let's go to the police station, then we'll come back and go to the tribal police. Do you want to go to the BIA?"

Sunny took her notebook from her purse. "Shit. That shirt made everything in my purse stink like Eva. We'll see what the cops say first. We might have to."

She kept quiet, hoping Gina was close by. She kept trying to contact her, but nothing was happening. She needed her now.

"What do you make of Jesse?" asked Barry.

"I'm sorry . . . about the Gerald crack. The *Indian Telegraph*, you know. I believe everything that's happened to us, from the hang-ups, the dead roses, the break-in, and especially my car getting rear-ended multiple times, are all Eva's doing."

"You might be right."

"I wouldn't be surprised if she's responsible for Gina's death."

"You mean, she killed her?"

"That's what I have to find out."

Oh, Gina, where are you? I hope you can hear me. I think we know how you died.

"Sunny. Are you all right?"

"Sure." She was upset she couldn't connect with Gina.

CHAPTER FORTY-NINE

Sunny and Barry walked up the wide concrete steps and made their way inside the Reno police station. Several long hallways with shiny linoleum floors went off in different directions. Sunny looked at Barry and shrugged.

He approached the information desk and motioned for the clerk to open the sliding glass window. He explained why they were there, and they were directed toward the hall to the right.

It seemed to go on forever because the ceiling, walls, and floors were all the same pale yellow. They found the door they were looking for and went up to the clerk. Sunny smiled. "Hi, I'm here to return the report form from a break-in last night. I have another report I want to file on the same person. I believe there's one on her already."

"Do you want to leave those with me or do you need to see an officer? What's the nature of your business?" asked the clerk.

"Yes, I'd feel more comfortable talking to one of your officers." She explained some of the things to the clerk.

"Why don't I take the form, and then you can go back down the hall on the left, to the detective division."

She motioned for them to have a seat in the row of padded chairs along the wall.

"Feels like I'm waiting to go into the courtroom at home," he said.

"I was thinking the same thing. As if we're at work." She smiled.

While waiting she tried again to contact Gina and wondered why she was having trouble finding a way to her.

A very tall, very slender man in dark blue pants and a light blue shirt introduced himself. He held out his hand. "Detective Long."

Sunny thought his name appropriate. They introduced themselves. Barry shook his hand and Sunny followed.

"Please step into the office. Have a seat." He pointed to the two chairs in front of his desk. "What brings you here?" Rubbing one hand over his white crewcut, he fumbled in his drawer for pens.

Sunny began telling him about last night's breaking and entering. How Officer Boyle had given her the form to fill out. She had given it to the clerk.

"The name on the form is the person we think did this, the same person who did all these things." She handed him the paper on which all the events were noted. "I also have Mr. Wilson's shirt with her perfume on it."

"What for?" the detective asked, frowning.

"Because when someone broke into the house last night, I smelled this same perfume. I'm a woman; I notice cheap perfume. I borrowed it from Jesse Wilson. She climbs all over him every chance she gets. I was hoping the officer who was at the house last night would be here to verify it. But I believe he works night shift."

"So, you think she was the one in your house last night? Or the guy with the shirt?"

"I'm pretty sure it was her. But, I don't know, it could've been both of them."

Detective Long looked at the papers and notebook Sunny had given him. "I can get your form and file that. As far as the other paper on the damages, we'll send someone out. We'll talk to her, this Eva person. Marshall, is it? Do you have an address? What about the brother-in-law?"

Sunny sat and crossed her legs, hands folded on her lap like a schoolgirl. "Eva lives on Ryder, one block before the reservation. Her brother-in-law's name is Jesse Wilson. He lives on the reservation, here in town."

The cop bounced his pencil back and forth on his desk. "Do you have a reason to think she'd do these things to you and your daughter?"

Barry and Sunny answered yes. Barry pointed his hand to Sunny, "Go ahead. You tell him."

Sunny uncrossed her legs and leaned in closer. "Yes, Eva's in love with her brother-in-law. They dated before he met her sister, Gina. Long story short, he fell in love with Gina and married her. They had two children together. After Gina died, Eva thought she'd get Jesse back. She sees my daughter as a threat, for no reason."

"I see. A love triangle. The other woman's name is . . ." said the detective.

"No! It's all in Eva's mind," answered Barry. "The love triangle was Eva, Jesse and Gina. My daughter was not involved."

"How did Gina die?"

"It was declared a suicide but I don't believe it. I've been investigating for the last few weeks. And I believe I have the proof you need." Sunny's neck started to get hot and her stomach tightened. "I'm an investigator for the Department of Social Services in San Francisco. Gina was my best friend. When I arrived for her funeral, too many things didn't add up. That's why I've come to you."

Her mind veered off.

Gina, are you here? Can you hear me? Answer me.

Yes, I hear you. I wouldn't leave my boys. Help me, Sunny.

"Mrs. Davis, are you all right? Would you like a glass of water?"

"Yes, please." She glanced at Barry and nodded. She drained the glass and returned it to the officer. They thanked him and stood to leave.

"I'll look into what I can. Go to the tribal police. Have you talked to anyone at the Bureau of Indian Affairs?" He walked them to the door.

"Thank you for your help. The tribal police is our next stop. I don't know yet whether we need to go to the BIA."

CHAPTER FIFTY

Sunny and Barry stopped by Rita's house for lunch on the way to the tribal police office. Sunny made sandwiches while Barry got sodas out of the fridge.

Over lunch they discussed what had happened at the police station and what the next step would be. Their meal was interrupted by the phone. Sunny got up to grab the receiver off the wall. "Let someone be on the other end, please."

"Hello."

"Hello."

"Hi, Gerald." She looked at Barry. A flush warmed her face. She looked away.

"Is Rita home?"

"No, Rita's at work. I'll tell her you called. Wait. Let me ask you, the day of the party at Gina's, did you leave before or after Eva?"

"Neither one."

"Was she the last one there?"

"No, we left together."

"What? Really?"

"Yeah, I took her home. Tell Rita I called."

"All right. Thanks. I'll tell Rita to get in touch." She sat back down in a daze, her hands pressing her chest.

"What was that about?" Barry asked. "What's the matter? Did he get out of line?"

"No, no worse. Let me catch my breath."

"What is it?"

"He said he took Eva home from the party. Gina was crying when they left. The back door slammed as they were going out the front, but he didn't know who came in. He thought it was one of the kids."

"If Gina was alive when Eva left, then she *could* have committed suicide."

"No, I don't believe that. She keeps telling me she wouldn't leave her boys. It has to have been Eva. Maybe she came back."

"You have those papers you put together. Let's take them to the tribal police and see what they think."

She wrote a note to Rita: *Call Gerald.* Then they left for the tribal office.

It was small compared to the Reno Police Station. The receptionist's desk was right inside the entrance. The department had cement floors which were scrubbed clean. Folding chairs sat against the wall. Barry gave the receptionist their name and the time of their appointment.

They'd just sat down when the tribal police chief came out into the lobby. "Good afternoon. I take it you're the Davises. I'm Chief Thomas." Sunny noticed his name plate: *Chief Dan Thomas.*

They shook hands. He was at least six feet tall, with golden brown skin, short black hair, a starched brown uniform with a brass badge, and shiny black shoes. He led them into his office and motioned for them to have a seat. "I understand this is about Mrs. Gina Wilson's death. Is that correct?"

"Yes."

"How are you related to Mrs. Wilson?"

"Gina was my best friend; like a sister or daughter. I picked her up from her foster home and brought her to live with my family the day she aged out. Her eighteenth birthday. I'm an investigator for the Department of Social Services in San Francisco, and my husband, Barry, is a probation officer."

"I'm glad to meet you. You told my secretary you have something very important regarding Mrs. Wilson's death."

Sunny took out her notebook, the cardboard with glued-on papers, and Jessie's shirt.

"You know, Mrs. Davis, we've already closed this case as a suicide. I know when this happens it's hard for family and friends to accept it."

"I understand that, Chief, but I want to give you what I have found. I also want to address what a neighbor overheard outside the Wilson home. A BIA agent came out and told another agent, 'As long as we say it's a suicide we don't have to do the legwork. Then that's it. Besides, it's only an Indian.' The neighbor asked the agent's name. It was Lyle."

"Hmm . . . yeah, I know him. Okay, Mrs. Davis, show me why you believe it wasn't a suicide."

"First, I want to tell you exactly how things happened."

Chief Thomas had his secretary hold all calls. "Before we begin, would you like coffee?"

Barry stood. "No thank you. If you don't mind I'll go outside and have a smoke."

"None for me, thanks." Sunny sat back and folded her hands on her lap. "When we came to Gina's home, her sister, Evil Eva we call her, was showing the ceiling where brain matter and hair was stuck."

Chief Thomas grimaced. "I've known Jesse Wilson since he was a little guy. And I've known Eva Marshall for years. I shouldn't say so, but that's a good name for her . . . Fits." He chuckled. "Sorry."

"Anyway, Gina's husband, Jesse, explained that they'd had an all-day party at the house. He left because Gina and Eva were arguing. Eva kept bullying Gina into drinking more and more . . ." Sunny let her voice trail off. "Jesse said he left and went down to his cousin's—you know, Louis, aka Moochie. He says he didn't know anything 'til the neighbor, Frank Allen, came and got him."

Chief Thomas picked up a pencil and wrote as Sunny talked. "Yeah, I know Frank. Good guy, him and his wife."

"Okay. The main thing was, I bumped into the wastebasket in the bathroom and tiny torn-up pink papers fell out of a tissue. Something drew me to those papers. I can't explain it, but it did." She shrugged. "Well, I could explain it, but it's not necessary right now."

She straightened and went on. "I put the papers in my pocket and told no one. I looked in her medicine cabinet; there were sleeping pills. And Jesse had a handgun under a floorboard. She would never use a rifle. She hated pain and despised guns. We went to the mortuary and I noticed an Indian burn on Gina's arm. Her skin was rubbed off, as if someone had held her arm down."

Barry came into the office and sat.

"I understand how you feel, Mrs. Davis, but that doesn't prove anything."

"Wait. Afterward, things started happening to my daughter and me, which we believe Eva did. Our car was rammed, over and over. And the front of hers is banged-up. I bet if you examine it you'll find paint that matches my rental car. Then there's the hang-ups. We get hang-up calls all the time. Jesse caught her using his phone and putting it down real quick when he came into the room. He said she looked guilty. My daughter was sent a florist's box of dead roses. The clerk at the florist's shop gave a perfect description of Eva as its purchaser. Also, after we saw Eva and her friend in the casino, my daughter's tires were slashed in the casino parking garage. A witness described two people who looked like Eva and her friend."

"Those are quite a few coincidences. Did you file a report about all this?" Chief Thomas asked.

Barry looked at Sunny, then Chief Thomas. "Yes, she did. In addition, there were the B&Es—breaking and entering. Both my daughter's house and her beauty shop were broken into and ransacked. I came home from dinner early and someone was in the house. They had cut the lights so I didn't see anyone, but the house reeked of that cheap perfume Eva always wears."

"Was anything taken? Were you hurt?"

"Nothing taken. I must have surprised them. I was knocked to the floor, so I guess it's an assault and battery too. But I'm all right. Jesse said Eva was at his house that night and had her arms around him and rubbed up against him. She was drunk so he sent her home, but she left him stinking of her perfume." She reached in her purse and pulled out Jesse's shirt. "Barry, would you get the cardboard out of the trunk, please?"

"Yes, I understand your reasoning." The chief handed the shirt back. "But I can't see where any of this has to do with Mrs. Wilson's death."

"You'll see. I took a lot of time putting those little pieces of paper together. I want to show you what I have. First, Gina left a letter, but there are different stories about it, depending on who you talk to. Jesse tells one story and Gina's coworker, Victor John, another. Jesse said she wanted peace; she was tired of fighting. I'm paraphrasing, but according to him, she said nothing about a divorce in the note. When Victor John told me what she told him, the papers made more sense."

Barry came in, bringing the cardboard with the pink bits of paper glued on. He laid it on the chief's desk. "I hope you don't mind."

"Do you still have Gina's letter?" Sunny asked the tribal policeman. "Jesse said your officers took it."

"I don't know. The BIA handles those things. I'll check." He went out to talk with his secretary.

A few minutes later he came back with a paper in his hand. "The BIA has the original. We've got a copy, though, if that'll help. Now, why don't you show me what you have there?"

Sunny took the note with shaking hands. "My God, these are the last words she wrote on earth. Oh, Gina, I'm so sorry."

"Mrs. Davis. Do you want to go ahead? I see this is hard on you."

"I'm okay. Let me show you the letter and what I put together . . . how I think it was done."

She laid the letter out flat. Goose bumps rose on her arms when she spotted a couple of droplets that looked like dried blood on the paper. It read:

Jesse—

I'm sorry, but I can't take the fighting and drinking and cheating anymore.

I want and need peace. If this is the only way I can get peace, then it's what I am going to do.

_____

Sunny pointed, "See the line on the paper under that sentence?" Tears slid down her cheeks as she leaned over the desk. The chief handed her a tissue. "Let me show you what I have."

The pink papers stood out against the board. The torn pieces, big, small, and tiny, all fitted together.

Sunny read:

I'm tak ing th e b oys a nd g ett ing a di vor ce.

The chief looked stunned. "You got all of that out of those papers?"

"Yes. Do you see where it could have been cut evenly across the paper and left to look like a suicide note?" She pointed at the line dividing Gina's words.

"Hmm . . . maybe. It might be enough for us to go question Eva and Jesse. We'll see what they have to say."

Sunny and Barry stood and shook hands with the chief. "Thank you for taking the time to see us."

Sunny felt as if a huge weight had been lifted. She sighed in relief. "Yes, finally they're going to arrest Eva. I know she did it."

"What about what Gerald said? That he took Eva home? And they heard the back door slam?"

"He had to be mistaken. Maybe he was drinking. I'm so glad it's over."

"Don't be too sure. It ain't over 'til it's over . . . and someone is convicted, babe."

"Well, I am sure. Let's go by the salon. Have Rita invite Victor for dinner."

Barry kept the car running while Sunny ran in to tell Rita all that had transpired.

CHAPTER FIFTY-ONE

The policemen drove down the gravel road to Eva's house. Two officers marched up the stairs and knocked at her door. No one was home.

MEANWHILE, A FEW MILES AWAY . . .

Eva knocked several times on Jesse's door, then let herself in. Boomer met her just inside, wagging his tail and rubbing his head on her thigh. She set her purse on the hall table, walked into the bedroom, and sat on the edge of Jesse's bed as he slept. The window shade was drawn. His shirt and Levi's were thrown over the back of the chair, boxer shorts and socks were heaped on it. Dusty boots were before the chair, one upright, the other on its side. His dresser was cluttered with keys, coins, crumpled receipts, a half-eaten Snickers bar, a screwdriver, and pair of pliers.

She waited patiently, watching him, smiling, listening to him snore. Boomer lay curled at the foot of the bed, watching her.

Jesse rolled over and rubbed his eyes, then bolted to an upright position. "What the hell! What are you doing here? How'd you get in?"

"I knocked, but you didn't answer, so . . ." She shrugged. "I used my key."

"What key? I took *my* key away from you."

She smirked. "Nope, I had extras made. In case you need me here in an emergency." She walked around the bed and straightened his blanket. "I mean to be prepared."

"Damn you, Eva." He slapped her hands. "I don't want you here."

"Oh, I think you'll change your mind. We are meant to be together. Always were. I'm willing to overlook that mistake you made with Gina."

"I married the best sister. It was no mistake. I loved her. You're too crazy for me."

"How can you say that after all I've done for you?"

"You've done nothing for me but be an arrow in my side."

"Now that Gina is gone we can be together. I can help you raise the boys. But you need to leave Rita alone. Then it can be you and me, like it used to be."

"Those feelings, such as they were, are dead. Dead, like your sister. Get it?" He balled his hands into fists. "What's this shit about me and Rita?"

"I know all about you and Rita. Sneaking around behind Gina's back."

"You're batshit crazy, Eva. Never happened. Rita was a little sister to Gina. We flirted, but it was hands-off."

"Yeah, well, I'm Gina's big sister, and that didn't stop you from banging me every time you got a chance."

Jesse just shook his head and mumbled, "Batshit crazy."

She shrugged. "Anyway, I followed you. I saw you bury the gun in the back lot."

"So what? Gina used a rifle. There's no goddamn law against me burying my pistol. I didn't want to use that gun, ever again."

"I told you, didn't I? Maybe you can't understand how I helped you. I've been calling and hanging up on Rita and Sunny. And I rammed into the back of their car. I sent dead roses to Rita, and then I went to Rita's salon and tore it up, all for you. I saw you go into her house and watched you looking for . . . whatever."

"What's this all-for-you crap? I don't want you to do nothing for me. Ever."

"I wanted to help you . . . confuse them . . . to take the blame off you. Wasn't that a great idea?"

"Eva, you're plain wacko. They'd blame you, not me. Sunny already knows it's you. Now get out and stay out!"

"No, I wanted them to get so scared they'd leave Reno and quit bothering us. The day of the party I saw you throw some scraps of paper in the garbage can outside. I took the pieces out and tore them into even smaller pieces. I threw them in a different wastebasket, in the bathroom. See how I helped you, Jesse? I meant to go back and get them. But . . ."

"What? Why? You got this all wrong. I haven't done anything."

"I wanted to help you, so we could be together. We don't need a big wedding, we can have a small one, or maybe we'll go with the boys to the justice of the peace. One of them can be best man, or whatever they call it. My friend at work can stand up for me. Or maybe I should ask Rita." She threw her head back and laughed maniacally.

Jesse swung his legs over the side of the bed and stared at her, jaws agape. "Get this through your thick skull," he shouted. "We don't need any wedding, any size, anytime, anyplace."

Eva's face scrunched up in misery.

His mind went back to the time Rita told him her mom was putting papers together. Could Sunny have found them? If she did, they weren't in her house so he didn't think she kept them.

"Holy shit, Eva! What have you done?"

"I love you, Jesse," she sobbed. "I just wanted to help you. Gina's gone. No one is in our way. She was going to divorce you. I'll never leave you, ever."

"Listen to me, Eva. For the last time, get this though your shit-for-brains head." He raised his voice. "I don't love you. I don't even like you. If you and I were the only people on this planet, I still would not friggin' want you. Get it?" he roared. "Now get out!"

Tears ran down her cheeks and into her mouth. She stood there, chin on her chest, arms against her sides. Mumbling, she turned and stumbled into the hall to get her purse from the table. "I gave him so many chances," she whispered.

"If I can't have him . . ." She pulled a .22 pistol out of her purse and turned back toward him. In the doorway of his room she pointed it at Jesse, just as he looked up. His eyes widened, his mouth dropped open.

"What the hell . . . ? Where'd you get my gun?"

"I told you, I saw everything you did. Everything. I dug it up." She giggled. "For you, Jesse, for you. We were meant to be together. I've waited for you, all these years. After all I've done for you, how can you treat me this way?"

He stood beside his bed. "Crazy bitch! Get out of my house."

Eva wiped her eyes with her left arm. She kept the gun trained on Jesse with her right hand. "I gave you so many chances. I kept quiet for you. I covered for you. But now it's over. If I can't have you, nobody's going to have you."

Jesse's eyes widened. He swallowed hard and lunged for her. "Remember, I love you." She shot him. The sound echoed through the house.

Blood spurted from his midsection and ran down his legs. Eva's bullet had found its mark in his stomach. He fell back onto the bed. She grabbed her purse from the table and left the house. A high-pitched scream emanated from her as she stumbled to her car.

CHAPTER FIFTY-TWO

IN THE MEANTIME . . .

Officer Long from the Reno police called the tribal police. "Hello, Chief Thomas? We need an escort to the home of one of your residents. We're looking for Eva Marshall. Need to talk to her." He explained the situation. "We understand she spends a lot of time at the home of a Mr. Jesse Wilson. We're on our way there now."

"My officers and I will meet you there."

As the Reno police and tribal police cars pulled up, Eva sat in her car weeping convulsively, taking in huge shuddering gulps of air, not bothering to wipe away her tears and snot. Through her open window they heard, "I killed him. I loved him and I killed him."

Quickly calling for backup, Chief Thomas sent an officer to Eva's car to talk to her. Then the chief hurried past her and into the house.

The cop approached her car. "Ma'am, are you Eva Marshall?"

Without answering she picked up the gun from the seat beside her. She raised it and pressed the barrel to her temple. Before he could stop her, Eva pulled the trigger. Thick red blood splattered over the car seat and dashboard, some landing on the officer's uniform. She slumped over, the .22 in her hand.

Chief Thomas heard the single gunshot. He'd found Jesse on the bed, blood oozing from a bullet wound in his abdomen, but still breathing. Thomas used his shoulder mic to call for paramedics. He grabbed a sheet from Wilson's bed to stop the bleeding, and applied pressure. Sirens screamed as patrol cars squealed into the driveway. An ambulance pulled up and three EMTs jumped out. One raced to open the back of the ambulance and yanked out the gurney.

As Chief Thomas ran out Jesse's front door he saw Eva in her car, collapsed over the steering wheel.

"What the hell happened here? The one in the house is still alive." He shouted to the ambulance driver. "Hurry! I don't know if he'll make it."

One paramedic stopped at Eva's car as the other two ran into the house. Another officer on the scene took charge of Eva. "Got a DOS here," he hollered. "Dead on site."

Patrol cars were parked zigzag in the yard. More sirens approached. Patrolmen hollered, sirens blared. Eva's car pungent with gunpowder and fresh blood.

Chief Thomas put a call in to the coroner while the paramedics pushed the gurney carrying Jesse into the ambulance. The chief had the other officers finish up with the tragic scene. For a second time in just a few weeks the area around the Wilson home was cordoned off. The yard and house swarmed with Reno and tribal police.

Stunned neighbors stood in the road outside Jesse's house gawking and mumbling.

"What happened?"

"Oh my God. Not again."

"Looks like a double shooting this time."

"Murder-suicide?"

"Looks like."

"Wonder who did what to who."

The ambulance drove with sirens blaring all the way to Washoe County Hospital. Jesse had trouble breathing while the paramedic worked to stop the hemorrhaging. The other paramedic hooked Jesse up to an IV and took his vitals.

"Hey, buddy, stay with me. Stay with me now."

"I can't feel anything. Listen . . . I'm not . . . going to . . . make it. Get me the chief. I got . . . I . . . killed . . ." He passed out.

The paramedic notified the police and Chief Thomas. He and another officer were waiting when the ambulance arrived at the hospital. Jesse awoke for a moment to talk to the chief as he walked beside the gurney. As they rushed Jesse into surgery, he made a full confession. "Chief . . . I got mad . . . came back . . . held her . . . arm down . . . used my rifle . . .cut letter . . . tore up . . . pushed Sunny . . . Sorry."

Back at the Tribal office, the chief dispatched someone to Jesse's mother to notify her of her son's bullet wound and his full confession.

Sunny, her family, and Victor were digging into their fresh-baked pineapple upside-down cake when someone knocked on the door. They looked at each other in dread. Barry looked at the clock: 11:12 p.m. "Kind'a late for visitors."

Rita pushed away from the table to answer the door.

"I'm Chief Thomas. Are Mr. and Mrs. Davis here?"

She nodded. "Come in."

Sunny and Barry, along with Victor, came into the living room. watching the chief. "Why don't all you folks sit down?"

"Did you arrest Eva?" demanded Sunny.

"No."

Sunny glared at him, still standing. "What? Why the hell not?"

He held up his hand. "Please. Just sit, Mrs. Davis, and listen." He looked around the room before announcing, "Eva Marshall shot Jesse."

Sunny gasped. "And you didn't arrest her?! What the—"

Rita asked, "Is he dead?"

"Please. Everyone, sit down and let me finish." He waited while they took their seats. "Eva shot Jesse. The officer heard her say, 'I loved him and I killed him.' Then she shot and killed herself."

Sunny put her hands to her open mouth and gawked at the chief. Victor put his arms around Rita. Barry hung his head.

"That's not all. Jesse's in surgery right now. At Washoe County Hospital. It doesn't look good. But he made a confession. He killed Gina."

Sunny and Rita shouted, "No!"

Sunny asked, "How could he have killed her? Why?"

Chief Thomas looked at the group. "He just said he was mad at her. From what I understand, he came in through the field behind the house, when everyone else had gone. He said she wrote him a letter. She told him she might as well be dead as stay with him. He said, 'That can be arranged.' So he held her down and shoved the gun under her chin. You were right, Mrs. Davis. He did cut off the bottom of the letter so it would look like a suicide note. As for the break-in at your house . . . it was him. He was looking for those little bits of papers. He's the one who pushed you down that night and him that stunk of cheap perfume."

"No, I wasn't right. It was Jesse." Sunny wiped her wet face. "I thought Eva did it."

Victor was holding a sobbing Rita. "I did too," she said.

"Eva did do things to you. Both of you. She admitted it to Jesse. I guess she thought she was helping him. But she didn't kill her sister. She thought she'd killed Jesse, and that, we assume from her last words, is why she killed herself."

Victor spoke up. "All this tragedy for something that wasn't necessary."

"Yeah," Barry chimed in. He shook his head. "Hell hath no fury like a woman scorned. That fits Eva to a T. Jesse dumped her for Gina and, all those years later, he paid the price for it."

Sunny nodded, then looked at the chief. "Can we visit him . . . Rita and me? Just for a few minutes."

"Do you think that's a good idea?" asked Barry. "Leave it be."

"I have to ask him why. I have to know, for my own peace of mind." *And Gina's.* Sunny looked at Chief Thomas. "And now Gina's poor boys end up with no parents." Her eyes filled with tears.

"I don't know if it's allowed. He's just out of surgery. We'll have to see how he's doing. Do you want me to call you here tonight? We can wait and see what happens in the morning."

Sunny glanced at everyone in the room. "No, we'll be up. Please call us tonight. We're not far from the hospital. Hopefully, we can go on over tonight."

A couple hours later, Rita answered the phone, then relayed the conversation to the others. "Chief Thomas said it's okay for me and Mom to go, but only for a few minutes. His condition is critical. He's out of surgery and in recovery, stable but still critical. He's in ICU. The doctors don't know yet about his prognosis. It's touch and go. They'll have to keep a close eye on him for the next twenty-four hours."

When they got to ICU, Sunny and Rita thanked Jesse's mom for letting them go in. She was there with the boys. Sunny and Rita were allowed only five minutes.

He lay on the bed, hooked up to an IV that was going to two monitors, one with green lights going back and forth across the screen and beeping, the other connected to the nurses' station.

He had tubes in his nose and abdomen, a heart monitor beside his bed. He looked pale. His long hair pulled back in a ponytail. Despite everything, he was still a good-looking man.

Tearful, Rita touched his hand. Sunny called his name. He moved his head toward her.

"I'm . . . sorry," he whispered, then coughed and winced.

Sunny looked down at this helpless man, surprised at her lack of sympathy. "How could you be so selfish? Did you even think about the boys? You took away their mother and now their father. If you're lucky enough to live through this, you'll spend the rest of your life in a federal penitentiary."

His eyes were filled with pain.

"Tell me, Jesse, why? That's all I want to know. Why?"

"She was . . . was leaving me," he gasped, then moaned. "She wanted . . . a divorce . . ." He grimaced. "No one leaves me . . . I do the leaving."

"You heartless, egotistical son of a bitch." She wanted to punch him in the stomach, where it'd do the most good. Her hand had balled itself into a fist. She forced her fingers to straighten and her hand to relax.

The door swung open and the nurse came in. Their time was up.

The drive back to Rita's was quiet. Barry had packed for the trip home. He and Victor were deep in conversation when Sunny and Rita returned and the subject changed to the latest events and revelations.

Sunny looked down at her cup. "You know, I never liked Eva at all, and at times I hated Jesse, but I never wanted this to happen."

Barry's hand covered hers to comfort her.

Rita said, "On the way home I was thinking that maybe later I'll sell my shop and move to San Francisco. Victor's got me thinking about going to law school. The girls at the salon want to go in together and buy my place. With everything that's happened, and you both gone, I don't want to stay here."

"What about Victor?" asked Sunny.

Victor leaned back in his chair. "Yeah, what about me?"

"You're my one good thing. We talked about this. He could transfer to PG&E and work in the Bay Area." She smiled at him. "He could take night classes at law school."

Sunny took her daughter's hands. "It's way too soon to make big decisions like that. This has been a shock to all of us. Wait awhile. Think about it, you can always do it later, or not."

"I think we're leaving you in good hands." Barry looked over at Victor. Victor kissed Rita on the cheek.

Sunny smiled and looked at them. "On that note, we're going to bed. It's been one helluva day."

Victor got up and, holding Rita's hand, walked to the front door.

"I'll say my good night," he whispered. "After your parents go back home, if you happen to be scared here by yourself, I'll come over and keep you company. You know, just for protection." He grinned.

Rita kissed him and playfully hit him in the shoulder. "Maybe." She turned around smiling and saw Sunny and Barry, hand in hand, watching from the hallway and grinning.

Late the next morning Barry and Sunny prepared to leave. The phone rang and Rita grabbed it. "What!" . . . "No." . . . "Okay, thank you." She hung her head and slowly put the receiver in its cradle. She looked at her mom and dad with watery eyes. "That was Chief Thomas. Jesse's dead. Died last night, not long after we left."

"Are you all right? Do you want us to stay a little longer?" asked Barry.

"No, I'm fine. It just took me back a bit. He's not the friend, or person, I thought he was."

"Rita, why don't you call Gerald? He needs to know what's happened. Ask Victor to come over. I'll feel better if you're not alone."

Barry looked at Rita, nodded, and winked. "Gerald should know about Eva. By the way, Rita, I'm fine with you and the Gerald thing. Don't think it hurts my feelings because it doesn't."

She nodded at him and smiled, then turned her attention to Sunny. "Mom, I dreamed of Gina last night. It was a weird dream. Victor was in it. I was there. Gina was a whirling blur, but she was smiling. She was swaying back and forth. She said goodbye."

"See, you're starting to be able to have dreams, like me and my mother," said Sunny.

Rita looked at her parents. "Wow! That is way cool. I didn't think it'd happen to me."

Sunny's eyes misted over. "I had the same dream, except for the Victor part. In my dream, I felt like I was wide awake, sitting on the end of the bed with her. We talked. She sat looking at me, her long hair flowing over her shoulder. But now I can't remember what we talked about. She was happy. She could finally start her journey and follow Grandfather Spirit to the next world. I pulled her close and we said goodbye. I also feel at peace."

"Wow," Rita said. "That was a great dream."

"There's more. The window was open partway and a breeze came in. As I looked at her she started to fade. Her hair blew around her face. She was smiling, and her arms reached out to me. A strong breeze came, lifting her and carrying her up. She faded more and more. And then she was gone."

"Man, that was a wonderful send-off," Barry said.

"When I woke up, I saw in the mirror that tears had dried on my cheeks." I said, "Goodbye, my friend. I'll always carry you in my heart. I hope my love will reach you, Gina. Let Grandfather Spirit embrace you in love."

Barry reached for the bags. "Does she know Jesse shot her?"

Sunny grabbed her small suitcase. "I don't know. Maybe it doesn't matter." They walked out the door. "As soon as it was solved, her journey began."

Rita walked them to the car. "I'm going to miss you. Maybe I'll see you soon."

"Take your time. I'll miss you too," said Sunny.

"Don't rush anything. Come visit anytime."

Sunny wrapped her arms around Rita. "Gina is at peace. She can move on. We can all move on. She can let Grandfather Spirit take her and continue her journey. She'll be wrapped in the love of her ancestors. I always believed what Chief Suquamish said: 'There is no death, only a change of worlds.'"

Sitting in the car, Sunny wiped her face. "My hurt I will tuck away in its own spot. I'll go on with my life, but I will never heal from this pain."

Oh, Gina, now you're gone from me. Now my ache begins.

ACKNOWLEDGMENTS

Writing was a long, slow process, helped greatly by the encouragement of the following people, to whom I am forever grateful:

My mentor, teacher, editor and friend, Carol Petersen Purroy. She had the foresight to keep me going.

Writers Unanimous, my first critique group: Mary Lee Fulkerson, Betty Johnson, Vonda Novelly, Audrey Cournia, Karen DeRocco, Celeste León, Marie Edwards, Helen Stevens, and Carol Purroy.

My critique classmates, whom I adore and from whom I have learned so much: my teacher, Janice Stevens, and fellow class members Linda Gannaway, Earlene Holquin, Bev Horsley, Hank Palmer, Gus Knittle, Tom Morton, Don Farris, David Elkin, Pat Shanley, Franz Weinschenk, Robert Eiland, Linda Robertson, Sue Bonner Martin, Courtney Webb, Joan Newcomb, David Creighton, and Jocelyn Speiser. And our member whom we loved and lost, Chuck Soley, R.I.P.

Thanks also to Larry Schram for his major help.

Writing is a solitary business and without help it can be very difficult. My thanks to CJ Collins, my mentor and friend, who was there for me daily these last years.

Special thanks go to my good friend, Rita Marie Betance, who read, reread, and re-reread page after page after page. She was kind enough to let me use her name for one of my main characters.

Not to be forgotten is Helen Ulrich, who always made me feel good about my book.

Finally, I want to thank my son, Leeland McMasters, for supplying the beautiful cover art.

ABOUT THE AUTHOR

Veronica Giolli's mystery stories have previously appeared in *The Poison Pen*. She was a founding member of Writers of the Purple Sage Publishing Consortium in Reno, Nevada. While living on a reservation Giolli acquired firsthand knowledge of tribal customs and spiritual practices. This in part provided the inspiration to write *Whispers in the Wind*. Giolli lives in California's Central Valley.

CPSIA information can be obtained
at www.ICGtesting.com
Printed in the USA
BVHW071712300119
538993BV00002B/8/P

9 781610 353298